BY SARAH ADAMS

The
MATCH

The
MATCH

A NOVEL

SARAH ADAMS

DELL BOOKS

NEW YORK

2024 Dell Trade Paperback Edition

Copyright © 2020 by Sarah Adams

Excerpt from *The Enemy* by Sarah Adams copyright © 2020 by Sarah Adams

Published in the United States by Dell, an imprint of Random House, a division of Penguin Random House LLC, New York.

Originally self-published in the United States by the author in 2020.

DELL and the D colophon are registered trademarks of Penguin Random House LLC.

LIBRARY OF CONGRESS CATALOGING-IN-PUBLICATION DATA
Names: Adams, Sarah, 1991–author.
Title: The match : a novel/Sarah Adams.
Description: Dell trade paperback edition. | New York: Dell Books, 2024.
Identifiers: LCCN 2023046614 (print) | LCCN 2023046615 (ebook) |
ISBN 9780593871713 (trade paperback; acid-free paper) |
ISBN 9780593871720 (ebook)
Subjects: LCGFT: Romance fiction. | Novels.
Classification: LCC PS3601.D3947M38 2024 (print) |
LCC PS3601.D3947 (ebook) | DDC 813/.6—dc23/eng/20231106
LC record available at http://lccn.loc.gov/2023046614
LC ebook record available at https://lccn.loc.gov/2023046615

Printed in the United States of America on acid-free paper

This book contains an excerpt from the forthcoming book *The Enemy* by Sarah Adams. This excerpt has been set for this edition only and may not reflect the final content of the forthcoming edition.

randomhousebooks.com

2 4 6 8 9 7 5 3 1

Title page art by Alsu Art © Adobe Stock Photos

Book design by Sara Bereta

This book is for all the four-legged superheroes
of the world, saving lives and giving love and
independence to those who need it!

And for my mother-in-law, Lesley,
who never stops inspiring me.

A NOTE FROM SARAH

Hello, darling readers! I am so grateful to you for taking a chance on my book, and I hope that it makes you laugh and fills your heart with warm fuzzies! This story is especially close to my heart because my mother-in-law runs a nonprofit service dog organization that breeds, trains, and places service dogs with those who are living with physical, mental, or emotional disabilities.

The amount of time, energy, and love that I've seen her and her volunteers put into their dogs and the recipients of those dogs is nothing short of inspiring. I wrote this book—through the eyes of Evie Jones—with her and her team in mind, to help bring awareness to the service dog community as well as to those living with epilepsy.

Thank you to all service dog trainers and volunteers who work endlessly to train four-legged superheroes to help change lives.

Although this story contains heavy elements, it is written to uplift you and leave you feeling nothing but happy and hopeful. That being said, I have provided a content warning below for those who need a little extra assurance before reading.

XO Sarah

Content warning: Please be advised that *The Match* portrays characters living with epilepsy; however, no seizures take place on the page. This story also portrays themes of parental neglect and divorce. In addition, there is a scene where the heroine evades an unwanted kiss from a side character; however, it is very brief, and the reader can be assured that she is not harmed. Finally, the story contains mild cursing and fade-to-black intimacy.

The
MATCH

CHAPTER 1

Evie

I wake up to the feel of Charlie's tongue grazing my cheek. I don't like being kissed like this first thing in the morning. Mainly because I don't like mornings, and I wish that he would get it through his thick head that I need my sleep. But just like every morning, he's persistent.

I am Sleeping Beauty, and he is the prince. Although, I'm pretty sure the prince didn't roll his tongue all over Sleeping Beauty's face like Charlie is doing now. What a different movie that would be.

"Can you please just give me five more minutes?" I ask while shoving my head under the pillow in an attempt to block his advances.

But he doesn't like this game. Never has. It worries him to not see my face. We've been together now for three years—and he's become the tiniest bit overprotective. But he's the best snuggler in the whole world, so I allow his slightly domineering attitude.

Plus, he really does know what's best for me. He's improved my life in more ways than I can count. It's why I adore him. It's why I let him lick my face at 6:30 A.M. It's why I sit up in bed and roll him over onto his back and rub his tummy until his leg starts shaking.

Oh, right. Charlie is my dog. Did I forget to mention that?

More specifically, he's my seizure-assist dog.

I was diagnosed with epilepsy when I was sixteen years old. It stole my adolescence. It stole my peace of mind. And more importantly—it stole my license. Turns out, the state doesn't like it too much if you randomly black out and convulse. Believe me, under no circumstances will they let you behind the wheel of a vehicle once they get wind of the E-word.

No one sympathizes more with the poor girl in the Beach Boys song about her dad taking her T-Bird away than me. Except mine was a 1980 slate-blue Land Cruiser with a cream-colored top. My dad bought it for me a month before my sixteenth birthday. Not even a week after that sweet sixteen, I had my first seizure. And my life changed forever.

Those next few years were hard, to say the least. I was scared of going anywhere or doing anything. One day I was a teenager, bliss-fully carefree about everything besides the chip in my hot-pink glitter nail polish. The next, I was painfully aware of how small a part I played in my own existence on this earth.

Charlie didn't come into my life until I was twenty-three and still living with my mom and dad because I was scared to live on my own. Actually, I thought I *couldn't* live on my own. But then I met a woman in a coffee shop who had an adorable white Labrador retriever at her side, a bright-blue vest strapped around its body with a patch sewed on the side that read *Working Dog, Do Not Pet.*

The first thought that went through my mind was wondering if this dog could do my taxes. Turns out, they don't do that sort of work. The woman was kind enough to field all my silly questions, because in her exact words, "*No question is too silly.*"

But I figured if she gave me enough of her time, I could manage to change her mind.

The rest was history. Joanna Halstead, the woman from the coffee shop—also known as my fairy godmother—quickly became one of my best friends. I learned that she owned a service dog company called Southern Service Paws, and she trained and matched dogs with people living with all sorts of disabilities. Disabilities just like mine.

That's how Charlie came into my life. It's how I regained my independence and security. It's how I decided to live on my own. It's how my parents came to hate the company that I adore and am being groomed to take over when Joanna retires next year.

Well, *company* might be a bit of a stretch.

Company implies monetary value. And money is not something that Southern Service Paws has. It's more like Jo is grooming me to take over her heart. Something that has a whole lot more value than money, but a shockingly low credit score.

I am the only other employee that is paid a salary—the rest are volunteers. And, actually, *salary* is also another one of those deceptive words. When you hear it, you think benefits, 401(k)s, and down payments on pretty little houses. When I hear it, I just think of my apartment that is the size of my thumbnail and my kitchen pantry that is stocked with ramen noodles and Froot Loops.

Luckily, I love Froot Loops.

I will eat nothing but sugary cereal for the rest of my days if it means I get to keep working for Jo and her company. Because I love what I do and the people I help. And as cramped as I am in this little place, I'm proud that it's mine—not my parents'.

In this new world I have carved out for myself over the past three years, I'm just Evie. Not Miss Evelyn Grace Jones, daughter to Harold and Melony Jones of the prestigious Charlestonian family that resides SOB (South of Broad, aka Snootyville, and where I was raised). That name might not mean anything to you, but around here in Charleston, it's everything.

My family comes from what's known as "old southern money." You know the kind: big historical houses, prestigious country clubs that only accept members with names that have been on the list since it was founded, garden cocktail parties served by men in white jackets, and a unique southern drawl that says, *I'm better than you.*

My dad is an attorney and partner at Jones and Murray Law, the oldest and most elite law firm in all of South Carolina, and my mom is on the board of the Powder Society of Revolutionary Ladies. What do they do? Mainly sit around in their finely tailored day dresses and drink martinis, planning more cocktail parties for their wealthy husbands to mingle and continue to pass their old southern money back and forth like playing cards.

Basically, how I'm living now is the exact opposite of how I grew up, and I couldn't be happier about it.

That thought reminds me of my schedule for the day, and I reach over Charlie, my ninety-pound golden retriever—who is more of a bed hog than any full-grown man—and pick up my phone. I do a double take at the time. That can't be right. It says it's 9:10 A.M. How can that be when I set my alarm for 6:45 A.M.? Oh, wonderful. I forgot to set it. And now I'm going to be late for my client meeting.

"No, no, no." I throw off my white comforter and jump out of bed.

Charlie sits up, ears at attention and body poised for anything, and watches me race across my studio apartment to the closet. I'm wearing a pair of cute new pink undies, and it occurs to me how sad it is that Charlie is the only male in my life to see them.

I trip over a shoe before I look in my empty closet and

remember that I put off going to the laundromat last night so I could finish binge-watching *The Bachelor.* Don't judge me. It's the only romance I have in my life right now.

Charlie walks up beside me and gives me a look that says, *I told you not to shirk your responsibilities.* He's so much more adult than me.

I put my hands on my hips and frown down at him. "I have twenty minutes before I need to be at the coffee shop, and I have nothing to wear, so quit giving me that high-and-mighty look or I'm going to shave your fur and wear it as a coat, like Cruella de Vil." *I'd never.*

He rolls his eyes at me. Some people might think it's impossible for a dog to roll his eyes, but that's only because they haven't met Charlie. I smile and rub his adorable head because I can never be mad at him for more than two seconds.

Thankfully, I spot the turquoise summer dress I wore yesterday. It's lying crumpled on the couch in a tight little ball that would make my mom gasp with disbelief. Her maid would never allow one of her dresses to crease. *How atrocious.*

Crossing the room, I shake out my dress, give it a good sniff, then decide that wearing it one more day won't hurt anyone. It smells a little too much like the burger I ate last night, so after pulling it on I douse myself in vanilla body spray.

Now I'm a walking ad for Bath & Body Works, and I consider requesting some sort of royalty from them.

The clock continues to race, and I look like I'm in the middle of a game show challenge as I rush around my apartment trying to gather everything I need for the meeting, take my meds, and get Charlie fed. *I better win a million dollars when I beat this clock.*

"Charlie, find your vest," I tell him while hopping on one foot and pulling my white tennis shoe on the other.

Another fact that would make Melony Jones gasp. Mom swears

that *this* is the reason I'm not married yet. I think it has more to do with the shockingly small pool of men who want a serious relationship with a woman who has to take a service dog with her everywhere and might drop down with a seizure in the middle of their dinner date.

And I just haven't been looking for a man all that much. My days are full of work, and I don't have much time to devote to weeding out the guys who only want to sleep with me from the ones who I could count on to show up if I made them my emergency contact. And at this point in my life, I'm ready for the emergency contact.

I check the time on my phone and then give myself two minutes to brush my teeth and wipe the mascara from underneath my eyes. I wish I had more time to spend on my face. There's nothing I hate more than feeling rushed for a meeting. It lends too much credence to my mom's opinion that I don't have my act together.

In record time, I swipe on some pink lip balm and knot a loose braid over my shoulder all the way to where it stops right above my hip. I've been growing my blond locks out for a few years now, and it's grown so long that I half expect a prince to throw a rock at my window and tell me to let down my hair.

Do I have a fairy-tale princess obsession? I blame it on those Wednesday cotillion lessons I had to attend in high school.

Charlie pulls me out of my wandering thoughts and keeps me on track by dropping his blue vest at my feet. He's better at finding things than I am. "I'm sorry about the 'turning your fur into a coat' comment. We both know I'd give my soul for you, Charlie boy." After buckling the vest around his golden body, I give him a quick kiss on his head.

Since the coffee shop where I'm supposed to meet my new client is right down the street, I plan on walking instead of calling a ride. Not being able to drive has been one of the hardest parts of living with a disability. There are so many nights when I wish I could hop into my car and run down to the drugstore to pick up a pint of ice cream. Or when I run out of tampons, it would be so nice to pop down to the store myself instead of having to call and wait for an Uber or order off of a one-hour grocery delivery service. Without fail, my delivery person ends up being a young guy. And every single time, he blushes when he makes the drop.

Evening, ma'am. Here are your military-grade tampons and overnight pads. I hope you don't die of anemia tonight.

At 9:20, Charlie and I are on the sidewalk, jogging toward the coffee shop. Literally, jogging. My braid is bouncing around my face, and I realize I probably should have worn bike shorts under my dress. Someone catcalls at me from somewhere across the street, and my suspicions are confirmed.

Somehow, I remembered to grab my binder full of information to share about our matching process as well as our training methods and fees before I darted from the apartment. I wish I could say that our dogs come free of charge to qualifying recipients, but we just aren't there yet. Right now they come with a hefty price tag. It weighs on me that there are so many people who could benefit from having a service dog but can't afford one due to the massive medical bills that also come along with having a disability.

But, hopefully, after the big fundraiser Jo and I are putting on in a couple months, that will all change. Several major businesses have agreed to donate their goods and services for our first-ever fancy-schmancy silent auction. If we make the kind of money we're hoping, we'll be able to give away our dogs one hundred percent free of charge to those who qualify. The recipients will have to prove that they are financially capable of providing food, necessary medications, and vet visits for their dog, but that's it.

If all goes as hoped, it'll become a yearly event.

I clutch my binder tightly under my arm as I race toward

Hudson Roasters. When a bead of sweat runs down my face, I wonder if it would have been better to just reschedule.

The man I'm meeting, Jacob Broaden, wanted to discuss having his ten-year-old daughter matched with one of our dogs. And maybe I would have canceled if it wasn't for her particular disability. *Epilepsy.* It's not as if we've never matched anyone who shares my same disability before, but for some reason, knowing how young she is makes me feel a kinship to this girl. I feel like I owe it to her to show up today.

The dad sounded nice enough over email—if a little . . . eccentric. Although, I think he might have been in a hurry when he sent off the email, because he misspelled a few words. His choice of five exclamation marks at the end of every sentence was intriguing as well. Actually, now that I think of it, I'm just hoping he's not a creep. I really don't want to get stuffed in someone's trunk today.

As we round the corner to the coffee shop, Charlie and I slow our pace. It's as hot as hell today. I'm sweating like I've been sitting in the desert wearing a parka, and my skin is emitting the vanilla body spray in toxic quantities.

My mom would be so proud. I'm really putting my best foot forward today.

Before I reach the door of the coffee shop, I come to a stop. I close my eyes and catch my breath, mentally reminding myself of all the major points I need to cover today and hoping I don't forget anything. It doesn't matter that I've been doing this for three years now; I'm always super nervous before these first meetings. I think it's because I know firsthand how much a service dog can change someone's life, and I don't want to say anything to deter them from taking that step.

I glance down at my dress and do a quick check that all my fun parts are where they should be and have not fallen out of the scoop neckline during my jog. But who am I kidding? None of my fun parts are big enough to move, let alone escape their confines. There are things I love about being tall and lean, but having a membership to the itty-bitty-*you-know-what* committee is not one of them.

I open the door, and Charlie walks through with a loose leash like a perfect little gentleman. During the first year after I adopted Charlie, my eyes were constantly glued to him and his to me. I used my face and hands, asking him to stay, wait, go ahead, or lie down at my feet. Now it feels as if Charlie knows what I'm thinking before I think it. He and I are so attuned to each other that sometimes I forget he's there. He's a part of me. My second skin. *A very hairy second skin.*

It's an odd thing when there's no one in the world you trust more than your dog. But that first time I had a seizure alone in my apartment, and Charlie did exactly what we had trained him to do—push the medical alert button on the wall that calls Joanna and then my parents, then turn me on my side and lick my face to help me regain consciousness—it sealed my trust.

And today I hope I can help a little girl and her dad find that same security.

The cool air of the coffee shop rushes over my heated skin, and I dab away the beads of sweat on my forehead with the back of my hand while looking for a man with a young girl. Mr. Broaden gave me a brief description of himself in his email, so I know to look for a tall man with "hunny"-colored hair. I really hope that his fingers hit the keys wrong, and he actually knows how to spell the word *honey*.

I'm scanning, I'm scanning, I'm scanning, and . . . bingo!

There's a tall man with dirty-blond hair, a to-go cup in each hand, walking toward a young girl sitting at a table. This has to be them. Charlie and I approach the two, and the girl notices us first. When she sees Charlie, her eyes light up with a look I recognize easily. It's the same one most people give my dog. It's a look that says she's seconds from lunging at him, and I'm going to have to gently ask her not to pet Charlie while he has his vest on.

Mr. Broaden notices that something has caught his daughter's eye, and he turns.

And then, *BAM*. The most spectacular pair of blue eyes hits me, and I almost feel like taking a step back. I'm staring into his eyes and dreaming of swimming in the shallow part of the ocean where you can still see your feet but the water is so blue that it looks like God dipped his brush in it after painting the sky. I immediately appreciate the way his eyes perfectly contrast the white cotton T-shirt that's straining over his chest and shoulders.

I mean, *wowza*. Is this what dads look like these days? Where do I sign up?

I'll take one dad with dirty-blond hair, tan skin, six feet tall, glittering blue eyes, and a chiseled body that makes my insides feel like molten lava, please. Actually, better yet, I'll just take this one. Thanks.

It's impressive how quickly my mind absorbs the information that his ring finger is blissfully empty. Not a tan line in sight.

"Mr. Broaden?" I ask, sounding a bit too excited for my taste. *Take it down a notch, Evie.*

"Yes?" He's tentative as he scans me, eyes dropping all the way down the length of my body until they land on Charlie and stop. He frowns, then those gorgeous eyes bounce up to mine again.

His hesitation is odd. There's a strange vibe, but I can't pinpoint the reason for it.

I tuck my binder under my arm and then extend my hand to him. "I'm Evie Jones. It's so nice to meet you in person!" My southern accent is friendly and inviting, and if we're being honest, a little bit adorable. I've been told I sound just like Reese Witherspoon more times than I can count. But he's not taking my hand. He's staring at it like he's just escaped from a deserted island he's been stranded on for most of his life. Human contact is foreign to this man.

My smile falters, and an odd feeling settles in my stomach. Finally, he seems to remember some sort of manners and accepts my hand. The moment his skin settles against mine, my body breaks out in chills. Until this moment, I've been completely unaware of how important it is to me that a man have hands so large they completely engulf mine. My hand looks like a tiny baby hand inside his, and I love it.

Mr. Broaden pulls his hand back, and I'm pretty sure he takes a step away from me. The bad feeling returns.

"I'm sorry, but . . . do we know each other?" he asks, his voice deep with only the slightest touch of a southern accent.

I'm not exactly sure how to respond to his question since we technically have met, but only over email. But he should know that already. He looks blindsided, like I'm a threat to his safety. He's concerned I'm going to try to kidnap his daughter and run away.

It's at this point that I realize the little girl at the table is biting her lip and focusing intently on the paper cup in front of her. She looks just about the right age to spell *honey* with a *u* and two *n*'s.

CHAPTER 2

Jake

A thousand alarms are sounding in my mind. Who is this woman? Why is she standing in front of me, looking at me as if I should know her? She's not a client of mine. I've definitely never met her before. Believe me, I would remember.

She's exactly the sort of woman I usually take one long look at and then mentally enter into my little black book of *DO NOT EVER CONTACT AGAIN*. I'm writing her name inside, shutting the book, wrapping a chain around it, bolting it, and dropping it to the bottom of a lake.

I can tell immediately that this woman would be trouble for me. Gorgeous, tempting trouble.

She's strikingly beautiful. And that immediately puts me on edge, because I just got off the phone with *Strikingly Beautiful*. Last night, *Strikingly Beautiful* was calling from Hawaii to tell me that she won't be able to visit Sam this weekend like she swore she would, because her new Hollywood boyfriend surprised her with a trip to some tropical resort. She said it as if I should be happy for her and her good fortune. I'm not happy for her. I kind of hope that the shark from *Jaws* swallows Natalie up while she's floating on a yellow tube in the ocean.

Fine, maybe not swallow her up—but definitely give her a good scare.

I haven't always been this vengeful. Not sure if that makes it better or worse, but I didn't get to my current level of anger overnight. It took months and months of watching my daughter cry in her bedroom when her mom didn't show up like she said she would, didn't call like she said she would, wasn't there for Sam like she promised she always would be. It's been two years since Natalie left us to move to Hollywood and pursue her dream of becoming an actress, and with each passing month it seems like we're becoming less and less of a thought in her mind.

My sisters are always encouraging me to *get back out there*. But as I look in the eyes of the first woman I've found *strikingly beautiful* since Natalie, I feel the opposite of ready to date again. In fact, I'm terrified at the prospect.

The woman's wide smile falters, and she looks at my daughter, Samantha, with a question in her eyes. This concerns me even more than the fact that I've already memorized the exact shade of green of Evie Jones's eyes.

Mrs. Jones—the woman I know I've never met before this moment—comes to some sort of conclusion, and she looks back up at me. Her smile finds its way to her mouth once again, and my stomach tightens. For one absurd second I consider finding the damn key to my black book and fishing it out of the lake.

"I'm guessing you're not the one who emailed me?" asks Mrs. Jones.

"Emailed you?" I feel like a patient learning he has amnesia. "No, definitely not."

She nods and chews her bottom lip briefly while casting her eyes down at her dog. *Her service dog.* There's a binder tucked under her arm with the words *Southern Service Paws* written across it.

Ah—and now I have it.

Sam has been leaving their pamphlets around our house for weeks. She's been begging me endlessly to let her get a service dog ever since she saw an interview of a woman and her service dog on an episode of *The Wake-up Show.* But I've been firm in my answer of no, and that answer still stands.

How should I proceed here? I'm frustrated that my daughter has evidently gone behind my back and contacted whomever this woman is without my knowledge, but I also know that she's had a hard couple of years with her mom leaving and then being diagnosed with epilepsy. I don't want to pile on by reprimanding her in front of this random woman. At the same time, it's not okay for her to be pulling stunts like this. Ever since she was diagnosed, she's been acting out in strange ways, and I'm not always sure how to handle her.

When I told her Natalie couldn't come into town for her birthday last month because she got the flu (reality: she told me she needed to keep her schedule open for a potential audition she heard through the pipeline *might* come), Sam told me to cancel the whole party. I wasn't going to, but she completely freaked out, crying and yelling that *birthday parties were stupid anyway* and she *didn't even want one.* She's quiet these days too—holing up in her room so much it worries me. She's gone through a lot of difficult change, and I don't know how to help her. I think it might be time to find us a therapist, actually.

I'm in way over my head doing this parenting thing alone. Sam needs her mom. Or rather, she needs a healthy mom, and Natalie hasn't been healthy in a long time. Even before our divorce was finalized, she had slowly started to change into someone I didn't recognize—not engaging with Sam as much and handing basically all parental responsibility over to me. And then she moved out, and now Natalie gives her image on social media more attention than she gives Sam.

The thing is, I'm all for Natalie pursuing her dream of acting. I even understood when she said she didn't love me anymore and wanted a divorce. Yes, it sucked and it hurt like hell, but it wasn't out of left field. We were married so young and didn't grow together over the years—instead, we grew in completely different directions. So, I understood and supported all of that. What I take issue with is how Natalie has made our daughter feel unimportant. How she never makes time for her. How Natalie's dream of making it big has completely taken over her life, leaving a hurting child in her wake. And each time I confront her about it, I'm met with a weak promise to do better next time. Even Sam's diagnosis hasn't seemed to affect Natalie much. It's like she's completely checked out as far as we are concerned, and it breaks my heart for Sam.

I turn to Sam and raise an eyebrow. "Did you email Mrs. Jones?"

"Miss," the woman corrects quickly and then smiles. "It's *Miss* Jones. Evie, actually."

I choose not to dissect exactly why she felt the need to clarify her marital status and instead fix my eyes on my daughter. "Did you email her?"

Sam dodges my gaze and looks down at her hot chocolate. She presses her lips together and then crinkles her nose. That's really not fair. She knows that's her secret weapon to get out of trouble, and she's using it now.

"If I admit to it, am I going to be in trouble?" Sam was born only ten years ago, but I swear she's sixteen.

I refuse to look at Evie. There's no need. I'll be done with her in five minutes, and she'll be on her way, and I'll never think of her and her cute accent again. "How about if you fess up to it now I'll only take away your iPad for one week instead of two?"

Most kids pout right about now. Not Sam.

"Five days and you have a deal." Her brown eyes find mine, and she's Natalie in the flesh. This girl is going to be trouble.

I can hear Miss Jones try to hide a chuckle from beside me, but I still refuse to look at her.

"One week. It was wrong of you to go behind my back, and you know it." I go easy on Sam because, honestly, she's a good kid, and even though she looks tough and rebellious now, she'll cry in her pillow tonight if she thinks she has disappointed me. And even though I'll never admit it to her, I'm impressed that she managed to hack into my email, impersonate me to set up this meeting, and then convince me to take her out for hot chocolate at the agreed meeting place.

I hope she channels this cleverness into curing cancer one day and not robbing banks.

"Okay," says Sam, tucking a lock of her dark-brown hair behind her ear. "I'm sorry."

Sam and I smile at each other for a moment, and I think I've handled this situation well. I don't always come out on top of these parenting moments, but this one feels like a small win.

Miss Jones clears her throat and reminds me that I've still got a loose thread to tie up.

Or cut off.

"I'm sorry to have wasted your morning, Miss Jones. But as you can see, there was a little miscommunication between my daughter and me. I'm sorry for any inconvenience." I'm just about to turn my back to this woman and join Sam at the table when Miss Jones speaks up.

"The morning doesn't have to be a waste. I'm already here, and

I have all my information with me. If you're interested, we could still—"

"I'm not interested," I say, cutting her off with a sharp tone.

I can tell I've startled her, because those glittering green eyes widen and her lips part. I don't want to be a jerk to this woman, but I'm also not in the mood to deal with her or her sunny smile. And definitely not her long legs that I'm refusing to notice. Is she wearing running shoes with a dress? Did she jog here? Never mind. I don't care. Miss Jones needs to go. She represents everything I don't want right now.

"It was nice to meet you, and again, I'm sorry for taking up your morning." There. I said it in a way that was firm but still nice enough that I could be cast in a children's television show where I pull on a red sweater and pretend to like everyone.

I glance at Sam, and she looks so disappointed that it physically hurts me somewhere in my chest. I know she thinks having a service dog is going to solve all her problems, but she's wrong. A dog can't keep her safe. But I can, and I will. I'm not about to step back and let a dog take on the responsibility that is mine. If I've learned anything this year, it's that I can't trust anyone else to love and care for my daughter the way I do. Definitely not an animal.

"Are you sure you don't want to hear just a little bit about the company or our process? I'll even go so far as to mention that no question is too silly." Is she serious with this? I clearly said no.

"In the email, it said that your daughter has epilepsy." Miss Jones's smile grows as if we are talking about a mutual favorite TV show rather than a life-altering disability. It grates on me. She looks down at her dog, and her smile grows more devastating. "This is Charlie. He's been trained as a seizure-assist dog, but he also alerts—"

I hold up my hand to stop her. I'm not proud of how condescending that makes me look, but she's just not taking the hint. I want her to go away. Far, far away from me and my daughter. "I don't think you're understanding, Miss Jones. We don't want to hear about your company or the dog."

"No, *you* don't want to hear about the dog," Sam says under her breath but at a volume that indicates she definitely meant for me to hear it.

I look at Sam and prepare to tell her to watch it because she's already on thin ice when Miss Jones pipes in again. "If Sam is interested, I would really love to tell you about Charlie and how he's—"

Now, here's the thing. I've had a bad week. Nothing has gone right. I've been looking into private schools for Sam to attend in the fall where they can give her more attention than she'd get in her large public school, and she's hated every single one of them that we've toured. She wants to stay with her friends even though I explained to her that it would make me feel more comfortable for her to be somewhere smaller. I've also had to tell her three times that she can't go to Jenna Miller's eleventh birthday party sleepover. Sam stormed up the stairs after her third try, with the words *I hate you* lingering in the air between us.

On top of all this, she had a longer-than-usual seizure last week that scared the hell out of me, and I haven't slept soundly in the past year since she was diagnosed. I can't stomach the thought of her having a seizure in the night and me not knowing about it, so I get out of bed at least fifteen times a night to check on her before I usually just give up and make a pallet on her floor. And the last thing I need to add to my plate is caring for a dog.

Because of all these things, I stand up so fast that my chair scrapes and everyone in the coffee shop turns to watch me be a complete ass to this woman.

"*Stop.* I told you we don't want to hear about your company's dog. I don't know if you're hard up for the cash or what, but you should know that you're coming across as an annoying car sales-man about to get fired if he doesn't meet his quota for the week."

Damn . . . that was bad. I immediately feel remorse.

Miss Jones shifts on her white-sneaker-clad feet, and her dog's ears shoot up. I'm prepared for all sorts of replies from her, includ-ing her siccing her dog on me for being so rude. I'm not, however, prepared for her smirk. "So, I'm a man in this analogy?"

I'm honestly not sure how to respond to that, so I settle for a very mature shrug.

She scoffs and shakes her head. I see pity in her eyes, and I don't like it one bit. Mainly because I deserve it, and I despise feeling like I need anyone's sympathy.

"Good luck to you, Mr. Broaden." She leans in close to me, speaking low in my ear and proving she smells as good as she looks. "You're going to need it when you try to walk out of here with your head shoved so far up your ass."

I'm a statue as I watch Evie Jones and Charlie walk out of the coffee shop, her sundress swaying with her hips, and my daughter's angry gaze burning a hole in the side of my face.

CHAPTER 3

Jake

Sam doesn't speak to me all the way home. Doesn't even take the bait when I ask if she wants to stop by her favorite ice cream shop and get a double scoop. Shawn Mendes's falsetto is blaring over the speakers, and I honestly have no idea how else I can redeem myself in her eyes.

I'm practically screaming *LOVE ME* to my ten-year-old daughter, and she's plugging her tiny little pierced ears, holding all the power.

How did this happen? How did I get here? Shouldn't she be the one begging me for mercy after the stunt she just pulled? Instead, I'm seconds away from offering to clean her room and do her homework for a month. I'm a total schmuck, but I don't care. Sam and I have always had a close relationship. Even before Natalie left, I was the one who Sam gravitated toward. I've always been able to see how brightly I shine in her eyes. But right now, they look dim, and she looks more disappointed in me than ever. I will do anything to see her smile right now.

"I've gotta stop off at the office real quick to pick up a few plans," I tell her as I pull up in front of Broaden Homes. It's my residential architectural firm—as in, I built this little company from the ground up. It's not the biggest firm in town, but it's not the smallest either. I'm doing pretty well for myself, and as I walk through the large light-oak doors of the historic downtown building I renovated and turned into our offices, I feel a shot of pride. Also a bit of longing.

Since I began shouldering the brunt of parenthood and learning a new way of life with Sam's seizures, I haven't been able to devote as much time to the business as I would like. The two other architects I have employed here are working double-time to pick up the slack I keep dropping. But being a single parent in the summertime is hard enough. Add in a newly discovered disability and an endless string of sleepless nights, and you get *nearly impossible*.

"Jake, what are you doing in here today?" asks Hannah, one of my head architects on staff, as she steps out of her office.

It's a smallish building with only three offices for the architects and one large common space for assistants and meetings. But it's beautiful, even if I do say so myself. A wall of windows lines the front of the building, the flooring is made of wide natural plank wood, and a massive fifteen-foot-long oak table for meetings sits in the center of the common space.

"I just wanted to stop in and grab those plans of the Halbert build." *And feel like myself again for a minute.*

Hannah levels me with a look before putting her hands on her hips. "I thought you were giving that project over to Bryan? Also, hi, Sam! It's good to see you, sweetie." She grins at my daughter, who has been brooding behind me but offers a smile to Hannah like it's an intentional jab to my gut.

"I was. I did." I run my hand through my hair, wishing I didn't have to get through a customs checkpoint before making it into my own office. "Last night I thought of a few ideas for the mudroom problem we were having, and I thought I might take a look at the plans again. I think if I move it—"

"That sounds like something *Bryan*—the man you handed the project over to because you were so exhausted you were falling asleep at your desk in the middle of the afternoon—should be worrying about."

I'm mad that she's right. I'm exhausted and stretched thin. It's why I decided to cut back my hours, delegate more projects to Bryan and Hannah, and devote more of my time to Sam this summer. But it's hard. I love my job, and I love giving my brain the opportunity to create. Forcing it to turn off like this feels like I'm cutting off my leg. I don't know how to walk anymore.

"Okay, you're right. Let me just look at those plans really fast, and then I'll be on my way."

Hannah gives me a flat smile that alerts me to what's coming. She steps up to me, puts her hands on my shoulders, and physically turns me toward the door. "Go home, Jake. This is your day off. Let us do our jobs."

I'm letting her push me through the door, but I'm not happy about it. "But you're not doing your job; you're doing *mine*. I don't like it, Hannah. I feel like I'm working you guys into the ground."

"Neither of us have kids or spouses, Jake. We like being worked into the ground by our taskmaster boss. It gives us something to gripe about when we go home to our families at Christmas," she says, pushing even harder now and nodding for Sam to follow us out.

"I'm going, I'm going." There's a good chance Hannah will lock the doors and not let me in again if I don't leave now.

I get back in my truck and look to Sam, waiting for her to smile up at me like she did for Hannah. She doesn't, and it's the most annoying thing in the world to have a ten-year-old give me the silent treatment. I let her, though, because I'm not entirely sure I don't deserve it.

Miss Jones's sweet southern drawl pulls at my memory. *You're going to need it when you try to walk out of here with your head shoved so far up your ass.*

Pulling into the driveway at our house, I click the button to open the garage and notice that my sister June is sitting on the front porch swing zeroed in on her phone, a box of donuts from her bakery on the seat beside her. June owns an iconic donut shop here in Charleston called Darlin' Donuts. She's worked so hard to make that place successful, and it doesn't escape my notice that she still makes time to spend with Sam. She's been a miracle for us, and today I arranged for her to come stay with Sam for a few hours so that I can go to the grocery store and shop in peace. And *wow* that statement makes me feel like the physical manifestation of my mom from twenty years ago.

But I don't know what I would have done without the help of June (and my other three sisters) this past year. At one point in my life, I lamented the fact that I had four of them—all younger than me. Growing up, it was like I was always sneaking into a sorority house, trying not to get noticed as I tiptoed past each of their rooms. It smelled like nail polish. They were either fighting ruthlessly or laughing hysterically. One of them was always stealing the other's stuff, and hell was always breaking loose.

But now that we are all grown adults, living our own lives, I wish they would move in with me and never leave.

June glances up when she sees us approach and smiles wide. But her grin falters when she sees Sam open the truck door and dive out before I've even had a chance to pull into the garage. It's as if I've kidnapped her and she would rather open the door and hurl herself out onto the concrete while driving seventy miles per hour down the interstate than live the rest of her life with me.

Sam's flip-flops slap the ground angrily, and her ponytail swings like a pendulum all the way into the house. She doesn't even look back at me, just slams the door shut behind her.

I wince a little and turn to my baby sister, whose eyes are now as big as saucers.

"What in the world was all that about?" she asks as I make my way up the front steps and join her on the porch swing. She offers me a donut, but I don't feel like eating right now.

"She's mad at me."

June laughs. "Yeah, I gathered that. But why? I've never seen her throw a fit like that. Usually, she just goes quietly and hides in her room." June is the only one of my sisters who isn't married yet, so she's been around this past year more than anyone else.

"Yeah, well. Unfortunately, those outbursts are becoming more normal by the minute. She even slammed her door in my face the other day. Nearly gave me a bloody nose."

"Yikes. So, what are you doing wrong?" she asks with a playful grin.

I know she doesn't mean it seriously, but the comment still stings me somewhere vulnerable. I feel so out of my element lately. I'm quickly approaching the day when Sam will enter puberty, and then I'll have a whole new pile of worries and insecurities on my plate. Right now I'm just obsessed with making sure Sam doesn't have a seizure while she's in the shower, where she could fall and hit her head. In a few years, I'll be worrying about seizures *and* the boy who keeps her out past curfew.

My hands find my face, and I rub my palms over my eyes and all the way up through my hair. "I wish I knew. I'm ninety-nine percent sure I'm failing at this single-parenting thing."

June shifts beside me and puts her hand on my back. "Oh, come on now, it was only a joke. You're doing a great job with Sam." She rubs circles on my back like I've done for her a hundred times. My reply is a halfhearted grunt.

"I'm serious!" She leans in and lays her head against my shoulder. "You're the best dad I know, besides our own. Top-notch, really. I can't think of anyone else in the world who could handle all that you've gone through this year with so much ease."

With so much ease? Last night, after Sam went to bed, I was so angry with how hard life has been that I tore a pillow in half. I'd never felt so powerful and masculine . . . until feathers went flying everywhere, making it look more like a scene from a 1990s slumber party movie.

I shake my head and sit up straight, dragging a deep breath into my lungs. "I feel like I'm losing her, June. She's only ten, but she's gone through so much heartache this year. It's like I can see her physically shutting down. And last night, Natalie called and bailed on her visit again."

June looks pissed. "What was the excuse this time? Another potential audition?"

"I don't think I should tell you."

"I swear, Jake, she better be bedridden with a hundred-and-three-degree fever."

I smirk. "Hawaii with some dude."

June's eyes look feral. She closes them and breathes through her nose to cool her temper. "I don't care how big of a movie star she becomes, that woman doesn't deserve to have a daughter as wonderful as Sam."

And that's the thing: Natalie *is* finding success in Hollywood. In the two years she's been out there, she's already landed a few minor roles in some big projects and has been filling her plate with commercials between auditions. She *is* reaching her dreams. It would be so much easier to be happy for her if she wasn't completely abandoning our child in the process.

June wraps her arm around mine, and we start to swing. "Listen, you've both had a tough couple years. And as much as I want to rip

Natalie's silky brown hair from her head, I want to squeeze you with hugs until you burst. Because I see you continue to show up for Sam time and time again, and it's because of your love and perseverance that I know she'll pull through it all. And eventually, Jake, you'll both figure out how to live with her seizures. I know it. It'll just take some time."

I nod and attempt to swallow the lump in my throat. "I wish there was something I could do to cheer her up, though."

"Well, maybe there is."

"I asked if she wanted to go out for ice cream, but she didn't seem too thrilled by that idea." Apparently, when your dad shuts down your masterful plan to con him into getting you a service dog, and you have to watch him act like a jerk to a perfectly nice stranger, you don't have much of an appetite for bubblegum ice cream.

"Hmm. Maybe there's something I can do with her while you're running errands. Any movies she's been wanting to see?"

"No."

"Does she need any new clothes? I could take her shopping."

"She hasn't been interested in clothes lately."

"Well . . . is there anything else you can think of? Anything she's mentioned lately that she really liked? Or wanted? Anything she's shown interest in that would get her excited about life again?"

I stop our swinging, and my gaze turns toward the house as if I've suddenly developed X-ray vision and can see right through the walls to the stack of pamphlets piled up on the kitchen counter.

The answer has been in front of me all along, but I dislike the idea now just as much as I did yesterday. I'm still holding tight to all the reasons I think getting a service dog is a bad idea, but I'm just desperate enough to see that maybe it's exactly what Sam needs to give her something to look forward to.

But more than anything, I really don't like that I'm about to have to eat a whole truckload of shit.

CHAPTER 4

Evie

"I don't think it's supposed to look like this," I tell Joanna, stepping away from my easel to inspect my work.

She leans around her own masterpiece (literally, it looks like it could hang in a museum somewhere) to look at my sorry painting. Honestly, it looks as if Charlie painted that bowl of fruit. *Not true—* Charlie would have painted a better version. His attention to detail is impeccable.

Six weeks ago, when Joanna announced to me that she was going to be heading into retirement at the start of the new year, she decided that she needed to seek out a fun hobby that could help occupy her time when she was a lady of leisure. Not sure why she felt the need to drag me along on her hobby-seeking adventure, since I'll be the one to absorb all the work she'll be giving up, but I've been along for the ride ever since.

So far, we've taken up power yoga (and then set it right back down), built a raised vegetable garden and planted ten different types of green plants before Jo decided that she didn't like being in the sun so much and wanted an indoor hobby, and took two improv

classes before the guy who never stepped out of his pirate character told me my hair was beautiful and that he'd like to see what it
would look like on one of his dolls at home.

Yeah.

So, when Jo suggested we take up painting in the comfort of her
kitchen while we sip white wine and listen to music, I was all for it.

Joanna scrunches her nose and shakes her head. "I don't know
how it's possible, but I think you might be gettin' worse." I love her
accent. It's thicker than mine because she's from the deep South.
Sweet home Alabama.

I give a short laugh. "No, don't sugarcoat it for me. Be honest
and tell me how you really feel, why don't you?"

Jo flashes me a sassy grin. "Honey, you know I love you more
than a stick of butter. I don't need to lie to you about your artistic
abilities to prove it."

And I do know that she loves me, which is why her honesty
never hurts. It's why I'm laughing at her comment instead of
silently brooding over it like I would if my mom would have made
it. Because if Melony Jones said something like that, it would have
been to show me exactly where I fell short in her eyes. Why I
needed to either hire the best private tutor and spend countless
hours a week perfecting my technique so she could hang the finished product above her mantel for her supper club to *ooh* and *ahh*
over, or hide it away forever, and for heaven's sake, never let anyone
know I have flaws.

By contrast, Jo stands up and fluffs her messy topknot—*seriously,
I want her long, gorgeous white-gray hair*—and tops off my glass of
wine before telling me to paint a line down the center of my orange.

"Then it'll look like a big round butt," she says with a satisfied
smirk. "And that, darlin', will make you laugh every single time you
look at it."

I nearly spit my wine back into my cup. Drinks are never safe with Jo around. There's no telling when she'll say something that makes you shoot it out your nose.

"Where's Gary tonight?" I ask later, after she and I have packed up our canvases and moved to the couch. Her painting is a masterpiece of bright, delectable fruit. Mine, a plump booty covered in an orange spray tan. *I actually wouldn't mind having this peach for an ass.* "And why doesn't he ever get dragged along on these hobby adventures?"

Gary is Joanna's husband, and he is just as likable as she is. He's a sixty-six-year-old journalist who can work from anywhere and loves his job more today than he did the day he started thirty years ago. Joanna and Gary Halstead are just the sort of people to make my mom and dad turn up their noses. *Gracious me, do you mean he had to work for his money?*

The Halsteads moved into the Charleston area about five years ago simply because they'd always wanted to live here. That was when Joanna founded Southern Service Paws. These people are as down to earth as the ground itself.

I aspire to have what Jo and Gary have—the kind of love where a man will still walk into a room and pinch my butt after forty years of marriage. And I know this from witnessing it a few too many times for my liking.

A mischievous glint enters Jo's eyes, and she wags her eyebrows playfully. "Gary's not invited because I don't like to mix my hobbies. And he already participates in a very favorite pastime of mine."

"Ew," I say, dramatically shoving my face into one of her oversized throw pillows.

Suddenly, I'm thirteen, and she's my mom telling me about the birds and the bees. Except the irony is that Mom never actually told me about the birds and the bees. She gave me a book and walked away, because Melony Jones doesn't have personal conversations.

I remove my face from the pillow and toss it at Jo instead.

"Gross. I don't want to know about your nighttime hobbies with Gary!"

She catches the pillow, laughing. I know she takes great amusement in the fact that I turn red easier than if I were on the beach with no sunscreen, because she always, always, *always* takes her inappropriate jokes a step further.

"I never said they are *nighttime* hobbies. Honestly, Evie, where's your creativity? Thinking like that is going to give you the most boring relationship on the planet one day."

La, la, la, not listening.

Don't get me wrong. I love a good inappropriate joke. But from the first day I met Joanna and Gary, they became the parents I never had—meaning, the parents I wish my current parents were. Because of this, I absolutely do not want to hear about my surrogate parents' bedroom endeavors.

I curl up in a ball in the corner of Jo's massive couch and shut my eyes. This day has felt way too long, and now it's catching up to me. "I don't think you're going to have to worry about the creativity in my relationship, because it's starting to look like I'm going to die a lonely old maid. Just me and Charlie forever."

I gaze longingly at Charlie curled up at my feet. There's so much comfort in seeing him resting. If he is resting peacefully, it means I'm safe too—no danger of a seizure.

"He won't live as long as you."

My eyes fly up to Jo, and I take in her smiling face. If I had another pillow, I'd throw it at her.

She laughs. "I'm sorry! I was just trying to lighten your heavy mood."

"By telling me my dog is going to die?!"

She shrugs. "My humor is dark."

I shake my head in a mock reprimand and sink back into my

corner. I wish my couch were this big and comfy, but that tiny love seat was hard enough to fit in my apartment.

"Joking aside, I have no idea how you're still single, Evie. You're gorgeous. Funny. Driven. Leggy."

Epileptic.

"As it turns out, men don't really like to approach a woman with a dog wearing a bright-blue vest with a patch sewn on it that says, *Hi, I'm single, and occasionally I lose consciousness and convulse on the ground.*"

I can see in Jo's eyes that she wants to make a sarcastic joke about the patch reference, but she refrains and instead says, "I wish there were something I could say to make it better. But I know there isn't."

Reason number 12,345 why I love Jo. She's been listening to people living with disabilities for the past five years of running Southern Service Paws, and she knows that sometimes people just need to talk and be heard—not fixed.

"Can we change the subject?" I ask, feeling a little too spent from this day to go down a deep, heartfelt tunnel.

"Sure." She pulls her legs up onto the couch to mirror my position. "Tell me how your meeting went today."

I groan. Maybe I should just go home. Apparently, there is no acceptable topic for me and my "I hate everything" mood tonight. "I wished him good luck trying to walk with his head up his ass."

Jo's mouth falls open, just as I suspected it would. "Gracious, girl! Why'd you say that?"

I screw up my face and then shove it into the collar of my T-shirt to hide. What I said to Mr. Broaden was so unprofessional and a drastic overreaction to what he said. Sure, he was a class-A jerk to me, but I shouldn't have responded the way I did. I should have smiled politely, thanked him for his time, and then gone home and stuck a hundred pins in the voodoo doll I made of him. Instead, I cast a bad light on our company.

"Well, in my defense, he was rude to me first. But still, I shouldn't have said what I did. And definitely not in front of his ten-year-old daughter."

"All right, here's what's going to happen. I'm going to pop some popcorn, and then you're going to start from the beginning."

And that's what I do. I tell her everything. Well, almost everything. I leave out the part about him being ridiculously hot and me replaying the scene in my head a hundred times, except changing the course our conversation took and ending it with us making out in the corner. She doesn't need to know any of that.

When my monologue is finished, Jo laughs and tells me she would have done the same thing. But I don't believe her, because she treats the company like it's her baby. She's helped train more than sixty dogs that have literally changed people's lives—giving them freedom in ways that medicine couldn't. She would never have let one stinging comment from an attractive guy undo her like it did me.

Jacob Broaden struck a nerve inside me. It still hurts.

Before I leave, Joanna and I discuss the plans I made that day for the fundraiser, and then I spend the rest of the night continuing to obsess over that five-minute conversation in the coffee shop. I teeter between being embarrassed of my actions or spitting angry that he would say something like that to me, because:

1) YES, I am hard up for money, and how dare he point that out.
2) Everyone knows that car salesmen are probably the most annoying humans ever, so I take great offense to that comparison.
3) He was right.

I *was* pushy and obnoxious. Not because I was afraid I would be fired if I didn't meet my quota, but because something in me is validated every time I can do something positive in this organization. And that same little something whispers that just maybe one of these days, my parents will see the grand total of people I've helped and finally say, *You know, Evie, I'm glad you took your own path in life. I'm proud of you!*

I pop that dream bubble and move on.

Later that night, after Charlie and I are back in our own little corner of the world, we spend our time curled up on my tiny love seat, watching *Friends* reruns while I eat sherbet out of a mug. I think Charlie has a crush on Rachel, because any time she comes on the screen his ears perk up. *Your ears never perk up for me like that anymore, buddy.*

And then I realize that I'm jealous of the attention my dog is paying a fictional TV character, and I decide I really need to get a life. As if my mom can somehow sense that I am at an all-time low and could possibly be swayed into becoming her mini-me as she's always dreamed, my phone pings.

MOM: Tyler told your dad that he asked you out again for this weekend and you turned him down. When are you going to start taking your life seriously and claim the future you're destined for?

EVIE: What a little tattletale.

Remember the name of my dad's law firm: Jones and Murray Law? Well, Tyler owns the Murray part of that title. He is two years older than me and the son of my dad's best friend (who used to own the company before he decided to retire a few months ago and handed the company down to Tyler). The law firm has been in the hands of our families for the past three generations. This match between Tyler and me has been in the making since our great-grandfathers shook hands on opening day of the firm.

Only families as delusional as Tyler's and mine would expect their children to marry in order to ensure that a business and all its money stays in the proper hands. I think the plan is for us to marry so I can immediately birth a son who they will both leave the entirety of the company to since my dad was never given a son. And not that I'd ever want that damn law firm anyway, but there's no way my dad would ever hand it over to me. He and my mom are of the mindset that a woman's only job is to look pretty, birth babies to take over her husband's empire, and help him close business deals by fluttering her lashes and making his colleagues the best old-fashioned on the planet.

The sad part is, I almost agreed to this life that I never fit in because I felt like I didn't have any other options. I was scared to live alone with epilepsy, and since I didn't have any men busting down my door to marry me (thank goodness), my only option was to agree to my parents' plan for my future.

That is, until I met Joanna and she gave me Charlie. Suddenly, a bright new future rolled out in front of me. One all sparkly and new, where I could live independently and work for my own living doing something I actually enjoyed. And most importantly, one where I didn't have to marry Tyler Murray.

I left home three years ago and moved into my Thumbelina apartment because it was all I could afford, but I didn't care one bit that it was tiny. It was all mine. My parents immediately cut me off in hopes that I'd starve and come running back to them wearing the patent-leather heels Mom has been polishing for me since I was in her womb.

I'd rather eat dirt.

To make sure I didn't have to do either of those things, I found a part-time job where I could work remotely from home, basically importing data for a healthcare company, and the rest of my week was spent working side by side with Jo, molding adorable little puppies into dogs that save lives. It was a monumental day when she told me I could move from volunteer into a paid employee position in the company.

> MOM: Evelyn Grace, why do you insist on being so childish? You are twenty-five years old. It's time you started acting your age and thinking about your future.
>
> *I'm twenty-six, but whatever.*
>
> EVIE: Because I like Froot Loops better than the grown-up cereals. Say hi to Tattletale Tyler for me.

I know she won't like that. Mom hates when I make jokes, especially during a conversation that she thinks should be life-changing for me.

Several minutes go by, and I turn off the TV and brush my teeth before climbing into my full-sized bed. My phone pings again. I groan and roll over to grab it off my bedside table, pulling Charlie in a little closer for the moral support I need before reading whatever biting comment my mom has texted me.

But when I unlock the screen, I'm confused to see a number I don't recognize.

> UNKNOWN NUMBER: Hi, Miss Jones. This is Jacob Broaden. I have no doubt that I am the last person in the world you want to be hearing from right now, but I was hoping we could talk.

I squeal and drop my phone like it's suddenly morphed into a hot coal. *Jacob Broaden is texting me?* Do I want him to be texting me?

Yes. No. Yes. No.

What could he possibly want to talk about? After our encounter this morning, I doubt he's wanting to shoot the breeze.

EVIE: Why? Are you in the market for a used car?

UNKNOWN NUMBER: I see what you did there, and I deserve it. That's actually why I was hoping to apologize in person. What do you say? Will you meet me at Hudson Roasters tomorrow at 9am and help me pull my head out of my ass?

UNKNOWN NUMBER: Was that joke gross?

EVIE: Very.

UNKNOWN NUMBER: I immediately regretted it. Will you meet me?

I'm biting my lip and smiling down at my phone like a fool. Charlie rolls his eyes at me again.

One minute ago, I hated Jacob Broaden and was contemplating adding a pin to a very special spot on his voodoo doll. Now I'm daydreaming of that corner in the coffee shop again. Which is exactly why I should decline his offer and suggest he meet with Joanna instead of me if he is considering getting a service dog from our company.

It makes sense. I mean, my body is breaking out in a flush just remembering his steely blue eyes. But then again, I have firsthand experience with the same disability as his daughter. Who better to advise him than little ol' me? Plus, it would be nice to hear an apology.

For no reason other than I'm a saint and only have the child's heart in mind, I pick up my phone and text him back.

EVIE: I'll meet you. But please try not to bite my head off this time.

UNKNOWN NUMBER: Where would the fun be in promising that?

CHAPTER 5

Jake

Walking into Hudson Roasters, I have the distinct feeling that I'm walking right to my death. I don't know why. It's not rational. I don't suspect Miss Jones is going to pull out a knife and stab me. It's more that I've been putting up walls around myself since the day Natalie left—big, ugly force fields of solitude that keep most women far away—and I'm a little afraid that the one I spent most of the night dreaming about might have a really tall ladder.

I woke up in a sweat the moment her pink lips touched mine. It was ridiculous, and I blame it on my late-night texting with her. I didn't mean to flirt. My only intention was to apologize and request a very professional meeting between the two of us to discuss the potential of purchasing one of her company's dogs. All business. Very buttoned-up.

But the moment I pictured her green woodland eyes, the flirtatious replies rolled off my fingers like it was a newfound superpower. I wanted to make her laugh. *Why?*

Because I'm weak, that's why.

But not today. Today I will be the epitome of professional. I am a neurosurgeon walking into the operating room. I've scrubbed up, gloves are on, scalpel is in hand, and I'm ready to extract only the information I need.

I open the door to the coffee shop and the scent of roasted beans hits my nose. I've already had two cups of coffee today because I woke up at 4:30 A.M. and couldn't go back to sleep after my dream about Ev—Miss Jones, but I still plan to get another because no one likes that guy who shows up to a coffee meeting and then says he already had his coffee that morning.

I fall into line behind a man in a nicely tailored suit and wonder if I should have dressed up too. Maybe it would have aided my efforts of being professional with Evie—*dammit*—Miss Jones!

I'm looking down at my jeans and gray Henley tee when I feel a warm hand on my forearm. I turn and my eyes collide with a woodland forest. "Mr. Broaden, good morning." Miss Jones is all business too. This is good. I'm definitely not wondering if her lips would feel as warm and soft in reality as they did in my dream.

"Miss Jones, thanks for meeting me. Can I get you a coffee?" I notice that she has the same binder from yesterday tucked under her arm. The dog is here again too. Maybe she brought him to give me a demonstration of his skills.

Something different, my eyes note without my approval, is that she's wearing a pair of jeans with a rip on the thigh that shows a sliver of tan skin.

It's fine. I'm fine. Moving on.

"I was actually going to ask you the same thing." I frown at her, and so she adds, "I buy all my potential recipients a coffee during these meetings."

"But did all your potential recipients insult you when you first met?"

She smiles and tucks her blond hair behind her ear. "Oh yes.

You'd be surprised the number of times I've been likened to a man."

I cringe, thinking back to that comment. The reminder that I was horrible to this woman hits me in the chest. "Right. In that case, can I get you a muffin as well?" I aim a smile at her, but when I realize it probably looks flirtatious I wipe it away.

"Chocolate chip, please."

Once we both have our coffees and pastries in hand, we make our way to a table by the window. We sit down, and I note that her dog, Charlie, lies down at her feet without her even having to ask.

I honestly had no idea dogs could be that well-behaved. He's huge. If he wanted to, he could be knocking over tables and swiping all the muffins off the barista's counter, but instead he's nearly invisible. It's impressive the way he tucked himself at her feet, with half his body under the table. I wonder if Miss Jones was the one to train him.

She must see me staring at him, because she smiles down at him. "This is Charlie. He's four years old and a major bed hog."

I'm choosing to pass right over the thought of Miss Jones in a bed.

"Is he a potential dog you would match with my daughter?"

"Only if I meet my sudden unfortunate end today." Her comment is so shocking that my eyebrows shoot up. She laughs and picks at her muffin, taking one small bite—a chocolate-chip-only bite. "Charlie belongs to me, not the company. He's been my personal seizure-assist dog for the last three years." *Did she say seizure-assist dog?* Charlie is *her* service dog? She sees the look on my face and continues, "That's partly why I was determined to speak with you yesterday. I know exactly what it's like to be in your daughter's shoes. Although, I really shouldn't have been so pushy."

Oh, well, great. Now I really am an ass.

"I had no idea," I say, still trying to absorb the information.

She laughs, and the sound trickles down my back. "Of course you didn't. How could you have known when you wouldn't let me say more than three words at a time?" Her smile slants.

I like that she's not letting me off the hook easily. "Yeah. About that. I'm really sorry for the way I treated you. It wasn't like me, and you kind of caught me on a bad day."

"Said every jerk since the beginning of time." Her mouth is still curved in the corner as she pinches off another chocolate chip.

"Is now a good time for me to start groveling?"

"It wouldn't hurt. I'm hoping I can squeeze at least one more muffin out of it."

Are we . . . flirting? And is it my imagination or is she giving me a look that says she's taken off her suit jacket and rolled up her sleeves. *Business forgotten.* I contemplate buying her the whole display case of pastries.

There's not one part of me that likes where my head is at. Miss Jones is capturing my attention like no one has since Natalie. It doesn't feel safe. In fact, this has got to be how a bug feels right before it gets zapped.

I clear my throat after a sip of coffee burns my mouth and nod toward her binder. "I feel like I should be honest with you. I'm not completely sold on the idea of a service dog for Sam yet."

"Okay." She draws out the word like she can sense there's more and doesn't know how to respond yet.

"I just don't want you to get your hopes up that I'm going to purchase a dog since there's only a small chance that I will. Today I'm just hoping to get more information."

She's smiling at me curiously. "Mr. Broaden, this is twice now that you've made a comment implying that I am desperate for you to buy one of my dogs. Why is that?"

I tell myself to not say what I'm thinking, but it doesn't work. "I've seen the average price of one of your dogs. They cost a fortune. I can only imagine that the commission is enough incentive for you to pressure me into buying one." *Wow.* I had no idea I could be any ruder to this woman than I already have been. Turns out, I had more left in the tank than I suspected.

Miss Jones's eyes are surprisingly full of amusement—looking at me like I just ate cat food, thinking it was caviar. She leans forward, resting her elbows on the table as if she's about to tell me a juicy secret.

"Jacob—Can I call you Jacob?" I consider telling her to call me *Jake* but decide against it and just nod. "To continue your metaphor, these dogs are not used cars I'm trying to move off a lot. They are highly trained animals that enhance the quality of—and often save—the lives of those living with disabilities. They do cost a lot of money to purchase, but that's only because it costs an enormous amount to care for a service dog. Not only do we have to pay a breeder, but the extra health tests that a service dog has to undergo are not cheap."

I open my mouth to say something—anything—but she's apparently revoked my talking privileges, because she plows on. "And then there is food, grooming, training equipment, and the teeny-tiny salary that my colleague and I make in order to eat. And if you still don't believe that I'm not making commissions off our dogs, I will be happy to show you my checking account, and you'll be impressed to see that the total is exactly the same as my age."

At this point, I'm wishing I could crawl under the table and disappear.

She still doesn't give me a chance to talk (not that I blame her). "I'm not in this for the money. I train and match dogs with recipients because Charlie gave me an independence and security that I thought I would have to sacrifice when I first started having seizures. I want others to have a chance at that same security."

I know she's telling the truth. I can see it in her eyes. They are like perfect open windows to her soul. Her passion is contagious, and I wish I hadn't made that stupid comment about the price of the dogs. I knew she wasn't making money off them. I think I'm self-sabotaging because I'm scared of how impressed I am by her. Trying to talk myself down from liking her too much or something.

I drag in a deep breath. "I'm not sure how many times I'm allowed to say I'm sorry to someone in a single sitting . . . but I'm going for the record. *I'm sorry.* I didn't mean anything I said a minute ago. I'm just . . . looking for reasons to not get a dog for my daughter."

"Can I ask why you're here, then? What made you text me and schedule another meeting?"

There are two answers to that question. I'll only give her one of them.

"Ever since Samantha was diagnosed with epilepsy about a year ago, she's changed. She used to be so vibrant and outgoing, and now she's closed off. She doesn't smile as much, and she's acting out in ways that seem too grown-up for a ten-year-old."

Miss Jones grins. "Like breaking into your email and impersonating you to get a meeting with a service dog company?"

I smile back and nod. "Like that. And yesterday, when I turned you down for the meeting, Sam wouldn't speak to me all the way home and then slammed the door on me after we got there." I can't believe I'm telling her all this. And the way she never looks away has me wanting to shift in my seat. "Anyway . . . this has been the only thing she's shown any excitement or interest in since learning of her condition, so I thought maybe I should at least hear you out."

Miss Jones holds my gaze. Her eyes narrow slightly, and I wonder what she's seeing. Her head tilts, and some of her hair spills over her shoulder. It's curled in long, loose waves today, and before I can tell my brain to stop it, I wonder if she's curled it for me.

No, dingus, she didn't.

"You're not sleeping, are you?" Her question is so out of left field that my head kicks back.

How does she know that? And why is she asking? I'm curious where she's going with this, so I answer honestly. "No. I wake up every hour almost to go check on her. I wanted her to sleep in my room with me, but she refused. Says my room is too boring."

In a desperate moment early on, I went to the home improvement store and almost bought three cans of bubblegum-colored paint for my walls before I chickened out.

"Does she spend most of her time in her room by herself?" she asks, and I nod, feeling so damn guilty. "And I'm guessing you've probably stopped letting her go to her friends' houses?"

How could she possibly know that? Suddenly, I'm in an interrogation room, and she's just grabbed the light and shined it in my face. It's searingly bright.

"But I still let her invite them over," I say, and there's definitely a defensive edge to my tone.

"But you're a single dad, so I'm guessing that some of the other parents haven't been too excited about that prospect."

Okay, who is this woman? Does she have a crystal ball shoved in her purse somewhere?

I lean forward. "Do you think that's why none of her friends have come over?" I never even considered that could be the reason.

Miss Jones smiles, but I don't feel patronized by it. More like, I feel as if she sees me and understands something. Something that even I don't know yet.

"Most likely, you're not doing anything wrong. What you just described about your daughter's actions is normal in my experience." Her words help me breathe for the first time in a year. "Samantha has had life as she knew it ripped out from under her. Her peace of mind is gone. Her friendships are gone. The small amount of independence she had probably gained from growing up is gone."

Her mom is gone.

"But it doesn't have to be that way," she continues. "I am a perfect example. Charlie has given me the ability to live alone with confidence that if I have a seizure, I'm going to be taken care of. And I know that thought sounds daunting to you right now, and you'd probably like to shrink your daughter and put her in your pocket so you can always watch over her, but believe me, you won't be doing her any favors. She needs freedom. She's not broken, and she can live a full, independent life like her friends with the help of a dog just like Charlie. If you give your daughter back some of her independence, she just might feel like coming out of her shell again."

Shoot. Just like that, Miss Jones becomes *Evie* in my mind.

CHAPTER 6

Evie

I've only seen Jacob and Samantha twice since the day, three weeks ago, that he filled out an application to purchase one of our service dogs. And both times were to introduce Samantha to one of our dogs and see if they were a good fit.

The first dog, Max, I could tell straightaway was not right for Sam. He's an amazing dog and very gentle, but even when Sam was excited and engaging with him, he looked as if he had a show recording on his DVR that he couldn't wait to get home to.

Sam and Jacob both seemed to get a little nervous at that point, thinking a service dog wouldn't work out for her like they had hoped. But I assured them it was normal to not match with a dog right away and that choosing one is a lot like choosing your life partner. You don't always find Mr. or Ms. Forever on the first date.

Or in my case, the second, third, or eighteenth. But I'm getting off topic.

The next option was Daisy. She's basically Charlie's twin, just a little smaller. When I brought her to visit, there was an instant connection. I let Daisy off the leash, and she went right to Sam and laid her head in her lap. It was that magical moment when I saw both human and animal sigh with relief that they had found each other.

It's hard for people who don't need the hope that a service dog can provide to understand the bond between a dog and a person. But as someone who knows firsthand what that feels like, it brings tears to my eyes every time.

And now today is the official start of what we call "training camp." It's a weeklong program where I help Sam and Daisy get comfortable with each other, teaching Sam exactly how to work with and utilize her dog.

I've instructed at least twenty of these training camps over the past three years, but never have I been as nervous as I am now standing outside Jacob Broaden's front door.

He and I have not interacted at all outside of updates concerning Sam's application and scheduling days to meet the dogs. No texts. No phone calls. And he's been all business when we correspond through email.

I had thought that he was flirting with me that night he texted (and a few times over our coffee meeting), but I guess I was wrong about whatever I thought I was picking up on. My antenna must be busted. And now I'm staring at the black front door of his gorgeous, expensive house, and I can see just how wrong I was that he would ever have been interested in me.

I knew from Jacob asking me to meet him and Sam at his office for the last two visits that he is an architect and owns his own firm—Broaden Homes. But this place is the physical representation of just how out of my league this man is. Like, he's playing for the major leagues, and I'm not even on the farm team. I'm in the nosebleeds eating a box of candy that I snuck into the game, just happy to have scored a free ticket from one of my friends.

I may come from a prestigious family with a fortune that could solve the nation's debt crisis, but none of it is *my* money. I'm just Evie. A girl floating from cereal box to cereal box, trying to figure out exactly what it is I want out of life (and also trying to collect all the prizes in those cereal boxes to get that free MP3 download).

I wipe my sweaty palms on the sides of my dress and then ring the doorbell. I'm armed with a service dog on either side of me (Charlie and Daisy), and I'm eager to get going on this day of training. Also really hoping there's going to be some snacks inside. My stomach rumbled loudly on the way over, making my Uber driver look even more uncomfortable than he did when I first got in his car with not one but *two* service dogs.

Why does this woman need two of them?!

While I wait, I assess the large modern swing on the front porch. My mind takes a speedy nosedive, and suddenly I'm sitting on the swing and Jacob is joining me. He's wearing the same Henley from the day in the coffee shop, highlighting the muscles in his shoulders and arms. His grin is playful as he takes a seat beside me, and he says he has wonderful ideas for groveling today, and next thing I know we're making out as the sun is setting behind us.

The door opens, and I jolt as if Jacob might have just caught me kissing him in my imagination.

Dammit. He looks good. Too good. He's wearing a black T-shirt (it fits him so well I'm skeptical that he didn't pay a fortune to have it tailored), brown chinos, and a watch with a leather strap around his wrist. How does this man manage to make wrists look sexy? It's not fair, and I'm worried that I might be drooling.

Nothing about Jacob Broaden screams money. At least not in the way Tyler's ridiculous suits do. But he has this air of confidence that says he should be taken seriously, and it leaves me feeling a little shaky-legged.

"Good to see you, Evie. Come on in."

Now, that is one thing that *has* changed. After our heart-to-heart at the coffee shop, Jacob has stopped calling me by the formal *Miss Jones*. Don't get me wrong, he's still polished and businesslike, but I like to imagine that maybe he sees me as a friend now. Not sure why that gives me hope, because remember, I'm up in the nosebleeds just lucky if my binoculars reach as far as the field.

"Good morning!" I step inside the house, and a choir of angels starts singing around me.

This place is . . . glorious. That's the only word I could possibly use to describe it. It's a big open floor plan with high vaulted ceilings lined with dark wood beams, and from where I stand at the doorway, I can see everything from the living room to the dining room to the kitchen. There are massive windows all around the house, letting in tons of natural light, and, oh look, there's a pool outside too.

I grew up in a mansion with a maid staff, and yet it never gave me the urge to dive onto the plush living room rug and make snow angels the way this house does. Everything is white and light-colored wood with contrasting black-steel trim on the massive windows. It's sophisticated yet homey, and it smells like vanilla and teakwood and something else that I'm realizing is Jacob's natural scent.

I'm really trying to control myself and not dive onto that big gray couch. What I wouldn't give to take a nap nestled into those puffy cushions.

And, *oops,* I apparently said that out loud, because Jacob replies with a grin, "Is there a naptime factored into the schedule every day?"

"There is now that I've seen your couch. I'd even be content on your carpet. It's so plush. . . . How is your carpet this nice?"

"I'm starting to think you actually weren't joking about the nap."

"What made you think I was joking in the first place?" He laughs as I continue running my eyes over every inch of the house that I can see. "Did you design this house?"

"Depends. Do you like it or not?"

"I love it."

He lets out a theatrical sigh of relief. "Then, yes. I did design it."

"I think I could fit twenty of my apartment inside it." I probably didn't need to say that. In fact, I wish I hadn't. It's only going to prove to him what a small fry I am compared to him.

I'm resisting the urge to open my arms wide and turn a full circle in slow motion. That's what living in a five-hundred-square-foot apartment will do to a person.

I turn just in time to catch Jacob's eyes dart up to mine as if he had just been checking out my legs.

It gives me a nice little boost of confidence until he says, "Your shoes . . ."

I look down at my scuffed-up white running shoes, and now I'm a ripe strawberry. "Oh. I'm sorry. Are you a shoes-off house?"

I'm frantically trying to toe out of my sneakers when Jacob's calloused hand lands on my forearm, but then he pulls it away just as quickly. "No, I wasn't insinuating you had to take them off. I was just going to tell you I like them."

I try to will my skin to cool as I meet his gaze. "Oh. Thanks. You'll be seeing a lot of them. I'm not able to drive because of the seizures, and I live close to downtown, so I usually walk most places. Helps to wear tennis shoes."

His expression looks a little too concerned for a conversation about sneakers. He runs a heavy hand through his perfectly mussed hair and puffs out a breath. "That's something I hadn't even thought of yet. Driving. Sam won't be able to drive, will she?"

I shrug, ignoring my sudden urge to wrap my arms around his

middle and tell him everything is going to be okay. And it *will* be okay. They'll find a new normal, and life will go on—just in a new direction.

But for now, it's important for me to be transparent. "Depends. If her medication helps and she goes the state's specified number of months without a seizure, she'll be able to drive. But if she's like me . . . then no."

I can see his mind processing that information, and it immediately triggers my memories of being sixteen and angry at my life too. But you know what? I got through it, and I learned to love my new life. Hopefully, Sam and her dad will too.

I turn around and face the main living area of the house again. Everything is so clean. Surely, a single dad doesn't have time to keep a house this clean all the time. *Unless he isn't single.* There is absolutely no reason why that thought should crush me as much as it does, but I feel as if I've been stuffed inside a trash compactor and it's turning me into a tight little square.

Wanting to escape my unjustified disappointment, I invite myself and the dogs farther into his immaculate house.

Seriously?! Where's he hiding the little knickknacks and doodads that prove they really live here?

I briefly consider lifting up the couch cushions to see if I find any crumbs or loose change living underneath. Would he think it's weird if I open that hall closet and have a little look around? I wonder if his bedroom is on this floor or up the stairs? Does he sleep on a king-sized bed? I think he would have to, otherwise those long legs of his would dangle off the end for the monsters to grab his toes.

"Evie!" Sam's voice breaks from the top of the stairs, and she comes barreling down, all teeth and sparkling brown eyes. She really is adorable. Her face is open and excited today. I remember that feeling well. Hope is in the air.

"Hey there, darlin'!"

For a brief moment I think Sam is going to run right up and hug me, but in the end she doesn't. She lost the courage at the last second.

I glance back at Jacob, and he looks puzzled—as if he is wondering the same thing. His hands are shoved in his pockets. An uncomfortable statue with no intention of ungluing himself from the front door. He's reenacting a BBC movie set in the 1800s where the gentleman is afraid of being caught alone in the room with the lady.

Don't worry, Jacob. You won't be forced to marry me.

Sam eyes me cautiously. "Can—can I pet her?" She glances down at Daisy, whose tail is wagging. Daisy looks as if the only thing she wants out of life is for Sam to wrap her up in a hug.

I know why Sam's nervous. Everyone is at first. They see the big, scary *Do Not Pet* patch on the bright-blue vest and remember me asking them not to pet Charlie on our meeting day. They all worry that they are going to be doing something wrong.

"Of course you can. Daisy isn't just any working dog, she's *your* dog. I want you to pet, snuggle, and play with her as much as you can."

"Really? That's not against the rules?" Her small freckle-dotted nose wrinkles.

I shake my head, trying not to smile too big and make her feel silly for asking. "No. Not against the rules at all. The more you and Daisy bond, the better care she will take of you."

Sam drops down to her knees in front of Daisy and reaches out to pet her. She's cautious at first, running her hand over Daisy's head and neck, and then something snaps in Sam and her restraint disappears. She wraps her tiny little-girl arms around Daisy's neck and shuts her eyes with a peaceful smile. The sight tugs at something deep inside me.

I know that relief.

Suddenly, my back feels hot, and I'm aware of a new presence. Jacob has peeled himself away from the door and is now standing right behind me, watching his daughter over my shoulder. I don't want to look at him. I'm afraid that if I do while standing this close, it'll be like throwing gasoline on that spark of attraction and I'll burst into flames.

Out of my league.

"She looks happy," he whispers close to my ear, doing nothing to help my buzzing nerves.

I cave and turn my head ever so slightly. He's watching Sam with an expression of such raw hope I feel like I could cry. Training camp weeks are always emotional for everyone involved, including me—but this . . . this feels different for some reason. Personal in a way that it shouldn't. Inexplicably, I feel what he's feeling.

"Can my dad pet her too?" Sam's voice is a bucket of water.

"Yep. He sure can. Seizure-assist dogs have to be working twenty-four/seven, and because of that, we want Daisy to be able to just be a dog sometimes too. It's best to not let other people pet her while you're in public because we want her to stay focused on taking care of you. But when you're home, she can definitely enjoy some TLC from your dad and friends."

We spend the next few minutes going over what we will work on that day, and Sam is jumping out of her skin with excitement.

And then Jacob says something that has me halfway falling in love with him.

"Oh, by the way, there are chocolate chip muffins in the kitchen if you're hungry."

CHAPTER 7

Evie

'm running behind. *Great.* Mom's going to love it when I show up to this swanky restaurant in my tennis shoes an entire (*gasp*) five minutes late.

I can picture her now, sitting at the table, tapping her French-manicured nails, apologizing to the waiter for her inconsiderate daughter causing such an inconvenience to him and his fine establishment. As if he really cares that I've delayed their ordering by five minutes. She's also probably given him at least one other example of when I've let her down during my lifetime.

As Charlie and I spring from the Uber and dash into the restaurant, I'm almost willing to bet all twenty-six dollars in my bank account that our waiter knows I turned down *the* Tyler Murray's hand in marriage.

I approach the table just in time to see my mom finishing up a monologue. The waiter looks at me with pity swimming in his eyes. I smile at the poor man who will have to wait on us this evening, because I know that no amount of money will be enough to erase the back-handed compliments my mom will offer our lowly servant tonight.

"Well?" I ask him. "Do you think I should have accepted his proposal or not?"

The waiter presses his lips together in an apologetic smile. *Listen, lady, I just want a good tip tonight.*

"Oh, for heaven's sake, Evelyn Grace, don't be so dramatic."

I turn my eyes to the woman I'm forced to call Mother and suppress my overwhelming desire to laugh. *I'm* dramatic? The very lady who has probably alerted the whole serving staff of this restaurant to the fact that I'm five minutes late is calling *me* dramatic?

"Hi, Mom. Dad." I pull out my chair and sit down, and Charlie takes his rightful place at my feet.

Dad gives me a halfhearted smile that doesn't reach his eyes and grunts, going right back to perusing the menu he has held in front of his face like it's Captain America's shield. He's been to enough of these "family" dinners. He knows how it's going to go down, and he is not excited about it. *That makes two of us, buddy.* I wish I could check out like he has since I was sixteen years old.

Charlie senses my tension. He lies on my feet and keeps glancing up at me.

"I assume you have a good reason for being late to our dinner?" My mom doesn't even wait for my butt to warm the seat before she begins her berating.

"Yep. I sure do." I lift my menu and begin reading. Goodness, I hope they are paying for dinner tonight; otherwise, I'll have to ask for a nice crisp water and a side of free cherries from the bar.

"Do you care to explain what that reason might be?" She's blinking at me so rapidly I consider suggesting some eye drops.

I set down my menu. "I don't think any reason I give you will be good enough in your eyes for my disgraceful tardiness. So, let's just pretend that I had to save a child from a burning building and leave it at that."

This does *not* make Melony happy. Her bright-pink lips are

pressed into a line. "Must you always act as if I'm the devil? Is it really so horrible of me to wish for my daughter to be punctual to an event one of these days?"

Got it. We've started the manipulative portion of the evening. That was quick.

I look to my dad, waiting to see if he's going to perform a miracle and intervene. His menu seems to have only become more engrossing. Stephen King has nothing on this restaurant's list of dinner options.

I sigh, knowing I need to just say what needs to be said to get through this dinner as fast as possible. "I'm sorry I was late. I was across town training a little girl and her new service dog today. It went a little later than I anticipated, and I had to return the dog to her volunteers for the night."

This is the part where a mother should say, *Oh, I'm so proud of you and the amazing work you do, darlin'!*

Not my mom. She looks bored to tears. "You wouldn't have to be doing all this silly work if you would just take Tyler up on his offer."

Silly work? I dig my fingernails into my palms to keep from crying at the table. "I can't believe we are still having this conversation. I'm not going to marry Tyler, Mom. You'll just have to find some other way to secure the family business, because I don't care to sacrifice my happiness for it."

"Again. So dramatic. Tyler would make you plenty happy."

"How? By parading me around on his arm at cocktail party after cocktail party for the rest of my life?"

She's giving me a look that says she sees no issues with that scenario. Of course she doesn't. We couldn't be less alike if I were an alien freshly beamed down from space.

"Your dad parades me around on his arm, and I happen to love it."

"Well, I'm glad for you, Mom. But I'm not the same woman as you."

She rolls her eyes. "Of course you are. You're a Jones just like the rest of us. Sooner or later, you'll get bored with this independent kick you're on and come to your senses. I just hope that Tyler still wants you when you finally wise up."

I want to scream. I want to stand up and shout a battle cry. Maybe then she would finally hear my voice over the crazy ones talking in her head. "This is not a kick, Mom. This is my life, and you need to get used to it. I don't want your money. Or Tyler's money. And I sure as hell don't want to spend the rest of my life having to pretend I don't see it when he grabs a cocktail waitress's rear end."

"Evelyn Grace, what a terrible thing to say about a man. Now, stop talking about Tyler like that before he overhears you."

I frown. "What do you mean *'before he overhears me'*?"

I look around, afraid that I'll find Tyler standing right behind me. Not because I'm afraid of him overhearing me say I think he would be a no-good, cheating husband (I'll say that to his face), but because I don't want to have to spend any amount of time with him. Ever.

"Quit craning your neck like that. It makes you look like a giraffe hunting for leaves. Tyler is running late too, but you want to look your best when he arrives."

"What?! You invited him tonight?!"

"Shhh. Lower your voice, young lady. We thought it would be a nice reunion for you two since you won't spend any time with him. I can't believe you haven't even seen him since he moved back to town. Really, Evie, we raised you to have better manners than that."

I am so angry my head might pop off my body. I push my chair back and shoot to my feet. Charlie does the same. He gives me the look that says, *Let's do this, girl. I've got your back.*

He was at my feet during my weekly hour with my therapist; he knows I have her approval to leave when Mom starts putting me down. "I cannot believe you went behind my back and invited him here. Actually, no. I can believe it." I shake my head. "I'm leaving. And until you can start learning to respect my boundaries concerning Tyler and me, our family get-togethers are over."

This is the scene in every movie where the mom realizes the error of her ways. My mom's mouth should fall open, and she should reach out to grab my hand to keep me at the table. She should apologize and tell me all she wants is for us to have a good relationship.

Nope. Maybe when hell freezes over.

Mom just sits back in her chair and lifts her brows in a taunting expression. "You're being childish again." That line should sting. It doesn't. She's used it too many times to count, so it just rolls right off my back. Or maybe it rolls right off my long giraffe neck.

I gather my purse and push my chair in to the table, not even bothering to reply to her. The brick wall outside would be more likely to understand my reasoning than my mom.

"Evelyn."

I hesitate and angle back toward the table. A false hope blooms in my chest that maybe she wants to make amends. How ignorant of me.

She continues, "And just what am I supposed to tell Tyler when he gets here to see you?" I stare at her, my mouth falling open a little. This woman is unbelievable.

"Tell him if he had been on time, he would have been able to watch my butt walk away himself." I shouldn't be the only one scolded for being late. But I know he'll get off scot-free because he's precious Tyler Murray. If we were to marry one day and he cheated on me, Mom would say it was because I wasn't giving him enough of what he needed.

Dad lowers his menu slightly to peek at me over the top. "That was a little too crude for my taste, Evie."

Okay. Where is that nice waiter? I need to find him and ask him to hold me back before I jump over this table and fistfight my parents. I've never been one to resort to violence to solve a problem, but it's never too late to start.

I turn around and raise a lackluster hand over my shoulder. "Have a lovely evening, you two," I say in a bland tone that conveys that I mean absolutely none of it.

On my way out, I notice our trusty waiter headed toward my parents' table with two drinks—the only two drinks my parents have ever ordered in the history of their lives: a glass of champagne and an old-fashioned.

I step into the waiter's path, looking like I'm a gunslinger from the Wild West. I wish I were wearing cowboy boots with spurs on the back so they could clink as I move. "Whoa, there. Are these going to the table I was just sitting at?"

I must have wild eyes, because the waiter nods skeptically. He *should* be skeptical.

I give him my best John Wayne smile before I take my mom's champagne off the tray and down it like I'm a college frat boy with major insecurity issues and something to prove.

After the bubbles have sufficiently burned my throat and threatened to come out my nose, I wipe my mouth with the back of my hand and charge out of the restaurant, just hoping to high heaven that I don't bump into Tyler.

Here's the problem with not having a car or a license. When you pull an epic move like storming out of a restaurant and drinking your mom's champagne on your way out the door, you're then forced to sit on the sidewalk with your service dog and find a ride home before you have to encounter the man you're avoiding. Not to mention the major buzz that's setting in because I forgot I hadn't eaten much since the muffins at the Broadens' house this morning.

I'm quickly scrolling through my phone, hoping to find that an Uber is only one street over and can pick me up, like, two minutes ago, but instead I'm met with a disappointing twenty-minute wait. *That won't do.*

I feel pathetic, small, and broken—basically, what I like to call the Melony Jones special—and I want more than anything to get in a car of my own and peel out of that restaurant parking lot, leaving glorious black tire streaks in my wake.

I dial the next best thing: *Joanna,* who will probably peel out just to make me smile.

She answers my call with, "It's going that well, huh?" She knew that I was having dinner with my parents tonight.

"Can you come get me?" Suddenly, I'm twelve years old at summer camp, and I want to go home because the popular girls are picking on me.

I hear some shuffling on the other end of the line followed by the sound of keys jingling. "On my way; just drop me a pin with your location."

I don't mean to cry. I really don't. But the fact that Jo knows nothing about the situation and is likely in the middle of dinner with Gary, and she stops everything to come to my rescue, does me in. She acts like my best friend, my sister, my mom, and my grandma all rolled up in one. Although, I would never liken her to my grandma to her face because, *hello,* I don't have a death wish.

I hear the sound of a garage door opening, followed by the closing of her car door, just before I notice a truck pull up and stop. The restaurant is on the main street, and the only vehicles that stop out front are either dropping someone off or picking someone up. Just then, the truck's reverse lights come on, and I realize it's backing up to stop right in front of me.

I might have been concerned that someone is clearly going out of their way to kidnap and murder me, but I think I'm a little too dizzy and buzzed to care. Instead, I openly inspect the lifted dark-gray truck and blacked-out wheels. The windows are so tinted that I can't see inside. It's not a bad truck to have to be abducted in.

Charlie's ears perk up when the window starts to slowly roll down.

"Evie?" says Joanna. "Where should I head to?"

"Hang on," I whisper, wishing that window would roll a little faster. "I think I'm being kidnapped."

"What?!"

"Shhh."

The window finishes its descent, and I peer inside the dark interior, not yet certain who my captor will be. A male voice calls out. "Evie?"

Imagine my surprise when the driver leans toward the passenger window, and I'm finally able to see the face of Jacob Broaden and his bright-blue eyes staring back at me. "Are you waiting for a ride?"

Of course he would drive a truck that only makes him look hotter. Of course he would. I wish he drove a minivan with an ugly stick-figure bumper sticker of him and his daughter wearing mouse-ear hats.

"Who is that?" Jo practically yells in my ear.

I pull my phone away with a wince, fairly certain I will never fully regain my hearing from that, and ignore her. "I—well, sort of. I was just in the middle of finding one."

"Lie!" Joanna shouts again. "You already found a ride, remember? Why are you lying to this man?"

"Shhh," I hiss at Joanna.

She makes a valid point, though. Why am I acting like I don't already have a ride?

"Hop in. Sam and I were just headed to dinner, but I can drop you off wherever you need to go first."

Hop in? Well, that's an idea. One that I should firmly decline. It wouldn't be good for me to get in that man's truck. I already have the teeniest bit of a crush on him (read: massive crush), and I know that nothing good can come of riding with him too.

All morning, I caught myself glancing at him when I should have been paying attention to Sam and Daisy. It didn't matter, though. He didn't catch my glances because he seemed to barely realize I existed. He hovered on the outskirts of the room, only participating when instructed. But even then, his attention was mostly zeroed in on his daughter and Daisy, which only made my attraction to him deepen.

He might have been flirting with me over those first few texts, but now he has made it perfectly clear that he is not interested in me. And why would he be? He's not old by any means, but he's definitely older than me. He's thirty-three to my twenty-six. (Of course I studied his age when I photocopied his driver's license for paperwork.) He has a daughter and a tidy, established life; meanwhile, I live in a disorganized matchbox and my life is mostly chaos. *It's fine, though.* I'm not interested in him either. And I almost mean that.

"Oh, that's okay! I'm good to catch a ride with my friend across town. You guys go on to dinner." My smile is all stars and butterflies, but inside I feel a little tremble. Why? Do I hope he fights for me? Or do I hope he drives off?

I am a human seesaw. Up and down I go. *Take me with you. Leave me be.*

"Who is this guy?" Joanna reminds me that she's still glued to my ear. "He sounds sexy." *You have no idea.*

"Come with us, Evie!" Sam bellows from the back seat.

I want to step closer so I can see her, but I know that's a bad idea too. I need to keep my butt over here, far away from this family that I can very well see myself growing attached to when I shouldn't. I'm already going to be spending every day this week with them; I don't need to heap more coals onto the already blazing fire.

"Come on," Jacob says with a cool-guy wave. His other hand is draped over the steering wheel, and he looks so effortlessly sexy. "Don't make your friend come all this way. We're happy to drive you."

His persistence is throwing me off. Just when I think I understand what's happening with him, he turns the tables. Earlier today, he was Mr. I-Don't-Care-About-You, and now I could almost swear I see a hopefulness in his eyes.

"Well . . ." I glance around and remember that Tyler will show up at any moment. I really don't want to be here when that happens.

"For Pete's sake, go with the hot man!" Joanna says, and I hear her garage closing again. What a pusher. "I'm officially retracting my offer to come pick you up."

I turn my back briefly to Jacob and Sam and cup my hand around the phone like I've seen people do in the movies. Apparently, this keeps anyone else from hearing what I'm saying. "Are you sure? I don't know if it's such a good idea." I haven't told Jo yet about my teeny-tiny, almost nonexistent attraction to Jacob.

"If he's half as cute as he sounds, I'd say it's a fantastic idea. And besides, you need more friends under the age of sixty. Honey, it's about time I kick you out of the nest. Fly, little Evie birdie, fly!"

I roll my eyes as she ends the call. I never get to end it first. One of these days, I'm going to end it mid-conversation just to throw her.

I turn around with a tense smile. "Well, my ride just bailed on me, so I think I have to take you up on your offer."

CHAPTER 8

Jake

How am I doing in my attempt to keep Evie Jones at bay? Not great, considering she's sitting in my passenger seat right now. I nearly ramped the curb when I saw her standing there with Charlie. She looked sad and concerned with her phone pressed to her ear. I threw the truck in park and almost sprang from my seat before I mentally grabbed myself by the collar and shook some sense into my sorry ass.

"How are you?" I ask after Evie puts Charlie in the back seat with Sam and buckles herself into the passenger seat.

This is ridiculous. I'm ridiculous. I saw this woman not even four hours ago, and I'm already feeling needy to know how she is? What she's been doing since she left our house? Why she looks so sad?

"Fine." She gives me the universal female answer for *everything is horrible,* but I resist asking any further questions, because I'm not her boyfriend. Never going to be.

Next time I date, it will be someone who doesn't take my breath away and definitely not someone seven years younger than me. (She told Sam her age. I was eavesdropping.)

"Thanks for giving me a ride." Evie crosses her legs.

"Happy to." And I am. Actually, I'm far too happy to have her seated beside me. "Where am I headed?"

"Oh, here, I can type my address into your phone." Her emerald eyes, along with her soft vanilla scent, hit me for the first time since she got in the truck. She's saying normal words, and her tone is completely casual. And yet, my heart is racing as if she just whispered something dirty in my ear.

I hand my phone over to her, and once she's done typing in her address, we set out toward her apartment. Because I have no idea how to talk to this woman without accidentally flirting, I do the same thing I've been practicing all day in her company: keep my mouth shut. I also squeeze the steering wheel, because out of the corner of my eye I can see an impressive amount of her tan legs, and I swear to myself that I will not give in and look at them.

I will not.

After a minute of silence, Evie adjusts in her seat to turn around and look at Sam. I'm not sure why this takes me by surprise. "What do you think about your first day of training with Daisy?"

Man, I like her southern accent. I grew up here. I'm used to women all around me having accents. Hers is different, though. It's sweeter somehow. Drenched in honey.

"It was great. I wish she could have stayed with me tonight," says Sam.

"I know. It's sad to have to say goodbye to them at night, isn't it? But until you've learned everything you need to know about how to interact with her, it's better to let her sleep at her volunteer's house. But you did so great today. I was really impressed with how quickly you caught on to all the techniques."

I catch Sam's eye in the rearview mirror and see the moment

Evie's praise hits her bloodstream. She wants to smile. She wants to soak every ounce of that compliment up, wring it out, then soak it up again. Other than my sisters, she hasn't had a woman offer her praise like that since Natalie left. I feel as if I can see the void inside her and watch Evie's words fill a small part of it.

"Thanks." Sam pushes away her unruly hair, which I have a hard time brushing behind her ear, and looks out the window. Only when her head is fully turned do I see the slight grin touch the corner of her mouth.

I'm torn. On the one hand, I want Sam to receive the praise she needs. But on the other hand, I'm scared to death of Evie. After this week she'll be gone, and it'll be just me and Sam again.

Evie turns back to the front, and I hear her take in a deep breath through her nose. She lets it out like it's the first one she's taken all day.

"How was your dinner?" I ask, proud that it sounded innocuous enough. Polite. Business talk between two colleagues.

"Dinner?" she asks with a furrowed brow.

"Yeah, weren't you just leaving that restaurant? I assumed you had eaten there."

"Oh." She looks down at her lap. "I was supposed to, but . . . my company wasn't so great, so I left before eating."

My eyes slice to her, and my mouth goes rogue. "Was the guy a jerk to you?" I have no idea why I said that. I don't even know if she was there with a guy.

One minute I'm driving Miss Daisy, and the next I'm a psycho-jealous boyfriend, fighting some random jackass in a bar because he looked at my girl wrong. I've never been that guy before. Not even with Natalie, and part of me wonders if we ever really loved each other.

I think Evie finds my comment amusing. She relaxes in her seat, and I can tell she's fighting a grin by the way she's biting her lips together. "I was actually having dinner with my parents. But someone was . . . never mind. It's a long story."

My grip on the wheel relaxes. I see Evie's fingers (and bright-yellow nails) creep toward the release button for the center console. For a second, I think she is going to open it and look inside, but she catches me looking at her hand and pulls it away. All day, I caught her peeking around corners of the house when she thought I wasn't looking. I think I even heard her open a cupboard in the guest bathroom at one point. She wouldn't have found anything fun in there. I keep all my personal items in my bathroom.

Maybe I should find it creepy that she was searching my house. I don't. Actually, it makes me smile, because I know she's as curious about me as I am about her—even though I really shouldn't be and need to put her out of my head.

Speaking of curiosity, I want to ask her more about her parents and this mysterious *someone* she stopped talking about, but Sam chimes in from the back seat before I get the chance.

"If you haven't eaten, you could come with Dad and me to dinner."

I try to flash Sam a look in the rearview mirror that says *no she absolutely cannot!*

Evie is not coming with us to dinner. I can't handle any more hours with this beautiful woman. After spending the first half of the day together, I feel like I've been staring at the sun. I shut my eyes, and the image of her face is burned there. I might never see properly again.

Also, she made Sam laugh ten times today. Ten. I kept a tally.

Yeah, Evie's not the only one being creepy.

I realize belatedly that Evie saw me give Sam that look. I try to play it off and smile at Evie, but she just chuckles like she's giving me the middle finger in her head. She thinks I don't like her all that much, and although it's kind of torturing me, I'm also okay with her thinking that, because I've been working hard to give her that impression all day.

"Thanks for the offer, Sam, but I'm actually pretty tired, and I think I heard Charlie's stomach growl earlier. I should get home and feed him."

"You sure? You're welcome to join us." I'm all politeness now that I know I'm in no danger of her accepting.

She makes a guttural noise that says she knows what I'm doing. I glance up at her in time to see her lips mouth *liar liar, pants on fire*. She smirks and turns her face to look out the side window. I like that she never lets me get away with my rudeness.

Five minutes later we are pulling up outside a classic Charleston-style tall and skinny house in the center of town. It's not bad. A little old and outdated, but it looks like a pretty nice place, all in all. I wonder what it looks like inside. Does she have colorful throw pillows sprinkled around the living room? Is she organized or messy? Somehow, I instinctively know that she's messy. Evie just seems like the sort of woman to kick off her shoes haphazardly as she walks into her apartment and drop her purse somewhere random that she'll forget by the morning. I definitely have her pegged as an "unfasten her bra, pull it out her sleeve, and toss it over the back of a couch before she's even made it fully into the house" kind of person. I've seen a few women do that move and it's always impressive to me.

I really want to walk her to her door and find out if I'm right.

Seeing me inspect her place, she says, "This isn't my house. I rent out their detached studio apartment around back."

Oh. Now I'm even more curious.

She gathers her purse and slings it over her shoulder. I notice that her hair gets caught under the strap, and before I realize what I'm doing, I gently lift her purse and pull her hair free. Evie's eyes widen, and I drop her lock of hair quickly, turn, and practically barrel out my door. My face is flaming because I just touched her hair like I've known her forever, and . . . *wait*, why am I getting out of my truck? What am I supposed to do once Evie comes around to this side of it? Do we hug? *Definitely not.* Do we shake hands? *That would be strange.* I feel like a teenage boy who has no idea how to act around a woman. This is awful.

I hear Sam call out a goodbye from the back seat and watch Evie wave when she and Charlie round the truck. If I'm not mistaken, she gives my truck one appreciative glance before meeting my eyes. *What would I do if she gave me that same look?* I'm officially losing it.

"Well"—she squeezes that damn purse strap again—"thanks for the ride. Should I Venmo you some money for gas?"

I shake my head and stuff my hands in my pockets. "Definitely not. Glad to help out."

She's fidgeting, awkward, and won't make eye contact with me. Charlie's eyes are very judgmental. Maybe she thinks I don't like her after that look she intercepted in the truck. Maybe that's for the best. "Okay. Well . . . I'll see you two tomorrow, then."

"Right. Yeah. Sounds good." I try to think of any way to stall. To spend just a few more seconds with Evie Jones and her beautiful green eyes that I should *not* be staring at. "Unless . . ."

"Unless?" Her tone shoots up.

I shift on my feet. "Unless you need me to walk you to your door?"

"Oh . . . *no,*" she says, tone lowering back down. "I mean, I'm good. It's well lit back there and safe. Thank you, though. Enjoy your night."

I wish she would smile at me—just want one for the road. She looks over my shoulder toward Sam's window, and then her face lights up with the smile I want aimed at me, but when she looks back it falls away. *None for you, jerk*. I get an awkward wave instead, and then she and Charlie disappear around the house.

When I'm back in the truck and buckling up, Sam says, "She saw you make that face, you know."

I sigh. "I know."

"Why didn't you want her to come to dinner?"

At least a hundred answers fly through my mind, but I can't tell my ten-year-old daughter any of them. "Because . . . I didn't want her to feel uncomfortable having to eat with us."

"I think she would have liked to come."

I flip my turn signal and move into traffic, pretending not to be overly curious about Sam's statement. "Oh yeah? Why do you think that?"

"Because she peeks at you as much as you peek at her."

Never mind that her statement makes me sound like a massive creeper . . .

I look at Sam in the rearview mirror and see her satisfied smirk. "We're just friends, kiddo. There's nothing else between Evie and me."

"Well then, you should have made her come with us. Friends eat dinner together."

The problem is, I don't want to be friends with Evie. I want to take her on a date, and run my hands through her long hair, and find out if her lips feel as soft as they look.

CHAPTER 9

Evie

This morning, I'm sitting at the venue Jo and I booked for the fundraiser benefit, waiting for the caterer to meet me so we can review the menu before I head over to Jake's house for training, when my phone buzzes.

> JO: You need to go shopping.
> EVIE: Because you hate my clothes?
> JO: Because you need a new dress for the benefit. Something short and black.
> EVIE: I was thinking I would wear my silver one again.
> JO: Exactly. That dress has seen better days. You need to go shopping. Let's go Friday.

Ugh. I hate that Jo is right. That silver dress is the last connection I have to my old life. I'm pretty sure when Mom bought me that dress, it cost more than my entire current wardrobe combined. But just because it was expensive back then doesn't mean it still looks expensive now—unless peplum dresses that have shrunk a few too many sizes in the dryer have suddenly come back in style.

> EVIE: Fine. You win. I'll buy a new dress. But it has to be from somewhere that I can use a 20% off coupon.
>
> JO: No way, missy. You haven't let me buy you anything all year. This is my treat.

That's true too. Jo is always trying to buy me things, but I don't let her. I can't exactly be a pioneer, forging my own path in life, if I'm constantly letting someone go in front of me and whack down all the weeds. I have to do it. I have to get my hands dirty.

But since the fundraiser is really important for our company, and I have invited quite an impressive list of people that I'm hoping will give us loads of money, I decide to give in this once and let her spoil me.

> EVIE: If I let you buy me a dress, does that mean I have to let you pick it too? Because anytime you dress me, I end up looking less like a lady and more like a lady of the night.
>
> JO: *Pretty Woman* GIF*
>
> EVIE: Does that mean yes?
>
> JO: *Another *Pretty Woman* GIF*
>
> EVIE: You're hopeless.
>
> JO: And you're more prudish than my grandma Sue.
>
> EVIE: I love you.
>
> JO: I love you too.

I hear the door to the venue open, and I look up with a grin on my face that immediately falls away at the sight of my caterer walking beside my mom, as buddy-buddy as I've ever seen two people.

They are laughing about something, and Mom gives the caterer a playful smack across the arm. "Monica, you're so bad. I had no idea that you were capable of being so conniving."

The woman beams at Mom. "That's only because you've never harassed my servers and then tried to get out of paying me for my services."

What in the actual hell is my mom doing here with my caterer?

I don't even bother trying to hide the scowl on my face as I stand. "Mom, what are you doing here?"

"Now, is that any way to greet your mother?" She's smiling like she does when she's trying to fool everyone around us into thinking we're a happy, do-anything-for-each-other family. We're not. And I'm so done pretending.

I cross my arms. "How do you two know each other?"

Poor Monica sees my face and starts looking worried. She backs up a small step to let my mother take the lead. "Did you not know? I've been using Monica's catering company for years. She provides the most delicious food for all of the Powder Society's functions."

I want to groan. Of course I picked the one caterer in town who is tied to Melony Jones.

"I think it's safe to say that I did *not* know that." *Or else I would not have used her.* "But how did you know we were meeting today?"

Mom smiles a syrupy-sweet smile at Monica over her shoulder. "Will you give us a minute, Mon?" Mon! Bleh. Excuse me while I go fire my caterer immediately.

Monica leaves my mom and me alone together. I spot the fire alarm only a few feet away, and I consider pulling it.

"Now, Evelyn Grace, can you please try, for one moment, to not treat me like some sort of almighty tormenter in front of my caterer?"

"*My* caterer! She's my caterer today! I'm just trying to figure out what the hell you're doing here." I'm as close as cat's breath to purposely spilling my coffee all over my mom's pink linen dress.

She sticks her nose in the air a little higher. "If you must know, Monica and I were together yesterday, discussing the menu for an upcoming Powder Society meeting, and she mentioned that she was meeting with a client today by the name of Jones and wondered if I was related to an Evie." Oh, yeah . . . Monica's got to go. "I told her you were my daughter, and she mentioned your fundraiser. Imagine my embarrassment when I had to pretend like I knew what she was talking about! My own daughter not inviting me to a fundraiser she is hosting!" She's shaking her head, and that pity card she's trying to fly in front of my face is looking pretty flimsy these days.

"Mom, you have made it perfectly clear that you do not support my decision to work for Southern Service Paws. So, excuse me if I didn't think it would interest you to be invited."

"We are the Joneses, Evelyn Grace! We go to every fundraiser in town. Imagine how it would look if word got out that I wasn't even invited to my own daughter's event?"

And this, ladies and gentlemen, is the mother that raised me. She is putting up a big fight, not because she's hurt that I didn't want her at the fundraiser but because she's afraid of what people would think. This is so classic Melony Jones. It's how she's acted every single day of my life.

Maybe I should move to a new town. Somewhere far away where the Jones name means nothing.

But I relent because I don't have the time to go eighteen rounds with her. "Fine, Mom. Consider this your official invitation. It's on the—"

Mom holds up her hand and then starts rifling through her purse. "Don't bother. I already have all the details on this *laser-printed* invitation I took off Deborah's fridge." She levels me with a frosty scowl. "Because *Deborah* and her family received one."

I knew she would mention something about the printing. Mom is the queen of event planning. She would rather saw off her arm to pay for the finest engraved linen invitations than have to settle for mere laser printing.

I gesture toward the invite. "So, apparently you didn't have to do too much acting when Monica told you about the event since you had already stolen that invitation from one of your friends. Remind me, do they teach theft in cotillion? It's been so long I don't remember."

Mom's eyes narrow dangerously. "That's enough sass from you, young lady. Like it or not, your dad and I will be at the benefit." She tucks her stolen invite back into her Coach purse.

She turns away and swings her hips as she walks toward the door, and without looking back, she gets one final punch in. "By the way, I already talked with Monica, and the drumsticks you originally ordered will never work for a black-tie event. I had her change the menu to salmon and chicken cutlets. If you want people to give like millionaires, don't expect them to eat with their fingers like cavemen."

I'm looking around for something I can throw at this woman, but because of my own bad luck, there's nothing nearby.

She pauses with her hand on the door. "Oh, and I expect you to send a proper invitation to Tyler and his parents."

"Sure. I'll get right on that as soon as pigs fly."

Mom swivels her lazy frown back at me. "Don't act like a back-woods bumpkin. This is proof you've been spending too much time with that Joanna woman."

I watch her disappear through the door and hear her chuckle with Monica on the other side of it. I wonder if this is how the rest of my life is going to be. Will I ever be outside of my mom's reach in this town? Is there anyone who works within the state of South Carolina who hasn't worked for Melony Jones in some fashion?

Southern Service Paws is usually my safe haven, but now it feels like Mom has wiggled her way in the back door somehow.

I despise the idea of accepting my parents' money or using their name in any way, but I do know that if word spreads around town that they are attending the benefit, all the other elitists will come too. No one wants to be the couple who didn't attend the same event as Melony and Harold Jones. And likely, if they see my mom offering up a check, the money will pour in like manna from heaven. Now that I think about it, it was selfish of me not to invite them in the first place.

For the sake of the company, I can lay down my pride long enough to add my parents' names to the guest list. But under no circumstances will I be adding Tyler Murray's name. I'll never be that selfless.

I pick up my phone and find that Joanna has texted me again. Just seeing her name on the screen helps my shoulders relax and my breathing to stabilize. She has given me a place in this world that I never expected to have; the least I can do is help the company she loves thrive.

JO: After we find you a dress, we need to find you a date.

EVIE: I have one. I need to buy Charlie a tux, though.

JO: I was thinking more along the lines of that sexy dad that gave you a ride home last night.

EVIE: You've never even seen him.

JO: I don't have to. When a man has a timbre to his voice like his, he has no choice but to be sexy. Bring him!

EVIE: No. He doesn't like me. Besides, shouldn't you be discouraging any fraternization between me and our clients?

JO: We're not a PR team for a presidential candidate. Fraternize
   all night if you want:)

Shoot. I was really hoping she would ban any thoughts of making out or otherwise with Jacob Broaden. It would be easier to
swallow his rejection if I knew I couldn't have him even if he *did*
like me.

CHAPTER 10

Evie

I sling my purse over my shoulder and gather Charlie's leash. It's been a long day of training at Sam's house, and she's done amazing. She's picked up the techniques so quickly that I'm considering asking her to drop out of elementary school and come work for me as a trainer.

Sam approaches me slowly as I gather my things, her bare toes scuffing the plush rug. She's after something. She glances toward the kitchen where Jacob disappeared a moment ago and then back to me.

"Spill it," I tell her when she works up the nerve to meet my eyes.

She smiles—something she's started doing more and more over the past two days—and asks, "Do you think . . . well . . . there's this birthday slumber party at one of my friends' house coming up . . ."

"Mm-hmm," I say, setting my purse down and giving Sam my full attention. "Go on."

"Do you think Daisy will be ready by then to go with me . . . you know . . . if I can convince my dad?"

"I don't see why not. I think you and Daisy are bonding quickly."
And that's the truth. I've been impressed with how attentive Daisy
has been to Sam. Anytime Sam simulates a seizure, Daisy has
snapped into action immediately, rolling Sam onto her side and
going to alert Jacob before returning to Sam's side and licking her
face until the "seizure" subsides.

"Oh, great." Sam doesn't look relieved, though. This conversation wasn't really about asking if Daisy will be ready or not.

"Are you sure that's all you wanted to talk about?"

"No." Sam gives me a crooked grin that has seriously started to
melt my heart.

I learned yesterday morning when I asked Jacob in private if
Sam's mom could come around sometime during the next week to
get acclimated with Daisy that she apparently left a couple years
ago. The way he made it sound, and how rigid his shoulders went
while saying it, I got the impression that his ex-wife is gone and
there's little chance of her coming back. Of course I wanted to ask
a million questions, but I didn't feel that it would be welcome, so I
just quickly moved on to another topic (but spent the rest of the
day obsessing over what kind of a woman would leave this sweet
girl behind).

"Actually, I was kind of hoping that maybe you could talk to my
dad about the slumber party for me. He doesn't think it would be
safe for me to go, but since you have epilepsy and live on your own
with Charlie, you could convince him that I would be fine, and he
would listen to you."

Ha! Listen to me? I think I'm the last person in the world that
Jacob Broaden wants to listen to. It's clear as day that the man is
only tolerating my presence because of Daisy. He doesn't meet my
eye when he's in the same room as me. He goes through ridiculous
feats to stand as far away from me as possible and only responds to
me in one-word answers.

I have no idea what I did to make this man not like me so quickly, but I wish I knew, because then I could bottle it and spray it all over myself before I go to the grocery store. Maybe then it would keep all those weirdos from hitting on me. Why can't the normal ones ever hit on me? You better believe that if a man is talking to me in a grocery store, he smells like body odor and Funyuns and is advising me on which foods will "enhance my hourglass figure." *True story.*

"I don't know, Sam." I look down at Charlie, and his eyes say it all. *Bad idea. Do not engage. Set down gently and walk away.* He's so smart.

Sam, however, does the dirtiest, meanest trick in the book. She reaches out and grabs my hand with big ol' Bambi eyes. *The little terrorist.* "Please, Evie. You're my only hope. I've tried, but he won't listen to me. I really want to go to this party. Everyone is going to be there, and I really miss my friends."

So, this is what it feels like to have your heartstrings tugged like a puppet.

Charlie whispers for me to stand firm.

"All right." Sorry, Charlie, I never stood a chance. "I'll see what I can do."

"Really? Thanks!" Her eyes light up, and you'd think I just told her she could eat ice cream every single meal for the rest of her life. But then I realize how badly I've been played when she starts pushing me toward the kitchen, where Jacob has been banging pots and pans around for the past ten minutes.

"Sam, no, not right now!" I dig my feet into the rug, but this little girl must be freaking Superwoman, because I'm no match for her. Suddenly, I'm being tossed into the kitchen, and I stumble forward as if I've just been shoved into battle.

Even better, Jacob saw the whole thing. The whole entire thing. My cheeks turn red under his blue gaze, and I consider doing a spin move around Sam and dashing out of the house. Screw the Bambi eyes; I'm not falling for her rotten tricks again.

But like every masterful con artist, she continues to hold the upper hand. "Hey, Dad! Evie wants to ask you something."

I thought we were friends, Sam!

His brows sink low, and he crosses his arms. I know, without a doubt, that if I were to ask him if Sam can go to a slumber party right now, he would take me by the shoulders and shove me right out of his lovely house. I'm pretty sure that he'd also tell me just where I can stick my advice.

I can't do that to Sam. I can't just sabotage her chances like that. So instead, I'm Katniss Everdeen. *I volunteer as tribute.*

"Actually, I was hoping that maybe I could invite myself to stay for dinner." And I was also hoping that a sinkhole could magically appear and swallow me up. "I'm . . . running low on food"—*oh gosh, make it stop*—"and since training went a little late today, I'll miss dinner if I have to go all the way to the store."

The only way I can describe how Jacob looks right now is *thunderous.* "Mm-hmm," he grunts through pursed lips, and I want to grab the frying pan off the stove and bang it against his head until he learns to be nice. How dare he make me feel terrible for inviting myself! *Have you no southern manners?!*

I backpedal as fast as I can. "Never mind!" I laugh, and it sounds shrill. "I just remembered I have a can of soup at home." Lie. I have a half-eaten pouch of Sour Patch Kids and an expired jug of milk in the fridge. "You guys have a good night! See you tomorrow!"

I whirl around and make a beeline for the door, grabbing Charlie's and Daisy's leashes in the process. Only problem is, I went the long way—out of the kitchen and through the living room toward the front door—and just as I'm about to make it to the entryway, I run smack into a hard wall. Not actually a wall.

A Jacob wall.

He took the shorter way and cut me off.

"*Oof,*" I grunt when my head comes in contact with his right pectoral muscle, and let me tell you, that man must work out every day, because I'm fairly certain I have a concussion now.

He grabs my shoulders to steady me, and when our eyes meet, he takes a big step back. *Do I need to change to a stronger deodorant or something?*

"Evie, stay for dinner," says Jacob, but his tone reads: stay at your own risk.

"No, thanks. By your reaction back there, it's apparent that my company would be nothing short of torture. So, I'll just be on my way." I try to go past him, but his hand catches my biceps before I can pass. His touch makes my stomach dip and my nerves sizzle like a drop of water on a frying pan.

His hold is tight at first, but when I freeze and look down at how his hand is wrapped completely around my arm, he loosens his grip.

Jacob lets out a long breath from his nose. "Please stay. I want you to stay." This man is nothing short of a mystery.

I'm plucking petals off a daisy. *He loves me, he hates me, he loves me, he hates me.*

Which petal will we end on?

I look up to Jacob and force a smile that I don't feel. I'm ready to give him a very polite "over my dead body" when I see the smoldering look in his eyes. He's serious. I don't know how I know that, but somehow I know that he really does want me to stay for dinner.

Because I'm not generally a masochist, my feet should be carrying me far away from this fickle mister as fast as humanly possible. But instead, my arm is burning wonderfully where he's lightly holding it, and I begin dreaming of that porch swing again. "Okay, I'll stay."

He smiles. Actually smiles. *There are crinkles beside his eyes!* "Okay, good."

We stand like that for a minute, and I'm not entirely sure what's happening or how to breathe anymore. Charlie must sense my heightened heart rate and think that Jacob is upsetting me, because he suddenly angles his furry golden body between us and looks up at Jacob with the most human look I've ever seen him give. *Hands off my lady.*

Jacob and I both chuckle at my little chaperone, and he releases me. I miss his touch right away.

Jacob turns on his heel and disappears back into the kitchen, and I'm left wondering what in the hell just happened.

I turn around and am bending down to unclip Charlie's and Daisy's leashes when I catch Sam's face across the room. She's leaning her hip against the side of an armchair, and her arms are folded, a smug grin on her face. I pull my eyebrows together in question, and as a response she waggles hers.

Oh no. What have I done?

CHAPTER 11

Jake

I'm standing across the kitchen, watching as Evie finishes painting the last fingernail on Sam's hand. Sam is smiling from ear to ear, and she keeps looking up at Evie with a studying look as if she's memorizing every tiny thing Evie does so that she can perfectly replicate her actions later. Sam adores Evie, that much is apparent. And honestly, I understand the sentiment.

The woman is gorgeous. Funny. Strong. Kind-hearted. She lives with a difficult disability and thrives. And she has the most tempting full pink lips I've ever seen. Okay, I doubt that Sam has noticed that last part, but believe me, I have.

Did I mention that Evie is painting a rainbow pattern on Sam's nails? That probably doesn't seem like a big thing, but for my little girl who has resisted everything happy and cheerful since her diagnosis, it's huge.

I was quiet during dinner, partly because I have no idea how to interact with Evie, but also because I was enjoying hearing my daughter talk. I didn't realize how starved I was for the sound of her voice. It wasn't heavy with sadness like it has been lately. She didn't give short, clipped answers. She told Evie things that I had no idea about. (Jenna Miller already got her first kiss?! Where have I been? And isn't ten years old a little young for that?)

Evie should have been bored by a young girl's monologue on preteen romance, but she wasn't. She was enthralled, sitting on the edge of her seat, one leg propped under her (I'm realizing Evie will never sit normally in a chair) and those emerald eyes wide with interest. I was floored when she asked Sam if there were any boys she was interested in. Even more floored when Sam said yes.

Note to self: hunt down Tate Bradley and explain to him in perfect detail what will happen to him if his lips get anywhere near my little girl.

After dinner, Evie helped me clear the dishes. When she came to stand next to me at the sink, every muscle in my body tightened with awareness of her. She feels like a magnet. I'm being pulled to this woman, and I'm helpless to stop it.

I want to stop it. I need to stop it. She's too young for me. Too wonderful. I bet she has drooling men trailing after her everywhere she goes. Her options are endless right now, and there's no way she'd ever want to settle for a guy with as much baggage as I'm carrying. When it comes to Evie Jones, I am nothing but a blob of insecurity.

But at the same time, I see what a good impact she's having on Sam. She has connected with my daughter in a way that even my sisters haven't been able to since Natalie left. I can't overlook that. Does this mean that I'm coming around to the idea of dating again?

"Dad, can Evie tuck me in tonight? I want to show her my room."

I sigh and rub the back of my neck. What's the protocol for this? Do I let Sam get attached? Do I protect her already broken heart? I don't know what the right answer is here.

"It's fine with me if Evie wants to. But I don't want to hold her up if she doesn't have time for it." I give Evie a questioning look.

I'm putting the ball in her court because I don't know what else to do.

She smiles down at Sam. "Plenty of time. Show me that room, cutie."

I hug and kiss Sam good-night and watch as the two disappear up the stairs, Charlie and Daisy following close behind.

While I'm rinsing the dishes and loading them in the dishwasher, I'm aware that I should feel nervous at the amount of time they are spending together upstairs. I don't. It feels right. Like this friendship between them was always meant to be.

And as I'm loading the last bowl into the dishwasher, Evie's white running shoes enter my sights. I know for a fact I've never been so excited to see a pair of shoes before now.

"You've got a great kid up there," she says, and that answers the question that's been flying around my brain for the last half hour.

I don't want to push Evie away anymore. I've been trying and it's not working. If she's up for a friendship, so am I. But *only* friendship. I need to dip my toes in and see if the water's warm before I'm ready to take a dive.

"I wish I could say I had something to do with it. But it's all Sam. She came out that great all on her own."

Evie smiles, and I want to let my eyes trace the outline of her mouth, but I don't because, yeah . . . *friends*. "Somehow I doubt that's completely true. I've seen how you are with her." We stare at each other for a moment, then Evie shuffles her eyes around the room. "Well. Thanks again for dinner. Have you seen my phone? I need to call an Uber."

She looks around the kitchen, and I wait until her back is turned to me to say, "It's a nice evening. Do you want to go sit on the porch until your ride gets here?"

Evie's body freezes. She looks uncomfortable. "Do you mean you want me to wait for my Uber outside and not in your house?"

"What? *God no.* I meant . . . do you want to sit on the porch *with me?* You know, talk together. With words."

I'm ten years old, and she's the cutest girl in class. I'm begging her to accept my Valentine heart, and she's staring at it like it's poison.

A grin finally cracks on her mouth, and she tucks her hair behind her ear. "Words? I wasn't sure you knew how to use those. At least, not outside of insinuating I look like a man or accusing me of extortion."

I smile and shrug. "Occasionally, I can find a few nice ones."

"And are you going to use those nice ones if I sit on the porch with you?" I hate that she's skeptical. I hate that she has a right to be. But I love the southern lilt to her voice.

I cross my heart. "The nicest."

She brushes past me with narrowed eyes as if I'm some feral predator lying casually in the tall grass and she's a doe, prancing by but cautious that I might pounce at any moment.

She doesn't know just how much I want to, but not in the way she thinks.

When we make it out onto the porch, I gesture for her to sit down on the swing first. I could swear she blushes before she sits. And then a secret smile hovers on her mouth. I briefly glance at my pants, wondering if my fly is down or something.

Still zipped.

I take care to sit as far away from her on the swing as possible, but my body still hums with awareness of her. We start swinging, and the dogs settle down on the porch by the front door. It's a deep swing, but I'm tall enough that my feet are fully planted on the ground. Evie's toes are barely touching, and for some reason that makes me smile.

Seconds pass, or minutes, or hours, I'm not sure. All I know is that we are both quiet and sitting stiff as boards, and I've never felt more awkward. I steal a glance at her and find her stealing one too. I'm not alone in this awkwardness.

"Okay. What are we doing here, Jacob?" she finally asks.

"Call me Jake. Everyone else does."

She laughs a little laugh that sounds borderline annoyed and pulls her legs up under her to face me. She's wearing a long burgundy skirt today that's kind of flowy and has a slit up to her knee. It's paired with a fitted white tee, but about an hour ago she got cold and pulled a gray crewneck sweatshirt from her bag and put it on. Her hair is down and wavy like she's been swimming in the ocean today and then let it dry in the sun. She looks casually beautiful, and *yes,* I realize I shouldn't be noticing any of this, but I freaking am because I have no self-control.

"Alrighty then, *Jake.*" She says my name almost like she's giving me a friendly shove to the chest. "Now I really want to know what we're doing out here. What's happening right now?"

I like that she's direct. That's not been my experience with relationships in the past. Especially not with Natalie, who one day woke up and seemed like she was a completely different person. I wonder, sometimes, if things would have been different if she'd just been honest with me about wanting more out of her life. I never even knew she had a dream of acting until she threw it in my face that she had lost that dream to raise Sam. It was so strange. Like she'd been sitting on it and feeling resentful for years but never voicing it.

If I'd known, would I have encouraged it? Or were Natalie and I always meant to break paths at some point?

"Well, Evie, this here"—I put on the same playful, sarcastic tone she's using and gesture between us—"is called friendship. It's a concept where two people—"

This time she really does shove me in the arm, and I break off with a chuckle. "I know what friendship is! I just want to know why you are suddenly feeling buddy-buddy with me, when it's been clear up until this point that you don't want me around."

It's time for me to be direct too. I purposely meet her gaze. "I've wanted you around."

That statement cracks through the air like a bullet from a gun.

She wants to smile—I know it because there's tension at the corners of her mouth—but she doesn't. "You have a funny way of showing that."

"Turns out, I'm . . . not good at having female friends since my divorce. Especially beautiful and single ones."

She lifts a brow, barely restraining her grin. "You think I'm beautiful?"

I laugh and meet her sparkling eyes, glad to know she's not making a run for it after what I just admitted. "Are you fishing for a compliment?" My tone is light—and probably too transparent that I'd be all too happy to shower her with them.

"Maybe. I've never gotten a compliment from you. I was just curious to see what one would be like."

I think we both realize the openly flirtatious ground we just stepped into, because I drop my gaze and Evie scoots around in her seat. She shifts forward and then bunches her long hair up on her head and wraps a hair tie around it until it's an oversized bun that somehow makes her look even cuter.

She clears her throat. "So, *friend.* Tell me something about yourself I don't know." She's deflecting, but I can still tell that her face is flushed.

"I started my architecture firm five years ago."

She scrunches her nose, shakes her head, then turns to fully face me on the swing. As she pulls both of her legs up under her, one of her legs brushes against mine. Her back is leaning against the armrest, and I couldn't get away from her gaze even if I wanted to.

"I don't want to talk work," she says, her gaze soft. "Tell me something personal about you. Like . . . what color Skittle is your favorite?"

"I don't like Skittles."

Her mouth falls open. I'm a serial killer in her eyes now. "You don't like Skittles?!" She shakes her head. "What's wrong with you?"

I laugh. "Many things."

"Wait. Do you not like *all* candy? Are you one of those guys who only eats lean proteins and greens? I mean, it would make sense based on the way you look, but . . ."

My smile is wide and cocky. "The way I look?"

"Now who's looking for compliments?"

I laugh fully and realize I could sit here and talk to her all night. That thought scares me as much as it excites me. "I like brownies—extra fudgy and with chocolate chips, slightly under-baked."

Her blond brow raises. "Really? Okay, I can respect that. I love chocolate."

Are we really having this conversation? It's so casual and sweet and unimportant and . . . exactly what I've been missing in my life lately.

"What's *your* favorite color Skittle?" I ask.

She rests her head against the back of the swing and pulls the sleeves of her sweatshirt down over her fists. "Red. Do you have any siblings?"

"Four sisters."

"Four! Goodness gracious," she says, sounding as southern as apple pie. "Are you close with them?"

"Very. I couldn't have gotten through this year without them." I can feel the conversation drifting toward the therapist's couch again, so I steer it away. "How about you?" Somehow, I can picture her fitting in with four sisters.

She shakes her head. "It's just me and my parents. And before you ask me that question, no, we do *not* get along."

"Really? Why not?"

She chuckles a little, but it doesn't sound like the happy kind. "They want me to be someone I'm not. They have very clear expectations for me and who I should be. From the day I flung my toddler beauty pageant crown in my mom's face, I've been letting them down."

"I'm sorry. That's gotta be hard." I can't imagine anyone ever being disappointed with this woman. I mean, she trains service dogs for a living. That's pretty saintly.

Her smile is soft, and her green eyes pin me in my seat. We are locked in a stare as the porch swing continues to sway us back and forth, and I never want this game to end. Except, it does when Evie's eyes fall to my lips. Did she look there intentionally? My stomach swoops, and I'm wondering how friendly it would be to tug her over to me and find out if her lips taste like strawberries. I've been dwelling on that important question since I saw her apply a pink lip balm earlier.

"Can I ask you something that's a little out of line for the business friendship we have?" she asks, her voice breathy and nervous.

"Sure. I'm all ears."

Her smile is tentative, and I wonder if she's going to ask me out. Do I want her to? Truthfully, I think she can do so much better than me.

"Will you consider letting Sam go to the slumber party with her friends?"

And just like that, I'm a popped balloon—air rushing out of me as I fall and land deflated on the ground.

In the tiny span of time between her potential and actual

question, my mind has taken a hundred different turns. None of which I can voice out loud because I'm too much of a gentleman— or at least I pretend I am.

"The slumber party?" Now I'm just stalling, feeling like I need a minute to reel my thoughts back in.

"Yeah. Sam told me about the slumber party at her friend Jenna's house. She really wants to go, and I think it would be good for her." She bites the bottom corner of her lip, and I realize that she's nervous. She's afraid I'm going to revert back to my caveman ways and beat the ground, telling her to get out of my house.

I've got news for her: I'm not going to be that guy again. I'm done being the jerk around her, so I smile and purposefully relax into the swing. "She gave you her doe eyes, didn't she?"

Evie's face lights up. "The biggest eyes I've ever seen! I think she even managed to let a single tear pool in one of them. How does she do that?"

I laugh. "She's an impressive human being. But honestly, Evie . . . I don't know about the party. I don't think I'm ready for her to do something like that."

"But Sam is." Her words feel like a hammer to my chest. "She and Daisy are doing great together. Trust Daisy to do her job. She's going to take care of Sam if she has a seizure, and she'll alert Jenna's parents, and they can call you." I don't respond right away, so Evie reaches out and lays her hand across my forearm that has been draped over the back of the swing. "You can't keep her in your pocket forever, Jake. Just because your daughter has epilepsy, it doesn't mean that she has to be treated like a toddler for the rest of her life. She's going to need to grow up and learn to live with her disability. Trust me."

I do trust her. Or at least . . . I'm starting to.

I puff out a breath, trying for once not to overthink anything. "All right. I'll let her go."

There's relief in her eyes as she squeezes my arm. I swear I'm going to lean across the swing and kiss her. I have to. Every inch of me is aching for it.

Honk. Honk.

Evie and I both jump, and she pulls away, springing to her feet and grabbing the dogs' leashes like we were just caught after curfew doing something we shouldn't. I wonder if she could read my thoughts a moment ago, because she seems suddenly reluctant to meet my eyes. Would she hate a kiss from me?

Get it together, Jake. You can't kiss her! You're not ready for this, remember?

"I think you're making the right decision about the party," Evie says as she's running down the porch stairs in a full gallop. "I'll see ya tomorrow!"

I'm watching her leave my house, and I hate it. I want her to stay—and that realization freaks me out. But just before she gets in the Uber a thought hits me, and I call out to her. "Evie, wait."

Charlie and Daisy jump in the back seat, and Evie pauses to look at me before getting in. "That's what Sam was trying to get you to ask me earlier, wasn't it? When she pushed you into the kitchen? She wanted you to ask me about the slumber party, but you knew I'd say no, so you covered by inviting yourself for dinner." I state this like I'm at a murder-mystery dinner and I've just solved the case.

A smile grows on her lips, confirming that she threw herself under the bus to protect my daughter's chances of happiness. "Night, Jake."

"Good night, Evie."

Tomorrow can't come fast enough.

CHAPTER 12

Training Camp Day 3

JAKE: Thanks for braiding Sam's hair tonight before you left. I
can never get it right.

EVIE: Not a problem. I love braiding. Maybe I'll quit the service
dog business and go to hair school.

JAKE: Can you wait to do that until after you've finished working
with Sam and Daisy?

EVIE: Bossy much? But okay. We only have two days left
anyway.

JAKE: Yeah . . . two days.

Training Camp Day 4

EVIE: Dinner was great. Thanks again for inviting me to stay. I
swear I really do have food at my apartment.

JAKE: It was nothing. Made sense for you to stay since training
went late.

EVIE: Which makes it even nicer of you to offer.

JAKE: Stop it. You're making me blush.

EVIE: I don't believe it. I need photographic evidence.

JAKE: Are you trying to get me to send nudes?

EVIE: What? NO. Now I'm blushing.

JAKE: I need photographic evidence.

EVIE: . . .

Training Camp Day 5

JAKE: Last day of training today.

EVIE: Yep.

JAKE: Sam's going to miss you.

EVIE: Sam can come see me anytime she wants.

JAKE: Good to know. Come hungry today. I'm going to feed you pancakes before you guys start your session.

EVIE: Do you talk this dirty to all your female friends?

JAKE: Just you.

CHAPTER 13

Evie

My intentions were noble when I set out for the bathroom. I swear it. Put a Bible under my hand and I will—okay, well, that's taking it too far because clearly my intentions were as noble as sin.

I'm standing in the middle of Jake's bedroom, looking around with hungry eyes. I'm a jewel thief inside Tiffany's, and I don't know where to start.

Jake was on a work call when I left him, and Sam was in the living room. I walked toward the downstairs bathroom, innocent as the day I was born, until I was out of Jake's eye line. Then I shut the bathroom door from the outside—I obviously missed my calling as a spy of some sort—and hurried down the hall to where I suspected Jake's room to be.

I don't know why I feel the overwhelming need to be in here. I think it's because Jake still feels like a mystery to me, and I'm hoping that if I have this inside look at his personal life, I'll stumble across the secret to who he is. During our last five days of training camp, Jake has been kind and friendly. But that's it. Nothing more. Nada. His attention is zeroed in on Sam or work or Daisy. He smiles at me. He asks if I want anything to drink. But that's it.

I wouldn't think anything strange about it if it weren't for the texts I get like clockwork every night. I've never been so glued to my phone before. It always starts with something innocuous and then quickly dips into flirtatious. It's like he has another Jacob Broaden stuffed in a closet somewhere and only lets him out after eight P.M.

I open his closet, and unfortunately, no one jumps out. It's so tidy, though. Everything hung nice and neat. By now, I've discovered that Jake is an obsessive cleaner. He puts things away as soon as he gets them out. And he must do a thorough sweep of all surfaces every night after Sam goes to bed, because by the morning everything is spic-and-span.

As I look under his bed, I realize I'm borderline stalker-woman right now. It's creepy that I'm tiptoeing around his room, running my fingers across his rumpled gray bedspread, and smiling that he makes it to perfection before he leaves in the morning. I really want to pick up his folded T-shirt and smell it . . . but I said that I was only *borderline* creepy, so I refrain.

The ugly truth is, I saw the signs saying *Beware: Crush Ahead,* but I blew right past them. Jake has stolen all my brain space.

He is all I think about, and it's really making me nervous. I don't want to fall for him. I still feel like he's too good for me. So, I guess by me tiptoeing around his room like this, I'm sort of just torturing myself with what I'll never have.

My eyes narrow on a book beside his bed, and my greedy little fingers snatch it up. What does a man like Jake read before he goes to bed?

Twilight?! No. You've got to be kidding me. This one life choice of his has me rethinking everything. There's no other explanation for a thirty-three-year-old man reading a book about teenage vampire love: he's a weirdo.

Yes, I realize that's rich coming from a woman snooping around a man's bedroom.

"Find anything interesting?" Jake's voice sounds from behind me, and I snap the book shut and spin around to face him, holding the book behind my back.

I'm caught red-handed. The jewels are behind my back, and it's incriminating enough to send me to prison for the rest of my life. I don't dare speak. *I have the right to remain silent.* I've seen enough cop shows to know that anything I say will be held against me in a court of law.

"Whatcha got there?" He's smiling, and I'm turning into a tomato.

"I was looking for the bathroom."

"In my bedside table?"

He's stalking toward me, and I'm quaking in my tennis shoes. Where's Charlie when I need him? *Attack, boy!*

Jake stops just in front of me, so close that I can feel the heat rushing off him in waves, and I have to tip my head up to look at him. It's doing nothing to help my flaming cheeks. I don't think he's ever stood this close to me before, and I'm wondering if maybe this is eight-P.M. Jacob Broaden, freshly escaped from whatever cell he's normally kept in.

He reaches around me, his arm brushing against my shoulder, and I think I accidentally shudder. No, I know I do because he notices and smirks. *Hello, eight-P.M. Jake.*

After retrieving the evidence from behind my back, he chuckles. I can't look away and neither can he. He's holding the book between us now but doesn't bother to look down at it. "Were you about to call Child Protection Services to have Sam removed from my guardianship after seeing this?"

"The number is halfway typed in my phone." I don't like how wobbly my voice sounds. But how else am I supposed to sound when I'm face to chest with a superhero who just finished fighting crime? Because that's clearly what Jake is. It's the only logical explanation for all the muscles.

He smiles. "Sam said she wanted to read it, so I thought I would read it first to see if it's appropriate for her."

"A likely story." I can't let him know that I think he's probably the best dad I've ever seen. The way he loves and cares for Sam only adds to my attraction for him.

"It's not at all an appropriate book for her." His eyes drop to my mouth. "Too much longing and wanting."

Between Edward and Bella, right? Because my mind is screaming that he's talking about us, and I have no idea what to do with that information. I want Jake to like me; I want him to *want* me. But I also don't dare believe that he really does. I don't have anything to offer him.

"By the way, your boss is here," he mentions casually, as if that isn't the most startling information I've heard all day. It has the same effect on me as a hypnotist snapping their fingers.

My head rears back. "Joanna?!"

He nods, but his eyes are still trying to tell me something. "That's why I came to get you. But I figured I should let you have a few minutes to creep around my room first."

My cheeks heat again. "You knew I was in here the whole time?"

His smile grows. "I don't mind. Snoop anytime you want."

"Why would you be okay with that?" It's a dare as much as it is a real question.

He's quiet for a minute, then he looks over my shoulder as if he can't look me in the eye when he answers. "I guess I . . . want you to get to know me."

"Oh."

His eyes hook mine again. "So, we can be real friends. Not just work friends."

Oh.

Again with this friend crap? I try not to let my dejection write itself across my face, but it's probably no use. I've never been good at hiding my feelings. He's probably reading a Post-it on my forehead at this very moment: *Hi, I'm Evie. I want you to like me romantically, but you don't, so I'll cry on my car ride home.*

"Do you know why Joanna is here?" I'm ripping the Post-it off and changing the subject. "She never comes to my training days anymore."

He shrugs his big shoulders, and I'm mesmerized by how the fabric of his shirt pulls tight. "I guess you're in trouble."

Not likely. If I had to guess, I would say that Joanna is going to be the one in trouble at the end of this day.

I try to step around Jake, but he cuts me off. Maybe Jake isn't the only superhuman, because I halt my body so fast that I almost knock myself backward. Thanks to my reaction time, neither of us are touching, but that doesn't help all the chills racing across my body.

"Wait. I want to know what you think of my room." His voice is playful, and this is seriously throwing me off.

He's like a bully who pulls my hat down over my eyes in the hallway and then keeps spinning me in reverse circles so I'm never able to catch my bearing. *Business. Flirting. Stoic. Friends. Flirting. Quiet.*

But he's very clearly not going to let me leave this room without an answer, so I sigh and take a long, exaggerated look around the room (as if I didn't already do a thorough investigation a few minutes ago).

"It's nice," I say and then get ready to leave.

"No, no, no. Tell me what's going on in your head. What do you think? What stuck out to you?"

"Why do you want to know?"

He smiles. "Because . . . I don't know. I just do."

"Okayyy. I like the vaulted ceilings." Ceilings are neutral, right?

"What else?" His smirk says this is some sort of game to him, but I haven't figured out the rules yet. Or the objective.

"You're being weird."

"Says the uninvited woman standing in my bedroom after going through my side table."

"Right. Well . . . I guess I like that you make your bed."

He chuckles, deep and full, and I'm pretty sure that if my hand were on his chest, I would feel the rumble of it all the way up my arm. "I knew that's what you'd like most. I wanted to see if I was right. And I was."

I narrow my eyes. "No you did not! How could you possibly have known that?"

He shrugs again. "I guess because I picture your place being messy." He's pictured my place?

"Should I take offense to that?"

"Not at all. I just mean that you . . . you're not uptight. Life moves too fast for you to take time to put your things away. It's refreshing."

Oh good. The claw of heat is creeping up my neck again, and I'm about to be full-on strawberry. "I haven't confirmed that my place is messy."

He looks down at me and lifts a brow. "Is it?"

My shoulders slump. "Yes. But I want to make my bed from now on like you make yours. This looks nice." I touch his bed-spread one more time.

He smiles, and those shoulders of mine are perking right back up. I need to get out of here. He's being strange, and I like it way too much. It makes me wonder if maybe his house is so clean because he needs someone else to help him and Sam live in it a little more. Someone like me. And maybe I need someone like him to help me keep my things in order.

"I need to see what Joanna is doing here." I move past him, and this time I don't avoid touching him. In fact, my arm brushes over his as I pass, and I could swear I feel his fingers extend to lightly fan against mine as I do.

CHAPTER 14

Jake

After Evie leaves my room, I give her a few minutes alone with her boss before I join them. Okay, fine, it was me who needed a few minutes alone to process. Evie was in my bedroom. And she looked perfect there. Too perfect. This room had never felt so bright before.

I watched her from the doorway for a minute before she noticed me, and I felt desperate to know what was going through her head. Did she like this space I've set up for myself? Or did she think it was dull?

She touched my bedspread. And thanks to how much I've read of *Twilight,* I can recognize longing when I see it. I mean, it's been a while since I've been around a woman who wasn't my wife, but I'm thinking that snooping through a man's room and staring at his bedspread can only mean one thing: she's attracted to me.

What the hell am I supposed to do with that thought?

Friendship was fine when there was only a small probability that a woman like her could be attracted to me—a single dad with so much baggage that I have to rent a U-Haul to hitch to the back of my truck—but after seeing her smile when her fingers landed on my bed, that complicated things.

I don't know what else to do, so after peeking down the hallway to make sure no one is around, I shut my bedroom door and pull out my phone to dial the one person I know can tell me what to do. "June! I need to talk to you," I say when my baby sister picks up.

"What's wrong? You sound weird."

"I feel weird," I say, scraping my hand through my hair. "I think she likes me."

"No way! Did she steal your baseball cap at recess?"

"Shut up. I'm serious. And I'm freaking out."

June chuckles a minute, then I hear her shuffling some baking pans around. "Okay, hang on. Let me go outside so I can talk to you and not have Stacy listening in. YES, I see you tilting your ear toward me, Stacy! Mind your own biscuits." June and her best friend, Stacy, co-own her trendy donut shop. The storefront looks like something right off a Pinterest page. Everything is white with pops of bright color, and each of their original-flavored donuts have names like Just Peachy for their peach-flavored donut, and Slow as Molasses for their cinnamon-molasses donut, and then my personal favorite, Kiss My Grits for their newest savory-grits-inspired donut.

"Okay, I'm ready. Spill."

I sigh and go into my bathroom and shut the door just in case anyone is in the hallway and can hear me. "Do you remember the woman, Evie Jones, I was telling you about the other day?"

"The hot toddy who works for the service dog company?"

"I never once called her a *hot toddy.*"

"You should. I bet she'd love it. Ladies love a sexy nickname." Oh my gosh. Why did I call her again?

I sigh loudly into the phone so she knows I'm done with her game. "Anyways, I just found her in my room."

"NAKED?!" I cringe hearing that word come off of my sister's tongue.

"No, you perv. Fully clothed. I just mean that she was in my room, looking around, because . . . I think she likes me. *Likes me* likes me." Wow, yeah. I hear how immature that makes me sound, but whatever.

June chuckles. "Okay, what's the problem? That seems like good news to me. Worthy of celebrating."

"It's not."

This time she sighs. "You're going to self-sabotage this, aren't you?"

"Most likely. Which is why I'm calling. I need you to tell me what to do so I don't jump out my bedroom window just to keep from having to face her again."

"Do you like her?"

I pause for a moment. "Yeah. A lot."

"Okay, good! Then just freakin' chill. No one is asking you to propose. Do you know how many guys' rooms I've snooped through when they weren't looking? It's how we make sure you're not a creeper with lots of—"

"Don't finish that sentence."

"Stuffed animals," she says, and I can hear her smile.

"That's not what you were going to say."

"Nope. It wasn't. But seriously, just chill about it all, okay? Don't push her away, but you don't have to decide anything yet either. I assume you guys are already something of friends if she felt intrigued enough to play spy in your room. So, maybe just keep being her friend until you're sure you want to take that next step into Relationship Land. And if the situation arises for you to play tonsil hockey—"

"And that's my cue. Goodbye, June."

"Byyyeee."

I end the call and plant my hands on my bathroom counter to stare at myself in the mirror for a minute. It's literally been more than eleven years since I've kissed anyone other than Natalie. These past two years have been so confusing with the divorce and Sam's diagnosis that I haven't even had a minute to think about being a normal male.

I'm thinking about it now, though.

June's right. There's no need to rush it. It's better for everyone if Evie and I just stay friends for a while. I can't do the dating thing the way a normal man my age would anyway. I have to be cautious because of Sam. Evie would be dating both of us, and since she's not even thirty yet, I don't know if that's something she would want. I need to inch toward the line. Feel her out.

I can hear June's voice in my head, saying, *I think you mean UP.* No, June, I don't mean *up*.

I'm going to take things slow with Evie. Christmas slow. Painfully slow. No-one-can-even-see-me-moving *slow.* And if she sticks around—if she can handle the lack of speed—I'll consider Relationship Land.

I walk into the living room just in time to see Evie physically pushing her boss toward the door. "Thanks for stopping by! You can be on your way now."

"But I only just got here!" She's digging in her heels and smiling ear to ear. I don't even know this woman, and I can tell she's messing with Evie.

"And you didn't need to come in the first place, so go before he comes back!"

"Too late," I say with a smile. "He's back."

Evie turns around with wide eyes—she might as well have a canary sticking out of her mouth. Sam snickers from her perch on the couch's armrest, and Evie narrows her eyes at her, which makes Sam burst into laughter and fall back onto the couch. What am I missing here? Why does Evie not want me around her boss?

Joanna gives Evie a smug look before crossing in front of her to get to me. She holds out her hand and smiles wide. "I know we met briefly a few minutes ago, but let me formally introduce myself. Joanna Halstead. I'm the founder of Southern Service Paws, and I'm pleased as punch that you chose us to provide a dog for your precious daughter."

Joanna is polite and engaging, and I still can't figure out why Evie looks like she's standing on pins and needles over by the door. Her hand is on the knob as if she's ready to thrust it open and shove her boss out at any moment.

"I'm the one who's grateful. Evie had every right to ignore my call and refuse my application after the way I treated her that first day."

Joanna waves away my comment with a good-natured smile. "Water under the bridge. Believe it or not, you're not the first parent to not want a service dog for their child. It's a little scary deciding to allow your baby's safety to be put in the hands of a dog—or paws, I should say. But believe me, those paws are more than capable."

"I see that now, and I'm excited to find out what Sam's new future will look like with Daisy. And it's all thanks to Evie. She's put in so much time here with my daughter, and I'm really grateful for all of her help."

Joanna beams at me like I couldn't have given a more perfect answer. She tosses a glance over her shoulder to Evie, who opens the door and gestures for Joanna to walk out. Joanna just turns back to me, a new devious smile in place of the previous businessy one. "Evie really is the best. Never have I seen a heart bigger than hers."

"Yep, I have a big ol' heart! Well, thanks for coming to check on everything, Jo! Tell Gary I said hi!" Evie's tone is shrill and panicked.

Joanna pays zero attention to her. Her eyes narrow on me, and I have a feeling I'm about to find out why Evie has been so adamant to get Joanna out of my house. "Mr. Broaden, has Evie told you about the benefit she's been planning? We're hoping to raise enough money to be able to give the dogs we are currently training to future recipients free of charge. It was all Evie's idea."

"JO, YOUR CAR IS ON FIRE!" Evie yells.

Joanna just bats her hand behind her and waits for my answer.

"No, she didn't. That is really incredible, though. When is it?" Why didn't Evie tell me about it? Suddenly, I remember our first conversation, where I accused her of trying to make a big commission off the dogs, and I feel even worse about my prior behavior. Is that why she didn't want to tell me? Because she didn't want me to see it as her being defensive?

"It's the Thursday after next. Going to be quite the shindig—a black-tie affair—and all the bigwigs in town were invited."

I nod, still wondering where this is going and how I play a part in it. "Sounds really nice."

"Oh, it will be! But you know what's not so nice?" She puts on a dramatic pout. "Evie can't seem to find a date! What a pity it would be for a pretty thing like her to have to get all dressed up and show up to the event all by her lonesome. Oh, wait! You wouldn't be interested in being her plus-one, would you?"

Ahhh, and there it is. Everything makes sense now.

Evie lets out a long, defeated sigh and shuts the door. Her cheeks are the color of a candy apple, and I'm suddenly enjoying Joanna's company more than I've enjoyed anything before. "Don't answer that, Jake. Joanna is a scheming old hen who needs to stick her nose back in her own business."

"Don't call me an old hen or I'll fire you, little missy."

"Don't call me *little missy* or I won't come to painting night Wednesday." I can't decide if these two women act more like sisters, friends, or mother and daughter. I like them, though. And I really like knowing that Evie needs a date. Also, *how* does she not already have one? That question perplexes me. Evie should have a line of men wrapped around the block, begging her to date them.

"It's black-tie, you said?" I ask, my voice making both of their heads turn and acknowledge me for the first time.

Evie's brows pull together. "*Yes*. Why?"

"Because it would be embarrassing to show up in jeans to a black-tie event."

Joanna's face grows into a smile, but Evie still looks skeptical. Honestly, I'm going out on a limb here by inviting myself as her date. I'm really banking on the fact that she and Joanna seem close and Evie would have told her if she already had one. But I'm painfully aware that this could all blow up in my face.

"You really don't have to come with me. I'm sure I can find someone to go if you're busy. Joanna never should have put you on the spot—" I cut her off because she sounds nervous but not entirely like she doesn't want me there.

"I want to go with you."

I am Ryan Gosling now. No one can touch my smoldering confidence. It's all fake, of course, but she doesn't need to know that.

"Really?" The hopefulness in her voice only boosts my confidence more.

I shrug my shoulders. *Yeah, no big deal. I go to fancy benefits all the time and definitely won't have to go out to buy a new suit.* "I do. I think it would be fun—if you're up for taking me."

She's trying to hide a smile as she tucks her hair behind her ear. "Yeah, okay, I guess that will work, then."

CHAPTER 15

Evie

"So, she's really mine now?" asks Sam.

"She's really yours."

"Like she gets to sleep with me from now on?"

"Yep."

Sam smiles and lets her toes skim across the pool water again. She's only dipping her toes in because she's wearing little-girl skinny jeans and could only roll them up to the ankles. I'm wearing my favorite yellow cotton dress, so I'm able to dip my legs in from the knee down.

The water feels like a bath, and the setting sun is warm on my skin. Charlie is lying down on the side of the pool to my left, and Daisy is lying down on Sam's right. Other than our different hair colors, we look like a mirrored reflection of each other.

I feel a tether to Sam that I can't explain, and I wonder if it's because I see her as a younger version of myself. We sit quietly together by the pool while Jake is inside putting out a few fires with a contractor over the phone. I glance over my shoulder and catch a glimpse of him standing at the window, phone pressed to his ear, but his eyes glued to Sam and me. His brows are pulled together, but he doesn't look angry—just thoughtful. My skin grows hot knowing Jake is watching me.

All I want to do is obsessively think about what took place this morning in his living room with Jo. Does he really want to go as my date to the benefit? Was it a pity offer? I want to murder Jo for asking him like she did—or kiss her, I can't decide. But when I get home and give my brain the free rein it wants to turn that conversation over and over and dissect it like a mad scientist, I'll know for sure.

"Soooo, my dad says I can go to the slumber party."

"I know! That's so great. Are you excited?"

Sam kicks some water. "Kind of."

I look down at her. "Just kind of? I thought you'd be super happy he gave you permission."

"I am." Except, she's not.

I bump her little shoulder with mine. "Tell me what's up."

She breathes in and out for a minute and then finally lets the truth out. "I'm kinda scared. I know I put up a big fight about wanting to go . . . but now that I can . . . I'm scared I'll have a seizure while I'm there."

I understand that, and unfortunately, the chances are pretty high that she will. Stress and sleep deprivation are triggers for a lot of people. "You might. But if you do, Daisy will be there to take care of you."

And I have no doubt that Daisy will. I've been working with them all week, and what I've seen leaves me with nothing but confidence.

Sam turns her face away from me to pet Daisy. "It's not that I'm afraid of the seizure. I'm . . . I'm afraid of what the other girls will think of me if they see me have one."

Unfortunately, this is the one thing regarding disabilities that service dogs cannot protect us from—other humans. People can be cruel, especially kids, so I understand Sam's worry.

"I wish I could tell you that everyone will always understand your seizures—but they won't. You can't control other people, but you can control who you surround yourself with. So, if you think that these girls will be mean to you if you have a seizure, don't go— they're not worth your friendship."

"Have you ever had anyone be mean to you after seeing one of your episodes?"

I don't like this question. It fills my mind with uncomfortable memories that I would rather never think of again. Ones I've buried six feet under the ground and promised never to revisit. Looks like I'm grabbing a shovel.

"Unfortunately . . . yes." I had a seizure during English class my junior year of high school. I am one of the lucky few who convulse during an episode (sarcasm intended). Let me tell you, the jocks of the school *loved* that. They spent the rest of the school year reenacting my seizures every time they passed me in the hallway, but they must have been very into drama since they made sure to take their reenactments way over the top.

And you know what? As it turns out, I don't think Sam needs to hear this whole story. It probably wouldn't make her feel much better. So, I keep it to myself but decide that, one day, if I feel she needs to hear it, I'll tell her.

Wait a second.

Why in the world am I picturing myself in Sam's life as she's growing up?

"I had some not-so-nice people say some not-so-nice things about me when I was young. But you know what . . ." I look down at Sam and brush her hair behind her ear. "I survived. It hurt at the time, but now I'm a strong woman who lives with a very scary medical condition, and I have every right to feel proud of myself for that. And you do too. Don't ever let anyone make you feel bad about who you are or scared to live your life. You're more than your seizures. And I'll be happy to remind you of that anytime you doubt it."

Sam smiles and then surprises me by leaning into me and wrapping me up in her darling little arms. "Thanks, Evie. I'm glad I emailed you that day . . . even if I did lose my iPad for a week."

I laugh. "Me too, darlin'."

A few minutes later, I hear the sliding door open, and Jake steps out wearing a pair of aviators in a way that would make Tom Cruise envious. "What are you two ladies doing out here?"

"Just enjoying your incredible pool," I say, holding my hand above my eyes to shade them from the sun. I should have put my hand in front of my eyes to shade them from Jake. I can't handle how good he looks drenched in the orange sunset. He's already tan, but the warm glow only adds to it, licking at his muscular forearms and making the man look downright illegal.

"I'm glad someone's enjoying it," he says, coming to sit down on the other side of Charlie.

"Yeah, we never use it," says Sam, a sad tone touching her voice.

"Never?" I'm shocked. What kind of crazy person would have a pool this glorious and never use it?

"Between work, and school, and doctors' appointments, we just don't have the time."

"Then make time!" He should be put in jail for owning a pool that could be featured on a design show and not finding time to use it.

He chuckles and shakes his head a little. "It's not that easy."

"It really is, though."

He's trying to sell me *adulting,* and I'm not buying it. The real problem has been hovering in Jake's and Sam's eyes all week. They haven't picked up the pieces of their life yet. They got hit with some tough stuff and haven't decided to move forward. I'm about to slingshot their butts into *moving on*.

"Life isn't worth it if you can't play a little. You've gotta steal fun when you can," I say as I stand up.

Jake looks up at me with a crooked smile. "Like when? What do you suggest when every day is booked solid and I can barely find time to tie my shoes?"

"Get some slip-ons." I flash him a haughty grin. "And allow me to point out that you're not busy right this minute."

His smile falters ever so slightly. "I don't have my swim trunks on."

Oh, silly little practical Jake. As you're about to find out, I don't give one hill of beans if your trunks are on or not.

I smile wickedly, and then, before he has time to process the evil about to befall him, I give him a solid shove from behind and dump his practical butt in the pool.

He comes up out of the water like a cologne ad that never made it to live television because it was too sensual. His navy shirt is clinging to his chiseled body, and his hair is dripping wet before he dashes his hand through it, sending glistening water droplets through the air—and basically, I've never been prouder of a decision in my entire life.

Sam has dissolved into a fit of laughter beside me, and I'm pretty sure that Charlie just called Jake a ding-dong under his breath. (Obviously, he likes Jake, but I think he's a tad bit jealous of our new friendship. He can go cry to Rachel Green.)

"Laugh it up, chuckles," Jake says with a heart-melting smile. "You're next."

I see what he's doing. He's inching toward the edge of the pool with a smirk that says *I'm coming for you*. Jake is so certain that I'm going to scream and run away like the girl who just got her hair done and would rather die than ruin her blowout. He doesn't know me very well yet, and my hair appointment is so overdue I think my hairstylist has given up on me completely.

I live by a very simple rule: if a sexy man is in a pool and smiling at me like Jake is now, I don't waste a single moment standing on the side.

Before he has a chance to make it to the stairs, I take off running and cannonball in right beside him.

CHAPTER 16

Evie

I'm wringing out my hair from my shower and listening to Leon Bridges croon over the speakers. I have a sweet-scented candle lit on my coffee table, and everything is right with the world. It's been a good week. A good day, especially.

I can't put my finger on it, but something about me feels different. I'm still working my same job; I still have my same thimble-sized apartment; there is still the same chance I'll have a seizure today as there was yesterday, but something feels different. It's like I had a pile of books stacked on my desk, and although I can't be certain, I think someone came in at some point and rearranged them. I'm rearranged.

Laughing in the pool tonight with Jake and Sam made me feel a sense of belonging. It scares me as much as it excites me, but I don't want to give in to the fear. I still feel like I'm sitting up in the nosebleeds, but maybe I'm ready to walk down a few flights of stairs to get closer to the field.

I think Jake might be having these same feelings. I could try to talk myself out of it—run a fake play on my own heart and choose to believe that he's not interested in me. But here's the thing: I catch him looking at me a lot. And it's not a normal look. It's a smoldering, knock-your-socks-off-and-carry-you-to-bed kind of look. He's at least attracted to me—I know that much.

So, what kind of dance are we doing here?

I've just finished squeezing the water out of my hair and neatly hanging up my towel on the drying rack (ha ha, just kidding! It's lying in a bundle on the floor, where it will probably live for the rest of the week) when I hear a knock at my door.

"Did you order cookies again?" I ask the lazy dog lying on my bed.

He gives me a look that says *stop blaming me for your poor nutritional habits* and then lays his head back down. It's a good thing he's so cute.

I open the door and then realize I should have looked through the peephole first. I could have just opened my home to a murderer, or a thief, or—*gasp*—my mom. But thanks to my incredible luck in life lately, I open the door to none other than Jacob Broaden.

"Jake!" I say, and *whoa* I need to simmer down because I sound *way* too excited to see him. Play it cool. I'm supposed to be walking down the stairs toward the field, not full-on sprinting and skipping steps.

He likes it, though, because he smiles until his eyes crinkle in the corners. "Hey, Evie."

Then his gaze drops and takes in my clothes.

And this is the moment that I remember what a lovely ensemble I am wearing. I have on an extra-large shirt that reads *Dolly is my fairy godmother,* which lands just above my knees, tall socks, and no bra. To make it worse, I'm wearing flannel pajama shorts under my shirt, but there's no way you can see those, so basically I look like I've opened the door without pants on.

Although I would never have worn this if I knew he was coming over, I also have to admit that I am enjoying the appreciative look in his eye.

No. Bad, Evie.

I fold my arms across my chest (but let's face it, my boobs are so small that this part is only for show) and feel the need to blurt, "I'm wearing shorts!" And if that wasn't stupid enough, I uncross one arm to lift up my shirt just enough to show him my green-and-red-checkered flannel bottoms.

He's so smug now. I swear he looks like a man who's just been told he won *GQ* magazine's Sexiest Man of the Year award. I'm squirming under his gaze, and he's loving the effect he has on me. "I like the Christmas trees on them," he says, and yes, I do wear Christmas PJs in July.

"It feels wrong to leave something in my drawer all year just because it's eighty degrees out. Do you want to come in?"

He nods and my heart races. Jacob Broaden is going to come into my apartment. My tiny, minuscule mousehole that really should be called a playhouse rather than an apartment because it looks like dolls could fit in here easier than humans. He ducks his head as he steps through the door, and *oh my gosh,* I just remembered that I'm a slob.

I quickly survey what I like to think of as my *boho* apartment through the eyes of Jake and see what he's seeing.

Unfortunately, since my whole apartment is only one room, he gets to see it all. Unmade bed. Cereal bowls stacked up on my itty-bitty kitchen counter (but the butcher-block top still looks adorable). Half-empty cups of old coffee sitting on my end table. Clothing dotting the hardwood floor. And is that . . . ? Yep! My bright-pink bra is definitely draped over the back of my couch from where I took it off as soon as I got home earlier.

I make a lunge to grab it before Jake sees it, but it's too late. He's looking at it now and smiling. I grab for it anyway and tuck it behind my back, aiming a tight smile at him. "Clearly, I wasn't expecting company."

"I'm glad. I like seeing how you live." He looks right at me, and I think I might fall over. This apartment is too small, and he's too big for it. If he moves, I'll bump into him.

I don't think I've ever been so nervous having someone in my space before. Jake is so grown and adult and hot. And I'm . . . well, I'm grown too, but I definitely don't feel adult. Never have. Probably never will. I've given up any aspirations of becoming the woman who rinses out her mug and puts it right into the dishwasher when I'm done with it. I don't need that kind of pressure in my life.

My nerves are sizzling like bacon in a frying pan, and I feel the urge to bounce. Why is he here? I only left his house about two hours ago. His presence in my apartment doesn't make sense.

"Did I forget something at your place?" I ask after a minute more of his quiet surveying. I want to blindfold him.

"Nope."

Oh great. Now he's walking fully into my apartment and sitting down on the couch. I want to laugh—no, I do laugh—because he makes my love seat look more like an armchair.

"Okaayyy. Well, don't take this the wrong way, but what are you doing here?"

He grins, his dimples come out to play, and now I'm way too aware that it's after eight P.M. He's not texting me. He's in my living room, breathing my air, and adding at least ten degrees of heat to the room.

"Do I make you nervous being in here?"

"No." I shift my weight to my other foot, shove my pink bra under the blankets on my bed, push my hair behind my ear—*don't like that*—untuck my hair. "Okay, maybe a little. Is this payback for me snooping around your room?"

He chuckles and moves his big arms to spread out over the back of my love seat. He looks mighty comfy there. Like a man who's in no hurry to leave. What the heck is happening?!

"Actually, I came by to bring you an invitation." He eyes me, and his brows pull together. "Are you going to stay over there all night?"

If this were a movie, this is the part where the camera would pan to me and I'd be gone. It would have to tilt up to find me plastered in the farthest upper corner of my apartment, like Spider-Man.

Why am I being so weird? I'm twenty-six years old and acting like I've never been alone with a man before. So what if Jake is here at my apartment? No big deal. Friends visit other friends' apartments all the time. I just wish this friend was wearing a bra.

"An invitation?" I ask, moving closer to Jake. He scoots toward one end of the "couch" and makes room for me.

Okay. I guess I'm sitting there. With Jake. That's fine.

I sit down, and we are so close now that I feel like I might as well be sitting on his lap. I adjust so that my legs are up in the seat with me and I'm somewhat facing Jake. Because having my feet touch his leg is way better than the whole right side of my body. Well, not better. Just friendlier and less steamy.

He reaches into his pocket, pulls out a folded piece of paper, and hands it to me. There is a very childish drawing of a girl jumping into a pool drawn on the front. "I had no idea you were such an artist," I say with a grin.

"I could say the same about you." He nods his head toward my fruit masterpiece leaning up against the wall. "Gotta say, I didn't take you for a butt girl."

My face flames and I laugh. "It was supposed to be an orange."

"Mm-hmm. Sure it was."

"Oh, go home and finish *Twilight*," I say while shoving his shoulder.

He laughs, and I love the sound. It echoes off the walls, and somehow my apartment suddenly feels safer and homier.

"So, what's this?" I'm opening the invitation and reading the few scribbled lines stating a date and time. SATURDAY, 12:00.

"Sam and I decided you were right, and we should make more time for fun. So, this is your official invite to our pool party this weekend."

I look up from the invitation, and I feel my smile growing too big. It's more appropriate for winning a new car off of *The Price Is Right* than accepting a pool-party invitation. "I love this idea. Count me in."

"Before you agree, you should know that my entire family will be there."

Okay, okay, okay. Just chill the freak out, Evie.

I want to dissect every part of what he just said and look for all the hidden implications. Meet his family? This has to mean something, right?! But instead, I answer, "How entire are we talking? Like distant-crazy-Uncle-Fred-who-drinks-too-much-and-might-try-to-cop-a-feel *entire*?"

He laughs and rubs his hands over dark-denim-jean-clad thighs. "Just my parents, sisters, and their families."

"That doesn't sound too bad. In fact, it sounds like fun." Someone sign me up for a movie deal, because I'm such a good actor right now that no one would suspect I'm completely freaking out. *Jake wants me to meet his family. Wants me to spend the day with his family.* Which reminds me of something.

"Wait, where's Sam right now?"

"My sister is at home with her. I had to run into the office for a little bit."

Right. The office. *His* office. The one he owns. I have to stop thinking of these things, because all they do is remind me that there is no way this guy should be interested in me. I'm the furthest from successful anyone could be. Just ask my mom. She'll vouch for me.

"So, work usually keeps you pretty busy?"

He sighs one of those heavy man sighs that sounds like he's literally holding the world on his shoulders. "Yeah. But I've delegated a lot of my work to the two other architects in the firm."

"You don't sound as relieved as a person normally does after a statement like that."

"I guess it's because I'm not really all that relieved. This is going to make me sound like the world's worst dad, but . . . I love my job. It's been hard for me to give up most of my work to be home with Sam."

I shake my head. "That doesn't make you sound like a bad parent. I think, if anything, it shows how amazing you are. You're giving up something you love to be there for your kid."

"Thanks. It was easier to balance it all when . . ." His words trail off, and I know what he's not saying.

"When you were married and had a second parent at home with Sam?"

His blue eyes lock with mine, and he nods. "Sorry. I don't mean to keep dropping that in every conversation."

"It's okay. Really. It's a part of your life, so why wouldn't I want to talk with you about it?" And then, suddenly, I realize I'm not such a good actor after all because I'm letting my interest in him show way too much. I clear my throat and look down at my knees. "How were Sam and Daisy getting on after I left?"

"Great. Sam is like a new kid with Daisy. She seems so much lighter and more excited about everything." He chuckles. "She even put a fake spider in my sock drawer earlier today. You have no idea how good it is to have her interacting with me like that again."

I smile. "That's wonderful, Jake. I'm so happy for you guys. I know what it's like to find that security, and there's nothing quite like it."

"Is that how you felt when you first got Charlie?"

I smile at the memory of those first few weeks of finding my new independence. My parents hated it, but I thrived on it. "Yep. It was pretty wonderful. I didn't move out of my parents' house until I was twenty-three because I was so scared of what life with epilepsy would look like living on my own. But Charlie and I clicked right away. My parents didn't support my decision to leave their house at all because . . . well, I think they liked being able to keep me under their thumb. So, when I moved out, Joanna became more of a mom to me than my own mother ever was. She helped me set up a landline here that attaches to a special button Charlie can push when I have a seizure."

I pause and point to the round yellow button on the wall by my bed. "It speed-dials Joanna's number. She usually waits about ten minutes for my seizure to pass and for me to regain consciousness and then calls me to make sure I'm okay." I pause and glance at my little furry hero. "And even though we can't technically train a service dog to alert before a seizure, he has. Charlie usually alerts me about thirty minutes before almost all of my seizures, and that gives me a chance to go lie down in a safe place."

"That's . . . I don't even feel like the word *amazing* is good enough. Do you think Daisy will do that with Sam?"

"Hopefully. But only time will tell. Just keep an eye out for Daisy doing anything out of the ordinary. It could be her trying to signal you."

Jake nods thoughtfully for a moment, and I think he's about to say something profound. "And to think we would never have found any of this new independence for Sam if it weren't for you telling me to get my head out of my ass."

He and I both laugh at the memory. I still can't believe I said that to him, but I don't regret it. Not if it got us to this place.

Jake's eyes land on mine again, and his playful smile dies away. Something is changing in the air, and my body is fully aware of it. He shifts his arm and gently grasps a lock of my damp hair between his fingers. "I'm serious, though, Evie. Thank you. I owe you." His low voice is rolling over me, and I'm a little worried his finger is going to brush against my neck and feel my hammering pulse.

"You don't owe me anything."

His gaze is unwavering. "I don't think you understand just how much you've helped us. It had been so long since I'd heard Sam laugh. And you helping her with her nails and her hair . . ." He shakes his head with a sad smile. "There are so many small things like that I'm not good at but worry she really needs from me. And it's clear she values those things more than I realized."

I bump his knee. "You're a great dad. I've seen it firsthand, Jake. And those things you're mentioning can be learned. Those are the easy parts."

"I've tried. But . . . I don't like learning on her. Natalie and I have already made so many mistakes that she pays for—and I feel even worse when I'm trying to fix her hair and just make her cry instead."

"Then practice on me." I say the words before I can decide if it's a good idea or not. And I don't pause to take them back either. "Come on." I tug him up from the couch.

"Where are we going?"

"Well, my apartment is as big as your eyebrow so we're only going about two steps to my bathroom to gather supplies. But after that! We're going five steps to my little kitchen island, where you're going to practice Girls' Day on me."

CHAPTER 17

Jake

She's loading down my arms with supplies. "What do you mean by 'practice Girls' Day'?"

There's barely enough room in this bathroom for the two of us, so I'm hovering half-in and half-out of the door. Evie keeps rummaging through disorganized drawers and pulling out little bags of stuff. She dumps one on the pile she's already made in my arms, unzips it, confirms it's full of nail polish, and zips it back up. "You know, Girls' Day. Where you get fun drinks and do your nails and hair and go shopping and pretend the worries of the world don't exist. It's a whole thing, and you need to be ready for it."

I'm Evie's pack mule, strapped down with cosmetic bags. She squeezes past me in the doorway, her body skimming over mine before she wraps her hand around my biceps and pulls me toward her tiny kitchen island.

"I'm not going to lie, I'm still a little lost."

"I told you. You're going to practice on me so you can feel confident when you do it with Sam."

She's on the opposite side of the island and leans across it to unzip the bag and dump out at least fifteen nail polishes. They clank together as she wildly rummages through them. She's a beautiful agent of chaos.

"You're going to let me paint your nails?" I line up her polishes side by side. It's a neat row of beauty soldiers.

Her hand brushes mine as she takes a pink from my grasp before I can line it up. "First, you're going to paint your own because I think it helps you understand the flow of polish better and what you don't want to happen when painting someone else's nails. You can graduate to me once you've learned the basics."

I give a cocky smirk. "You don't have to worry, Evie. I'm a master at the basics. Been practicing those on myself since I was a teenager."

She presses her lips together against a laugh—it grumbles behind her closed mouth anyway. "Interesting. I thought you would have had plenty of volunteers to help you practice," she says with a taunting smile of her own. "Since you have four sisters and . . . oh wow . . . no, wait. That inappropriate joke really fell apart at the end."

My face is a look of horror as I laugh. "I have found your only flaw. Evie Jones is not good at innuendo."

"Oh, I have plenty more flaws where that one came from. Just call my mom and ask—she'll list them off one by one for you."

"I remember you saying you're not close with your parents. What happened there?"

She stares at the line of nail polishes. "They're . . . we're just different people." Her eyes snap back up to me and she smiles. "That's enough about the Joneses. You can sit there."

I pull out the small barstool and take a seat. Evie rips off a square of paper towel and sets it in front of me. A makeshift drop cloth. She selects a blue polish, shakes it, and hands it to me.

"Who's this for?" I frown at the color.

"You. I thought you'd want it."

I grimace. "I prefer yellow, with a glitter layer please."

Her eyebrows raise in a look of happy approval. "Glitter is intermediate. Let's focus on the base layer for now and see how you do."

It takes all of ten minutes for me to screw up my fingernails. I look like an actual toddler. No—I'm sure toddlers paint nails better than I have. It's all over my cuticles and clumped up into sticky patches that will never dry in certain places. Evie has lost it laughing at me more than once, and I blame my terrible painting skills on her distracting smile. On the fact that I can't look away from her for more than thirty seconds before my eyes trail back in her direction.

I'm eating up every second I get alone with Evie. I never want it to end.

"Here," she says on a laugh, making me extend my hand across the island in her direction. And then she takes my hand in hers, dips a cotton ball in some polish remover solution, and starts brushing it over my nails. "This is embarrassing. I can't let you leave here like this. I thought architects are supposed to be good with details."

She leans over my hand, and her messy bun of blond hair wobbles a bit to the right. Pieces are falling all around her face and down the curve of her neck. I want to trace them with my fingertips.

"I'm better with a pencil." I'm trying to focus on my hand and not the place where her oversized shirt has fallen off her bare shoulder. Her skin looks as soft as velvet, with a light golden-brown tint that makes my mouth water. I want to kiss that patch of skin. I want to taste it.

"Let's hope you're better at using your basic skills on other people than you are using them on yourself." Evie's voice pulls my gaze from her shoulder to her laughing eyes. She's finished removing my polish and is now holding out her fingers for me to paint.

I force myself to breathe and pick up the polish she's chosen for herself. Hot pink. "Look at you, already improving on your dirty jokes."

"Let's hope you're as quick of a learner as I am," she says while wiggling her fingers in front of me.

Focus, Jake.

I do a pretty decent job of it this time, managing to keep most of the polish on her nail rather than her skin. And when I'm done, there's only a few smudges. She assesses them with a smile that I want to drink up. "Much better. I think you're ready to move on to hair."

I frown. "I'm not even going to pretend to not be terrified of that. Last time I tried to brush Sam's hair it ended in literal crying. Like tears pouring down her cheeks. I don't want to put you through that—because you seem to have twice the amount of hair as Sam." My eyes instinctively creep up to the blond bun on top of her head.

She waves me off, though. "I have a hard head. You can't hurt me. I'm the best test subject." Careful not to smudge her wet nails, she plucks the hairbrush from the counter. "Let's go to the couch."

I sit down first and then freeze as Evie steps right in front of me between my legs. For one glorious second my brain imagines all sorts of things. Placing my hands on her hips and spinning her to face me. I'd lift her shirt and kiss her stomach. I'd—

She sits on the floor, and I quickly blink the desire out of my eyes. Because I'm sure my pupils are so blown out right now I'd look like one of those vampires I've been reading about.

"You'll have to take my hair tie out for me." She holds up her nails to remind me that they're wet.

I fill my lungs before carefully taking the scrunchie between my fingers and unraveling it from her knot of hair. It tugs once and I hiss, afraid I've hurt her. She just laughs. "I told you; I have a hard head. You can't have hair as long as mine and be sensitive."

Of course I immediately imagine dipping my lips to her neck and seeing if she's sensitive there or not.

I swallow my attraction and get back to work. Finally, her hair loosens and falls down over her shoulders and back. It's long and beautiful—even in this wavy, tangly state, I'm gripped by it. But to be fair, it could be any length or color and I'd still think the same thing because it's a part of her.

A hairbrush enters my line of sight. "Here. Use this."

I take it from her and my nerves twist. "You really want me to brush your hair? I'm telling you—"

"Stop being so timid and brush my hair, Broaden."

I chuckle and take her challenge. Starting with the brush at the top of her head, I sink it into her hair and start pulling it down. It's ripping through so many tangles, it sounds like Pop Rocks. I stop midway down. "I'm really so—"

"I thought so. You're doing it wrong."

She reaches behind her, gathers all of her hair into a ponytail, then raises it to me. "Hold this," she says, and I just stare at it. This feels . . . intimate. Should holding all of her hair in my hand feel seductive? Has it just been that long since I've had sex that I'm overthinking the most basic of touches?

Trying to act as natural and unaffected as possible, I take her hair in my left hand. She then covers my right hand, holding the brush with hers, and moves it to the end of her ponytail. "If Sam has a sensitive scalp, you're going to want to keep her hair gathered up like this in one hand while you work the tangles out from bottom to top like this." She guides my hand through the movement as she talks—and *damn* this is hot when it absolutely shouldn't be. It's not sexual in the least, but it feels like the most sensual thing that's ever happened to me.

"Okay, I got it," I tell her after a minute, gaining confidence and guiding her hand away so I can do it myself. And now that I'm getting the hang of it, working in small sections up her hair like she suggested, I'm able to just enjoy the experience. I soak in the sweet scent of her shampoo. I'll be smelling it all night in my dreams.

"Jake," Evie says, when her hair is nearly free of tangles. "You may feel like you're in over your head with Sam, but you're not. You're a fantastic dad to her. I hope you know that."

I pause, feeling her words like an arrow to the heart. "I'm trying."

"And that's what sets you apart from the rest." Her voice sounds sad. I wish I could see her face. "My dad would never have cared enough about me to learn to brush my hair the right way. I'm not even sure he knows what color my eyes are. But he definitely knows when I'm going to say something to anger my mom, and he leaves the room before that happens."

I set the brush aside and run my fingers through her hair—feeling the silken locks slide through like water. The backs of my knuckles brush her warm neck, and I notice she tilts her head a little, arching against my touch.

"I pity him. He's a fool to have missed out on getting to know you."

She turns her face to me over her shoulder and our eyes connect. I smile warmly and she returns it. I'm still playing with a lock of her hair, running it back and forth between my thumb and index finger. But something about her look is undoing me slowly. Effortlessly drawing me in.

Before I can stop myself, I push all of her soft hair over her shoulder, exposing the side of her face that's turned to me. I'm not totally sure what I'm intending here—my body seems to be on autopilot.

I touch the bottom of her chin, tilting her face up.

"Evie." I whisper her name like a question. Silently begging her to stop this if it's a bad idea. I'm hoping she's thinking rationally, because I'm not. I'm drunk on her attention.

But she doesn't stop me; she twists her body a little more in my direction. My hand slides from her chin, down her jaw, to cup behind her neck. I brush my thumb over her pulse and feel it hammering under her skin. She doesn't know it, but the rhythm of my heart matches hers. It's frantic.

I dip a little closer, giving her all the time in the world to pull away, but she doesn't. Her lips part as her gaze drops to my mouth. There's fire in her eyes that ignites my skin.

"I owe you a compliment," I say quietly. Almost afraid if I speak too loudly it'll burst this moment.

"A compliment?" she asks, her voice little more than a breath too.

"The other night. You said you wanted to know what it was like to get one from me. And I changed the subject because I was too scared to tell you what I was really thinking." She waits, her chest rising and falling faster as I run my thumb up and down the side of her neck. "You are *so* beautiful, Evie. Gorgeous, actually. But more than that—I can't . . . I've never met anyone like you."

I lean in even closer, hesitating just before my lips touch her cheek. She can ask me to stop and I will. Instead, she leans into me.

"I can't get you out of my head." Her skin is so warm and soft against my lips as I kiss a little closer to her mouth. "I like the way you laugh. It's . . . mischievous almost. Like you're always planning something." She chuckles and I kiss the corner of her mouth—not wanting to cut off the sound of her laughter but needing to feel it against my lips.

"And your eyes. Damn, Evie, your eyes are so pretty I can't handle it. Deep emerald green—I've never seen a color so vibrant before."

"Jake . . ." she whispers, closing her eyes. "What are you doing?"

"And your *mouth*." I inch my hand up so I can touch my thumb against her bottom lip—tracing it *oh so lightly*. I can barely contain my heartbeat now, it's kicking against my chest so hard. "Does it freak you out to know I've been dreaming of kissing you since I met you?" I shouldn't be saying any of this. But I can't stop myself either.

"That depends." She rises up to her knees, fully facing me, bracketed by my legs and sending a bite of need down my spine. "Does it freak *you* out to know I've been thinking of kissing you since I met you?"

"Liar." I grin. "You hated me when you first met me."

"You don't have to like a person to want to kiss them. And I have dreamed of it every single time I've been with you. And even when I'm not with you."

Any hesitation I have is gone. I don't know if this is a good idea, and I don't care anymore. All that exists is Evie. I'm not Sam's dad right now or Natalie's ex-husband. I'm simply Jake, the man about to kiss Evie Jones.

"Then maybe we should kiss?" I say, tilting my head. "Just once to get it out of our systems?"

Something flashes in Evie's eyes. A small frown tugs between her brows, and before I have time to consider it she presses forward, taking the kiss I've been dangling in front of her for minutes. I suck in a sharp breath as her lips crush against mine. And just as quickly, she pulls back. The separation is so abrupt our lips make a popping sound, and I'm momentarily stunned.

"There," she says, slightly breathless. "Is it out of your system now?"

Ah—I see. She called my bluff. "Point taken."

"You've been holding back since you met me. Why? And why now when I know you don't want only one kiss?"

I hold her gaze and debate just how honest to be with her. "I . . . haven't dated anyone since Natalie. I haven't even been with anyone else since her." *All the way honest, Jake.* "It's more than that, actually. I haven't been with anyone at all besides her. She was my first and my last." I push Evie's hair behind her ear. "Those are my deep, dark secrets. And I want to kiss the hell out of you, Evie, but I don't know if I'm ready for anything more physical than that tonight."

Part of me expects Evie to be repulsed by that truth. To look awkward and start scooting away because that was quite the honesty bomb I just dropped on her.

Instead, she smiles one of her trademark soft smiles, puts her palms on my knees, and leans in to kiss my cheek. Just as gently as I kissed her the first time. "Thank you for telling me. We'll go slow. Do you want to kiss a little?" she asks, and the sweetness of what she just said, how kindly she treats me, it tears me into a million pieces.

I cradle her face in my hands and kiss her. Firmly and fully. No holding back and no buildup this time. Just my mouth slanting over hers and taking the kiss I've wanted since I saw her walk into the coffee shop. She wraps her arms around my neck, settling in closer. My nerves rise to the surface of my skin to accept every small touch she gives me. Maybe I'm rusty—maybe my kissing is outdated. But Evie kisses well enough for the both of us. Her mouth moves against mine in seductive caresses that have me gripped with need.

I drop my hands from her face to wrap around her lower back, tugging her in close to me. Her mouth opens and I take the invitation, sliding my tongue between her lips as she sinks her hands into the back of my hair. I groan from her silkiness and how sweet she tastes. *Dammit, I need more.*

The tension between our bodies smolders. If our clothes don't come off soon, they'll set fire and burn us both to ash. Her teeth bite my lip into her mouth, and I can't get enough of her. Her hands are on my shoulders, my neck, the back of my hair. They roam up under the back of my shirt, hot against my skin as my tongue sweeps over hers. With my hands around her back, I tug her to my chest and lift her off the ground, sweeping us both onto the couch.

She squeaks and breaks the kiss, jumping off me and pacing three steps away while pointing an accusing finger in my direction. "You said you only wanted to kiss!" Her eyes are bright with desire. I'm hypnotized.

"I changed my mind." I stand up from the couch, and she steps backward, her back hitting the wall beside the TV. "I want more if you do."

"*Yes,* I want more. I mean, no! You can't." She shakes her head. "I won't let you. You're in a sexy haze and not thinking straight."

"I love a sexy haze." I press her hips to the wall with my hands and drop my mouth to her neck. "I need to hear a consensual yes before I continue."

She whimpers. "*Jaaake.* I'm trying to be strong for you."

"I don't need you to be. Yes or no, Evie?" Sure, maybe all my fears have magically disappeared now that sexual desire has taken over, but either way, I'm not worried about being with someone new anymore. The jitters are gone. The wanting is unbearable, however.

"It's a yes from me, but . . . but I won't be able to keep talking you out of . . . oh gosh—" Her head lulls back against the wall. "I can't process good decisions when you are sucking my neck like that."

I trail a line up her throat with my mouth until I make it to her lips. This kiss is hungry and frantic. Searching quickly for new angles and new parts of our bodies to touch and press together, and just as I find her hands and push them against the wall above her head, she slips out of my loose grip and out of my arms altogether.

She's bouncing on the balls of her feet like a fighter in a ring. "A few minutes ago you sat there and told me you weren't ready for anything more physical." I look to the ghost of the man in question and mentally flip him the bird. "We're not doing anything but kissing tonight, Jake. I care about you too much to wake up tomorrow and see regret in your eyes."

I puff out a heavy breath and run my hand through my hair.

"Thank you for caring about me," I say reluctantly, even if I'm annoyed at myself for suggesting it in the first place.

She opens her mouth to say something else when we're interrupted by a knock at the door.

Evie frowns.

CHAPTER 18

Jake

I try not to smile as Evie adjusts her T-shirt and runs her hands through her wild hair that I had smoothed out and then immediately messed up. While she goes to answer the door, I sit back down on the couch, rest my elbows on my knees, and scrape my hands through my hair in an attempt to settle myself. *What the hell just happened?* Was that a bad idea? I haven't fully decided yet. As the height of the moment is wearing off, though, I do think I'm grateful she put a stop to it. I'm not just Jake. I have a daughter to consider before I get too tangled up with anyone new.

And believe it or not, what happened a minute ago is *not* why I came over here. I only intended to give her the invitation and run. *Just your friendly neighborhood postman.*

But no. I saw her, and my body suddenly had other plans. Plans to kiss her. Plans to do a lot more than just kiss her, apparently.

What now? I wanted to move slow. This little action just changed things. Now I have a conversation on the horizon that I'm not at all prepared for.

Well, maybe I'm a little prepared for it. The more time I spend with Evie, the more I can't imagine not dating her. But I don't know if I can trust myself. I've made a poor decision concerning a woman before, and look how that turned out. Although, I know I don't want to spend the rest of my life alone . . . so I'll have to face my fears at some point. Looks like that point is now.

I hear Evie open the door, then gasp. I turn toward the door just in time to hear her say, "Mom. Dad. What are you doing here?"

Oh, super.

I shoot up from the couch, and in a split second—because Evie's apartment is made for ants—I'm standing beside her at the door. Her mom's eyes are wide as they look from me to Evie and then slowly down Evie's body in the same way one might look at a nudist they've just encountered on the sidewalk.

I don't know why I suddenly have the urge to defend our current state. *She's wearing shorts!* I'm a grown man, and Evie's a grown woman. Even if she weren't wearing shorts, that's our business.

But Evie's mom has the look of a woman about to chew out her daughter. Instinctively, I move to shield Evie. "Hi," I say, sticking my hand out toward her dad first. "I'm Jacob Broaden."

He shakes my hand with all the gusto of a dead fish and cocks one eyebrow. "Harold Jones."

Wait a second. I pause mid-handshake. Harold Jones? As in, *the* Harold Jones from the long line of Joneses that have made up the majority of our city's wealth for generations? I knew Evie's last name was Jones, but I guess I never thought to ask her if there was any connection because she just seems so . . . normal.

I slide my wide eyes to Mrs. Jones, and she rolls her eyes at Evie.

"I can see you haven't told him who your relatives are." The woman sounds like she's never been more bored in her life. She looks at me again but doesn't even offer me her hand. "Melony Jones."

Oh yeah. I know who she is. Everyone in Charleston knows who this woman is. And she's just as off-putting as I had imagined.

Suddenly, I feel like laughing. Here I was, thinking that Evie would be impressed with my little architectural firm and two-thousand-square-foot house, when she grew up with the leading socialites of Charleston in a twelve-million-dollar home. I know this because I read the magazine article about it last month. I feel embarrassingly ignorant.

She gave up all that to live in this shoebox? I have a whole new appreciation for Evie. Not because she came from money but because she turned out so down-to-earth despite her entitled upbringing.

Mrs. Jones turns her sharp eyes to Evie; apparently, she's done with me. I'm just a small fly, and I've been swatted away. "Evelyn Grace, are you going to make us stand out here all night?"

"I'm entertaining a guest right now," Evie says through her teeth. I'm impressed by her backbone. She's not cowering under this woman's haughty glare—and believe me, it's more than a little intimidating.

"Clearly," Mrs. Jones says with another accusatory glance at Evie's bare legs.

I take one more look too, because *goodness* she has amazing-looking legs.

"But you've been taught better than to leave your parents standing out in the heat like this." Mrs. Jones pushes past both of us and steps into Evie's place uninvited. It's shocking. I don't think I've ever seen anyone do that before.

Mr. Jones pulls out his phone and frowns down at it. He answers it, turns around, and walks back out without so much as a glance to the rest of us. *These people are something.*

"I can't do this right now, Mom. I don't want to inflict our drama on an innocent bystander." Evie gestures toward me.

I have no idea what to do right now. Do I jump to her aid? Do I act as her bouncer and throw these people out? I'm not prepared for this, but I want to help somehow.

Mrs. Jones acts as if she doesn't hear Evie's comment. "We won't be long." She runs her finger across the small entry table and then examines it for dust. "Honestly, Evelyn, what has happened to you? This place looks like a pigsty."

I expect Evie to take offense to this, but instead, when I look at her, I notice that she's looking at me—and she's amused. No, not amused. She looks like she's about to crack up laughing. And then I realize she's looking at my hair.

I glance in the mirror on the wall and find that it's sticking up in all directions. Possibly from where I ran my hands through it while Evie was getting the door. Possibly from where Evie ran *her* hands through it while I was licking her neck. *Who's to say.* But this, coupled with Evie's outfit, looks more than incriminating. I quickly smooth it down, trying to hide my own laugh now.

"If you're just here to comment on my cleanliness, Mom, you can walk right back out. I'm happy with the way I live."

"That's not why I'm here. Although I do feel compelled to mention that if you would stop being foolish and accept Tyler, you would be able to move out of this cardboard box."

Wait a minute. Who's Tyler?

"I don't live in the 1800s, Mom. I'm not going to accept a man's proposal just because he has a big estate. Am I the only one who thinks this idea is ludicrous?"

Proposal? Apparently, Evie's not as unattached as I thought. . . .

Mrs. Jones's eyes suddenly shift to me, and I can see her sizing me up. "Is *he* the reason you're not accepting Tyler?" She's looking at me, but it's clear that she's not talking to me.

"Okay, this conversation is over." Evie walks back to her door and opens it. "Time to go, Mom."

Mrs. Jones turns a smirk to me. "If my daughter won't answer me, I'll ask you. Exactly who are you to Evelyn?"

"He's a friend," says Evie before I have a chance to open my mouth.

Mrs. Jones makes a guttural noise and then starts to stroll toward the door at a leisurely pace. "I only came by to inform you that your cellphone bill is overdue. If I don't see your payment in our account by the end of the week, I'll be forced to have your phone turned off."

Turned off? Is this woman high on something? She sounds more like a villain in a movie, threatening to bash Evie's kneecaps in if that AT&T money doesn't show up soon.

This reminds me of something Evie said the first time we had coffee, about her bank account balance matching her age. At the time I thought she was kidding. But now I'm genuinely concerned.

"Of course," her mother continues, "if you decide to have a relationship with Tyler, all of those ugly bills will go away. And you are welcome to come live in the guest house for free until you and Tyler marry."

"Great, not going to happen," Evie bites out. "Message received. You can leave now. Tell Dad I said thanks for stopping by to check on me." Her sarcasm is thick, and although I've never seen her like this, I understand it. Admire it, even.

A protective energy courses through my veins, and I'm powerless to stop it. If this villain in the baby-blue pantsuit doesn't leave in the next minute, I'm going to end up throwing her out myself.

Mrs. Jones shakes her head at Evie. "You're making a mistake, dear. I just want the best for you and your future." That almost sounded nice. And maybe it would have been a kind parting had she stopped talking right there. Melony casts a disgusted glance over Evie's appearance one last time. "And for heaven's sake,

Evelyn Grace, you shouldn't be so easy. It looks bad on the Jones name."

Okay, that's it. I'm hot on Melony's heels, but Evie reaches out and catches my chest before I can follow the monster out. She shuts the door quickly and puts her back to it like she doesn't trust me to not wrench it open and go after Melony Jones. Probably for the best. Not sure I trust myself right now.

I stare at Evie for a minute, waiting for the floodgates to open or her fury to burn hot. Instead, her dimples pop, and she smiles. "Can I bring anything to the pool party on Saturday?"

My mouth falls open. "How are you so calm?!" I feel like the Hulk, ready to rip my shirt off and burst through the ceiling; and she's just standing there, looking like a springtime fairy. "How are you not spitting angry right now?"

She shrugs and steps away from the door. "I stopped letting that woman steal my joy about fifteen therapy sessions ago. Where do you think all my money disappears to?"

I don't know what else to do, so I walk over to Evie and wrap my arms around her. I want to hold her close because, somehow, I get the feeling she and Sam share more than just the same disability. I think Evie is tough as nails, but she'll still cry into her pillow the second I leave.

For a moment, she seems shocked. She doesn't move. Her arms are limp noodles beside her body. But then they finally lift up and wrap around my waist, and she squeezes me back as tightly as I'm squeezing her. It's all I can offer her.

"They suck," I mumble into her hair, and she laughs.

"Yeah. They're not the best parents."

"Why didn't you tell me what family you were from? I had no idea."

She pulls away from me and starts busying herself by packing up all the nail polish. "Because number one, how weird would it have been if the second I met you, I said, 'Hi! I'm Evie Jones. You know? Of the famous Joneses who practically own this city?' And number two, I'm trying to make my own way in life without riding their coattails."

She moves on to a fluffy blue blanket, which she aggressively folds.

"I understand that." We're both quiet for a moment, and then, when I can't take it any longer, I finally ask the question that's been eating at me. "So, who's the Tyler guy your mom was talking about?"

Evie grins like she can tell I'm jealous and likes it. "Have you heard of my dad's law firm? Jones and Murray? Well, Tyler is Tyler Murray. He just inherited his dad's half of the firm. Our parents have been planning on our marriage since we were kids so that they could always keep the company in trustworthy hands. The problem is, I'm the only one who doesn't want the marriage."

Only one?

"So, that means Tyler *does* want the marriage?"

Evie shrugs like it's not a big deal. Like this relationship I was beginning to picture between us didn't just grow fuzzier and more unclear. Is there even a chance for us now? If Tyler is one of the Murrays, I've no doubt he's a millionaire. By society's standards, he would be a catch. How do I stand a chance against someone like that?

Then again . . . I'm here with Evie in her little apartment that she chose to live in because she didn't want the same life as her parents. So, that's something. Isn't it?

"Tyler wants a pretty wife on his arm who will help him climb the social and economic ladder. Marrying a Jones is exactly what he needs to ensure that happens. He doesn't want me. He wants what we would represent together. A unified company in more ways than just business. Investors would love it and it could be a boost to the company."

"And you don't want that?"

Evie laughs, and the sound makes my heart lighter. "I sent that idea down the toilet a long time ago. Honestly, Tyler and I dated for a while in high school, and that was enough to make me never want to be attached to that man again. And he's only gotten worse since we broke up."

I don't say anything for a minute. I'm not sure what to say. Evie accurately interprets my silence and goes on. "Jake. I don't . . . I don't know if it's necessary for me to say this to you or not, but there really is no chance of me ever wanting to marry Tyler Murray—or any man like him, for that matter."

I really want to let those words soothe my fears, but it just isn't helping me feel better about wanting to date her. If anything, it adds to my terror about a million percent. What if we get serious and then she changes her mind and finally takes Tyler up on his offer? I don't know. I can't think about that right now. I need to change the subject before I self-sabotage. "Did they say you're still on their phone plan?"

She gives me a look that says, *Don't you dare make fun of me.* "It's cheaper that way. I hate being beholden to them, but I can't afford it without the family-plan discount." Right. This reminds me of something.

I walk into her "kitchen"—meaning I take two big steps to the right. I'm not sure you can actually call this a kitchen. It's really just a fridge and a sink and a one-foot-square slab of butcher block that, if you squint, might be able to pass as a counter. I open the top cupboard, and it's just as I suspected.

"What are you doing?" she asks, sounding a little panicked.

I reach in and push aside the box of colorful cereal and an open pack of sour candy. When I spot a tumbleweed blowing across the back, I move on to the fridge. I pull it open and find a carton of milk with a questionable date and a Tupperware container that's half-filled with what looks like egg salad, but I don't dare open it and find out.

She runs up and shuts the fridge door like I was peeking in her lingerie drawer instead of her fridge. Her cheeks are burning red, and suddenly she looks like she might bite my head off. "If you're hungry, we can go down the street to a diner that stays open late."

"Evie, do you have money to get groceries?"

Her cheeks burn deeper. I could fry a pancake on them. "Yes! Of course I do."

"Do you have money to buy more than a box of cereal?"

"I'll have you know that a serving of that cereal has *half* the recommended intake of fiber for the day."

She's trying to play, but I'm not having it. I'm the bad guy now. *Stop fooling around; things just got serious.* "Come on. Get your shoes."

I grab her hand and start pulling her with me toward the door. Charlie darts off his perch on the bed and grabs his vest. For once, he gives me a look that says he is on my side. Evie deserves to have someone on her side, and I've just decided that that someone is going to be me.

She hits the brakes and digs her heels into the floor. "STOP. Where are we going?"

I swear, I will pick her up and carry her over my shoulder if I have to. "The grocery store." She's fighting, but I'm a big bully, and she doesn't stand a chance against my size. "I'm buying you some food to go in that fridge."

"No! Jake. I'm fine, I swear. *UGH.* Charlie, attack!"

Charlie trots beside me. I pause at the front door long enough to scoop up her tennis shoes. "Evie. You can't live on cereal. And I will never be able to sleep at night knowing that the woman who helped change my daughter's and my life for the better is at home with no food. Now, either you can hop in my truck on your own or I will pick you up and put you in myself, but either way you're going to the grocery store with me." I pause and then tack on, "*Please let me.*"

I can't tell if she wants to smack me or smile. I think there's a hint of both on her face. "Can I at least put on a bra first?"

I smile. "I guess."

She stares me down, and her eyes narrow in contemplation. "I don't need a sugar daddy, Jake."

"Good, because that term has always creeped me out, and I really don't want to be associated with it."

"I'm serious. I'm not helpless. I'm just a little broke until I get paid again, because my insurance went up again this month, making things a little tighter."

"When is payday?"

". . . Two weeks."

"Yeah. Come on." She looks so torn. If I don't want to throw her over my shoulder, I'm going to have to reason with her. "Please, Evie. Let me help. I promise this won't make you beholden to me. I can just help you with this one little thing to get you on your feet, and then I swear I'll never force my money on you again."

She grins a little. "All right, fine." She's crossing in front of me, headed for my truck. Bra forgotten. "But we're also buying the ingredients for your favorite brownies so I can make them as a thank-you." She pauses at the right bumper and looks over her shoulder. The wind catches her hair, and she looks way too cute in that oversized T-shirt. "Except, I'm going to have to make them at your place because I don't have an oven."

CHAPTER 19

EVIE: I opened my pantry this morning and felt overwhelmed.
I've never had so many breakfast choices before.

JAKE: Mix them all together.

EVIE: EW! Are you one of those people who stacks all of your
food on top of one another at Thanksgiving?

JAKE: It all goes to the same place.

EVIE: *GIF of a woman yelling "murderer!"*

JAKE: So, you're a gif girl, huh?

EVIE: I prefer them over words.

JAKE: *GIF of a person walking across the street*

EVIE: What in the world was that????

JAKE: I thought you preferred them over words. That was me
saying I'm leaving to come get you soon.

EVIE: Wait, why?! I can call an Uber.

JAKE: I know. But I want to come get you.

EVIE: Stop being so nice to me all the time.

JAKE: Just making up for calling you a car salesman.

CHAPTER 20

Evie

I'm sitting in Jake's truck, feeling baseball-sized butterflies fill my stomach. It's the day of the pool party, and in approximately ten minutes I will meet every member of Jake's family. This still perplexes me. I honestly don't know what I'm doing here. I do know that I'm holding a tin of extra-fudgy brownies in my lap . . . but only because I spent the evening at his house yesterday making them. Sam helped while Jake hovered and kept trying to stick his finger in the batter. I swatted him no less than three times, and the whole thing felt oddly domestic.

I want to love it. I want to let myself be ridiculously happy with what seems to be blooming between us. But I can't seem to silence the loud voice in my head that won't stop screaming, *What the hell is blooming?!*

What am I to Jake?

What is he to me?

We kissed once (granted it was a knock-your-socks-off kiss). But was that a fluke? Neither of us has brought it up, so the longer we go without mentioning it, the more it feels like it never happened.

"What's going through your head over there?" Jake's voice makes me jump.

"Huh? Oh. Nothing."

"Not nothing. You look like you're about to throw up in the car."

I laugh, and it sounds silly and put-on like a theatrical dame on Broadway. *Ha ha! Oh, Jake, you're too funny!* But yes, I'm totally going to throw up. Nerves are overtaking me. I'm about to meet Jake's family. I almost chickened out this morning and said I was sick, but Jo texted me before I got the chance and basically forbade it.

> JO: I better see photographic evidence of your cutie little bootie in a swimsuit poolside, or I will revoke your use of my washer and dryer.

Rude. She knows my weakness too well: clean underwear.

"I'm fine," I say, but of course my voice wobbles.

"Are you nervous? My family's going to love you." *Really? 'Cause mine doesn't.*

A few minutes later we are pulling into Jake's driveway, and there are already five other cars parked outside, and I'm mentally reminding myself how much I love having clean underwear, otherwise I would be hightailing my ass out of there.

Jake gets out, and I stay put. I don't mean to, but the superglue I poured on the seat before sitting down is really doing its job.

He looks at me through the window and grins. The door opens. He's not just being chivalrous; he knows I'm not leaving if he doesn't pry me out. "Come on, goose. They aren't going to bite, I swear."

I hand him the brownies and slide out. My cover-up drags against the seat, and a substantial amount of my leg is revealed in the process. Sure, I'm wearing a bathing suit under this cover-up, and it's going to come off soon anyway. But in a driveway where Jake is still completely covered and there is not a drop of water in sight, it feels a little scandalous. Sexy.

Jake thinks so too, because he's trying and failing to hide his wicked grin. His thoughts are all over his face. This is the distraction I needed, though.

I whack his arm. "Can you at least *try* to be a gentleman?"

"I could, but I don't really want to."

Charlie jumps out behind me, and I think he finds this flirting between Jake and me annoying, because he grunts and then sits down right beside us, staring up with the most unamused expression I've ever seen.

"All right, Charlie. We're going." I wasn't the one to say that. It was Jake. Which means Jake is now interpreting Charlie's facial expressions too, and *wow,* this thing is getting real. There's no way it can be only in my head.

Speaking of real, Jake takes my hand and guides me into the house. We're holding hands and walking into a family event. This doesn't feel like friendship. This feels like dating. But are we? I've never felt more confused in my life. I also love Jake's hands. You would think from all the calluses that he's a contractor instead of an architect.

We walk through the front door, and Jake only drops my hand to take the brownies from me and set them on the counter. He made fun of me for putting up a big fuss about taking the brownies back to my place so I could bring them over again today. That way everyone would see that I was contributing something to the party. I'm disappointed that no one is here to witness my contribution. Now it just looks like the brownies were here all along!

"Wait. Let's go back and ring the doorbell so everyone can see me bring in the brownies."

"You don't have to come bearing brownies for them to like you."

"But when has bringing brownies ever *hurt* anyone's chances of likability?"

In the next moment, the back sliding door opens, and I'm out of time. I lunge for the brownies so I can hold them in front of me like a peace offering, but Jake is one step ahead and blocks the brownies. Now it looks like I'm lunging for him. Wonderful. He takes it in stride, though, and wraps his arm around my shoulder, holding me pinned to his side. *Must get to the brownies.*

"Jake, you're back!" says a little blond woman in a voice that is southern and sweet as iced tea. I don't know why, but I did not imagine Jake's mom sounding like Jo. Probably because Jake barely has an accent. But it's clear from her teased-up hair and drawn-out *r*'s and *a*'s that she's as country as bread pudding at a church potluck.

"Oh, and Evie, honey! You made it!" I don't think anyone has ever sounded so pleased to meet me in my entire life. Even when I was still wrapped up in my parents' world as a socialite, no one seemed happy to have me around. I was just another pawn to move around the room. Another person with money and influence to watch their back around. Even when someone was smiling at me I felt loathed.

"EVERYONE! EVIE IS HERE!" she bellows toward the back door.

I'm glad I'm only wearing a bathing suit under this cover-up, because there is definitely some back sweat starting to happen.

"Hi! It's so nice to mee—"

"Evie!" Sam bursts through the door with Daisy at her side and throws her arms around my waist.

Jake doesn't let go of me. So, I'm just standing here with one Broaden wrapped around my upper half and another Broaden wrapped around my lower half. And then, suddenly, *all* the other Broadens are watching, and I'm hyperaware of the picture we must be painting.

"Who's here? Oh, Evie!" says a happy middle-aged man who comes to stand next to Mrs. Broaden. He looks a lot like Jake.

There are now four other women filing into the kitchen, followed by a trail of various-aged children and spouses to look on too. They are all saying hi and smiling so brightly, and the room is spinning. Why do they all look so happy to meet me? And how does my name sound so comfortable on the lips of people I've never met before?

But when Jake squeezes my shoulder, I feel like everything shifts into place. Like one glorious line of Tetris when you can get all the shapes to fit perfectly together. He *really* likes me. Jacob Broaden likes *me*. He's told his family all about me. He's standing proudly beside me and not letting me go.

Maybe our kiss really was the beginning of something.

The introductions are complete, and I have been given a moment to catch my breath by the pool. Jake and his dad are over by the grill, tossing hot dogs and hamburgers on, and Sam and a few of her cousins are swimming in the pool.

Turns out, Jake has the sweetest family on the face of the earth, and I had nothing to worry about. Who knew that there were people out there with families who actually love one another without secret agendas?

I pull my towel out of my tote bag and drape it over a pool chair. I find myself smiling at the sounds of splashing and laughter. Growing up as an only child with two very formal and career-driven parents meant the only sounds that usually filled our house were that of Dad typing on a laptop and Mom gossiping with her other elitist minions on the phone. Exciting stuff.

"Soooo," says Jake's sister June as she plops down, stomach first, onto the pool chair beside me. She has a beautiful big sunflower tattoo that caps her shoulder. "You're the hottie with the body that my big brother keeps talking about."

My eyes are the size of oranges.

A shadow falls over me. Jake appears out of nowhere, towering beside my lounge chair. "I never called her that!" he says to his sister before looking down at me. "I never called you that."

June huffs an offended sound. "So, you're saying she doesn't have a hot body? How rude, Jake."

He gives June a look, and now I'm stuck between two siblings in a game of monkey in the middle. "Cut it out, June."

"You're not helping your case. Evie is going to leave today completely sure you don't think her body is hot. But she looks like she knows better than to care what you think anyway."

I'm struggling so hard to keep a laugh from bursting free.

"She's not going to think that." I like the way Jake's face is turning the tiniest bit pink, and I wonder if I can push it over the top to red.

I give him a pouty look and decide Jake needs to be the one in the middle now. "I am sort of feeling like you think I'm a troll under a bridge."

He's glaring at me but clearly trying not to grin. "Fine, I'll give. Evie . . . you've got a hot body." *Bingo!* Jacob Broaden is capable of turning bright red, folks!

I laugh, enjoying the feeling of victory far too much. Jake just rolls his eyes and goes back to the grill with his dad.

"He's too easy to mess with," June says, shaking her head with a smile while watching her brother walk away. I like her. She's spunky and a little wild in the best kind of way. And her watercolor flower tattoo makes me wonder if I would look as cute as her with one. Probably not. Plus, I really don't like needles, so I dismiss the thought instantly.

"So, are you guys dating?" My eyes shoot to June, and I must look like a deer in the headlights, because she laughs. "You don't have to answer that."

"No. It's not that I don't want to answer. It's just . . . I don't know *how* to answer." I fish around in my tote bag for my sunscreen to give my hands something to do. "I think Jake and I are friends right now."

"Eh, I wouldn't be so sure. He's never talked about any of his friends like he's been talking about you lately." Not sure what to do with that statement other than try to hide the wings I just sprouted from that surge of joy.

"Oh. Well . . ." I laugh and shrug, letting the conversation dangle out on the line because I really don't think I should be having a DTR conversation with Jake's sister before I have one with him.

"What are we talking about, ladies?" Mrs. Broaden rounds our pool chairs in her daisy-printed kimono, gives June a little pat on her bikini-clad rear end like affectionate moms are known to do, then takes the third seat beside us.

"Just trying to figure out if Jake and Evie are dating or not."

"What!" says Mrs. Broaden so loudly I think the whole neighborhood heard her. All of Jake's sisters definitely did, because now they are swarming me like a frenzy of sharks. "Honey, of course you're dating. He brought you around us, didn't he?" says Mrs. Broaden.

"Oh, well, I—"

Jake's oldest sister, Jennie, squats down beside my chair. "Isn't he taking you to a benefit or something next weekend? Sounds like dating to me."

I open my mouth, but it's useless because yet another sister, Julia (Mr. and Mrs. Broaden apparently have a thing for *J* names), leans over the back of my chair. "I don't know. Jake is pretty friendly in general. It doesn't necessarily mean anything that he asked her to the benefit. I can totally see him thinking this is nothing but a friendship thing."

Do I even need to be here for this?

June sits up and crosses her legs. "Have you guys kissed yet? That would totally help us figure out his intentions."

HA. What?! I'm definitely sweating.

"All right, all right. Everyone shoo," says Mrs. Broaden, riding in on her white horse. Forget Jake and Charlie; she is my new knight in shining armor. "Evie doesn't want all these questions, and our meddling is going to do nothing but scare the poor girl away. Go play with your children in the pool and let her catch her breath." She's waving them away, and they all disperse.

"So, Evie, you're the one I get to thank for bringing some happiness back into my son and granddaughter's life."

"I can't take that credit. That's all Daisy's doing."

"Oh really? And did Miss Daisy teach my Sammie how to make brownies last night? Did Daisy convince Jake to have a little more fun in his life and throw a pool party? Did Daisy teach Jake how to paint fingernails?"

I laugh. "Jake's quite the sharer, isn't he?"

"It was hard to miss the yellow polish." She smiles. "But actually, no. Jake's pretty private about his life. Sam is the open book, and she and I talk every night on the phone. She's been keeping me apprised of all things Evie Jones." Her smile turns a little more serious. "She really likes you. And my Sammie is a good judge of character."

"I think Sam is pretty amazing too."

We are both quiet for a moment, and I decide I need something to do, so I peel off my cover-up, revealing my bright-yellow polka-dot high-waisted bikini, and apply sunblock to my arms and legs. Jo made fun of me when I picked this swimsuit out in the store, saying that she owns sexier swimsuits than this one, but I don't care. I like it. It's cute and sporty, and I don't have to worry about all my parts falling out during a game of water volleyball.

Yes, I know . . . I'm once again pretending that I have big enough parts to fall out of something, but I can dream.

Mrs. Broaden—or Bonnie, as I've now been bid to call her—and I spend the next five minutes shooting the breeze and getting to know each other. No, not true . . . She only wants to talk about me. But I like her. I like her a lot, so I answer all her questions. She's encouraging and cheerful, and I think she and Jo would hit it off right away if they get to meet one day.

When the conversation winds down, though, she throws me a curveball. "Your mom must be so proud of you, Evie. You're quite a woman."

I have to look away as soon as she says those words, because I can feel tears prickling my eyes. This is *so* not the place to cry over my mommy issues. It's just that I've always dreamed of hearing my mom say something like that to me—and I don't think I ever will. I've had to learn to appreciate myself without her help. To see myself living with epilepsy and recognize that I am strong, not helpless and broken the way my mom has always treated me.

Before Bonnie has a chance to notice my change in demeanor, I turn my head to find a bare-chested man with a gorgeous six-pack and tanned, defined shoulders rushing toward me. I only have time to blink at the vision of sexy masculinity before Jake's arms go under me and he scoops me out of my chair.

I scream and kick like a child as he jogs us toward the pool.

"What are you doing?!" I yell.

"This is payback, Evie Jones," says Jake before he jumps off the side and plunges us both into the pool.

CHAPTER 21

Jake

Evie is lounging beside the pool like a golden suntanned goddess. She's put her oversized shirt back on and added a massive straw visor and big sunglasses. A picture of her hanging in a dermatologist's office as an example of sun safety would have every container of sunscreen sold out.

The best part of Evie: she's laughing. She's always laughing. Her smile lights up her whole face in a way that looks like she might explode from joy. She's talking to June right now about a date that June went on last week. I was hanging out nearby until my baby sister started talking about the guy kissing like a slimy wet fish and I decided it was time to go.

But the weird thing is, Evie fits here. My family gave her the ultimate hazing of no personal space and a rousing game of a hundred questions right out of the gate, and Evie accepted it all with that adorable dimpled smile of hers. I don't want to be that guy who's constantly comparing every woman he spends time with to his ex-wife, but I can't help it. The picture is a stark contrast.

Natalie never fit in with my family. She didn't like them. She thought June was childish and that everyone else was too involved in our life. I don't remember the last time we had a pool party like this, because honestly, Natalie wouldn't have wanted to spend the afternoon with them. In the interest of making my marriage work, I went along with it. I had lunch with my parents by myself most Sundays, and for holidays we got in and out of family functions as fast as possible.

I've missed having them in my life, and I can't help but notice that I don't miss Natalie one bit.

"Well, I think this pool party was a success, Jakey," says my mom, using my shoulder to help her sit down beside me on the edge of the pool. My mom is cute. She's about five feet tall standing on her tiptoes, with the voice of Paula Deen and a personality like a shot of Fireball whisky mixed with sunshine.

"You think? I'm glad. And I'm glad you guys could come."

Evie's voice carries across the pool and distracts me. "Sam! When's the last time you put on sunscreen, darlin'?"

Sam pauses her descent down the pool steps and looks over to Evie. "Oh. Not since this morning."

"Come over here and let me lather you back up before you turn into the world's cutest lobster."

I watch my daughter smile from ear to ear and then rush back up the steps to go perch in front of Evie on the lounge chair. Evie's sitting cross-legged now, smiling and talking away to my sister while thoroughly applying sunscreen to my daughter's back. I'm mesmerized by this scene. I couldn't look away if I tried.

I am the person who loves Sam the most in this world . . . and I forgot to reapply sunscreen to her back. But Evie remembered. What does that mean? It feels significant.

My mom leans close to me, and from the corner of my eye, I can see her smile. "I think you found a good one."

I take in a deep breath. "Yeah. I've thought that before, though."

"True. But you were just a kid back then when you met Natalie. You didn't know the first thing to look for in a woman besides her bra size. And Natalie didn't know what she wanted from her life either besides what was in your pants."

I grimace. "That was disturbing to hear. You're starting to sound like June."

She chuckles and rolls her eyes. "You kids think I'm so out of touch, but I'll have you know that I watch *The Bachelor* every week." She says it like that fact in itself should knock fifteen years off her age. "But that's not the point. The fact is, you're a grown man now who's lived a lot of life, and you know what kinda woman it's gonna take to hold your hand through the rest of it." She pats my back and then shimmies off the edge of the pool into the water to go swim by my dad, who, at this moment, has approximately five grandkids leeched on to him in the shallow end.

I turn my eyes back to Evie just in time to see her stand up, empty glass in hand, and head toward the house.

Next thing I know, I'm on my feet and striding after her. I suddenly feel like there is some unfinished business between us.

I step into the house, and the cool air hits my bare chest. I probably should have grabbed a shirt, but there was no time. Everyone else is outside, and Evie's alone in here, and I didn't want to waste this moment.

Turning the corner, I find Evie in the kitchen, pouring herself a fresh glass of lemonade and shoving a brownie into her mouth. She spots me and covers her mouth to keep the crumbs from spewing out with her laughter. "Caught red-handed," she says from behind her fist.

I round the island to get closer to her, and I notice her chewing slows and her body straightens a little. I stop just behind her, hoping she'll turn around to face me. "You're allowed to eat the brownies, you know. You're the one who brought them."

My plan works, because Evie turns around, and now she's trapped between me and the counter, and I'm loving how close we are. I can see the freckles dotting the bridge of her nose and the perfect bow of her full top lip.

"Yeah," she says with a final swallow, "but am I allowed to have *four* brownies?"

My eyebrows lift. "I'm impressed. Did you really eat four?"

"What? Me? No. I was kidding. I'd never eat half the pan of brownies I brought for other people. That would be soooo rude." That means she actually ate five.

I smile and lean in and set my hands on the countertop behind her—one on either side of her, pinning her in. Her eyes widen. I know this is bold. Other than that ridiculously amazing and unexpected kiss we had last night, our relationship has looked nothing like this. And speaking of that kiss, neither of us has even acknowledged it.

I'm ready to acknowledge it now.

I've been watching Evie all day, and there's not a chance that I'm letting this woman leave my house with us stuck between friend zone and something else. I get closer and breathe in the scent of Banana Boat suntan lotion mixed with the sweet strawberry balm I've seen her apply to her lips. Let me tell you, it's a ridiculously good combination.

"*Jake,*" says Evie in a slightly nervous, playful voice as she looks over her shoulder toward my hands. She takes a tiny step back toward the counter and puts her hands behind her to grip it. "What's going on right now?"

I smile because I like how frank she is. She doesn't try to play games. She's straightforward. What you see is what you get—and *goodness,* I like what I see.

"What's going on is . . . I can't stop thinking about our kiss from last night." *I can be frank too.*

She sucks in a breath and blinks before pursing her lips. She looks over both of her shoulders before her green eyes hit mine again. "Do you think *this* is the place to discuss that?" She's cute when she's nervous.

"Yeah. I do."

"But what if Sam walks in here?"

"She'll probably be scarred for the rest of her life."

"Jake! I'm serious."

I smile and inch closer so our bodies are touching. "Me too."

Evie's eyes drop to my mouth and then lower to my chest. She swallows, and her cheeks pinken, and I swear I've never felt cockier than at this moment.

She looks back up at me. "You can't just switch gears on me like this in the middle of the day at your family pool party. I mean . . . one minute you're giving wholesome PG dad vibes and the next you're pinning me against the counter and kissing me while you're half-naked? You're not allowed to do that. It gives me whiplash."

I smile bigger and move my hand up to her neck, enjoying the way her skin is still hot from the sun. "It's been a little while since I've brushed up on the rules, so you'll have to forgive me. I want to kiss you again, Evie, even though there's a pool party outside. And I don't want to be just friends. Or friends with benefits."

A full smile curls her lips, and I can't stand it any longer. I've gotta kiss her. I'm leaning down, and her hands move up to rest on my bare chest. The sudden skin-to-skin contact is electric, and it short-circuits my brain. I've been dead for the past year, and she just put two paddles to my chest. I'm alive now.

My lips touch hers, and I immediately want to groan from how good she feels. But of course we get interrupted.

"Whoa!" says my dad from the doorway. Evie and I split apart.

"Sorry, you two. I didn't realize there was something going on in here." But his smile says he knew very well.

I lean my back against the counter opposite Evie and give my dad an unamused smile. "Impeccable timing, Dad."

He shrugs and struts right on over to the fridge to fill his glass with ice. "I've got four daughters, son. I've had loads of practice to perfect my timing." He looks at Evie and winks.

One minute ago I was a cocky son of a gun, and now I'm fifteen with a face on fire, and my dad is embarrassing me and my pretty girlfriend. How can I recover from this?

Dad is taking his sweet time, adding one cube of ice to his glass at a time, filling it with water, taking a sip, and topping it off again. This goes on for two minutes, and I can see that Evie is trying hard not to dissolve into laughter.

I give her a look that says, *Enjoying this, are you?* That forces her to cover her mouth with the back of her hand so a laugh doesn't spew out.

All right, enough.

I'm not fifteen, and this is my own damn kitchen. "Okay, water boy, I think you're well hydrated. Why don't you take this outside now and stop doing whatever it is you're doing in here."

My dad laughs as I'm pushing him from the kitchen. "I'm going, I'm going . . . but you should know that we can all see you out there." He points toward the glass sliding door just off the kitchen . . . and yep . . . it's a straight shot to where Evie and I have been standing. Everyone is gathered and watching like their cable got canceled months ago and they're starved for entertainment.

Once I forcibly remove my father from my house, I turn around and go back into the kitchen. I find Evie giving in to her laughter with both hands covering her face. I take one of her wrists and pull her out of the kitchen and into the hallway—*away* from the prying eyes of my creepy family.

"Are you going to sneak me away to make out in the hallway now?" she asks while laughing.

I stop and turn around when I know we are clear from the audience. "No. The moment's over."

"Boooooo," she says with a big smile.

I'm laughing now too, and I can't believe how bad I am at this flirting thing. Turns out, it's something you *can* get rusty at.

"What are you doing Friday night?" I ask.

Her smile goes a tad serious. "Friday?"

"Mm-hmm."

"Well, nothing that I know of."

"Come over Friday night, then."

Her smile peeks out again. "Come over?"

"Are you just going to keep repeating everything I say?"

"Only if you don't start explaining what you mean in full sentences. I know we just kissed again in the kitchen, but I don't want to misconstrue anything." Gosh, I like this woman. I want to kiss her more, but I refrain because I can't handle another interruption, and the potential for that happening is way too high.

"Sam has her slumber party that night, so I'm going to be off dad duty. I was hoping you'd come over and let me cook you dinner . . . as a date."

"A date?"

"You're still repeating."

She smiles wider and leans her back against the wall. The shadowy hallway blankets us—only adding to the flirty look she's giving me. Evie is *not* rusty. "So . . . a *date* date? Like . . . you *like me* like me? Not just a friend or attraction thing?"

"Didn't you get the note I passed you in science class? I *like* you. Check yes or no if you like me too."

She scrunches her nose and pulls me even closer by wrapping her arms around my neck. "I check yes."

"So, does that mean you'll come?"

"You said you're cooking?"

I nod.

"Count me in."

She raises up on her tiptoes and kisses my cheek before breaking away and darting back out toward the pool.

CHAPTER 22

Evie

"Where do you want to go dress shopping this weekend?" Jo asks me around a bite of salad.

"Doesn't matter to me."

"Just prepare to get something skimpy to show off those legs for Jake."

I give Jo a flat look. "First of all, I want a man who likes me for more than my body. And second, shouldn't *you* be the one telling *me* this? You're in your sixties. How am I the mature one here?"

Jo shrugs and steals a fry from my plate. "Now, why would I tell you something you already know? I'm pretty sure all you ever think about is how to be upstanding. Think of me as your fairy godmother." She waves the fry like a wand over my head. *"Bibbidi-bobbidi, do yourself a favor and live a little."*

I shake my head at my fairy godmother and take a bite of my burger.

My phone buzzes on the table with a new text, and I see the name *Jake* written across my screen. Jo sees it too and wags her eyebrows suggestively while reaching for my phone. I snatch it off the table and clutch it close to my chest before she gets a chance to swipe it open. "No one likes a Nosey Nelly."

"Even fewer people like a Boring Bessy." She steals another fry, and I smack her hand playfully.

I angle myself away from Jo, and I swipe open my phone.

JAKE: Only two more days until our date. It's been way too long since I've seen you.

I smile because it *has* felt like a long time. Jake and I haven't seen each other since the pool party last Saturday. It's Wednesday now, and I've never felt like a week has gone by slower. It's not that I haven't been busy. In fact, I've been crazy busy training a new group of volunteers who signed up to be puppy raisers. Our newest litter of pups will be ready to leave their mom and go into a volunteer's home to start learning their basic manners: potty training, don't chew the rug, sit, and lots and lots of socialization.

Our company literally wouldn't survive without these volunteers and the time they sacrifice in helping train our dogs. But these weeks of breaking everyone in and teaching them the rules is always exhausting for me.

Not only have I been teaching classes for the volunteers, but I've taken three dogs to the vet, had two match meetings with potential recipients, reviewed five new applications, and ignored three texts from my mom reminding me that I need to quit fooling around and do something useful with my life. Something like join the Powder Society of Revolutionary Ladies and drink martinis in the afternoon.

But, in the meantime, Jake and I have been texting every day and talking on the phone almost every night. The more I get to know him, the more I really like him. He's thoughtful, funny, tender, and truly and completely *ripped*. I could have chosen to say something sentimental there, but I didn't, because thoughts of Jake's ridiculous body keep running through my mind. All intelligent thoughts have melted into steamy nonsense.

This morning I got lost in a fantasy of what would have happened the other night if I hadn't stopped us, and I accidentally overflowed my coffee all over the counter. If this date on Friday goes well, I'm afraid my brain will be permanently fried.

EVIE: Oh. Is our date in two days? I totally forgot.

JAKE: You're not funny.

EVIE: *Screenshot of countdown timer, titled: Days until date with Jake.*

JAKE: Better. What time should I call you tonight?

EVIE: I'll be home by 7.

JAKE: I'll call you at 7:01. I mean . . . I'll call you at some vague time after that so you don't realize how much I like you.

"Oh, he's good," says Jo from over my shoulder.

"Hey!" I lock my phone screen again and give her the stink eye. "Mind your own beeswax."

"My beeswax is boring today. So, tell me, are things going good with you two?"

I can't hide my smile. "Really good. Too good, actually."

She rolls her eyes. "Only you would say that when a hot man is being attentive and flirting with you."

"I know! I don't want to feel this way, but . . . I have too much experience that's taught me it won't last long. Every guy I've ever dated has moved on to less epileptic pastures. They're all in with me until they see one of my episodes and it scares them right out of my life."

"Yes, and do you know what you oughta say to those types of guys? *Don't let the door hit you where the good Lord split you!* Because if you don't know it already, honey, you've been known to date duds."

My mouth falls open. "What?"

"It's true. The few guys you've dated in the past have all been a few eggs short of a dozen, and *way* below your level. It's like you're so desperate to not end up with anyone like your parents that you swing completely the opposite way. Jake is the first man you've ever been interested in that even comes close to being on the same tier as you."

"Ha! You think I'm on Jake's level?"

"No." Her eyes slide to mine, and I see a twinkle. "I said he's close to being on your level. I don't think anyone will ever measure up to you. But I get the feeling that Jake will actually try."

I don't know what to say. The fact that Jo thinks so highly of me makes me feel weepy. There's nothing else to do but lean over and wrap her up in a hug and then slide my phone onto the table in front of her.

"Just for that, you get unlimited access to my texts for the next five minutes."

She wastes no time in picking up my phone and scrolling through every text Jake and I have ever exchanged. While she's giggling like a teenager, I decide to occupy myself by refilling my water.

I stand up, and Charlie does too, but with a big yawn. Poor guy has been bored to death the past few days. Or maybe exhausted from all the running around and meetings we've been to. Either way, I need to devote some special time to take him to the park and throw the ball.

I'm filling up my water at the drink station and mentally planning on taking Charlie to the park on Friday morning so that he won't feel slighted during my date with Jake—*Don't worry, Charlie, you'll always be my first love*—when I feel the presence of someone else beside me.

I cut my eyes to the side to get a look at whatever weirdo is entering my personal space, and I find an attractive man smirking down at me. He's not Jacob Broaden attractive, but I'm still human enough to admit he's good-looking.

"Hi," he says.

"Hi," I reply, and I'm a little embarrassed to say it sounds more like a mouse squeak.

Come on, water. Fill faster!

"I'm Garrett."

Okay. Nice. Cool. So, what's going on here? This never happens to me. I briefly glance down, worried that maybe Charlie ran away, because men never approach me when Charlie is around. He and his blue vest are a giant man deterrent.

"Evie," I say with a polite smile and then turn to set my cup on the counter and put the lid back on. *Annnnnd* then Garrett is beside me again, doing the same with his lid.

"What's your dog's name?"

Huh. Okay, so he did see Charlie. And he's not scared off? I don't know how I feel about this. Actually, yes, I do. I'm not interested in this guy. Maybe a month ago, before I met Jake, I would have felt flattered. But right now, I just kind of want to extract myself from the conversation as quickly and politely as possible.

"This is Charlie."

"Sup, Charlie," he says, and I smile instead of telling him not to distract my dog while he's working. "Are you from around here?"

Alrighty, then. I guess we are going to do the chitchat thing now.

This is so bizarre. Do men have some kind of scent tracker that helps them sniff out the women in town who are unavailable? Because, I swear, I never got hit on by cute, normal-seeming guys before Jake asked me out.

"Yeah, I am. Are you?"

"Kind of. I just moved here a few months ago, so I'm still trying to get my bearings in the city."

"That's nice."

"I'm actually a physician's assistant over at Roper Hospital." *Cool, cool, cool. Didn't ask you, but that's all right.*

"That's a great hospital."

"Yeah? You've been?" He's asking like we're talking about a hot new club that just opened or something. *No way, I love that place! Maybe we could go together sometime. I know people who can get you one of the good gowns without stains on it.* It's a strange topic of conversation, but I give him slack because I'm betting he's just trying to find ways to keep me here talking and will likely want to punch himself later for asking that question.

I laugh lightly. "A few times, yeah." I glance down at Charlie, and Garrett follows my gaze to the patch that says *Seizure-Assist Dog.* A look of dawning understanding hits Garrett's face, and I expect him to start moonwalking away from me any second.

He doesn't. "Ah—I see. So, look, Evie, this is really forward of me and probably going to creep you out a little, but . . . I think you're really attractive, and I'd like to take you out sometime if you're free."

If I'm free? Does he mean if my schedule is free? Or if my relationship status is single and I'm free to date other people? Because I don't know. I mean, Jake and I talk every day, we flirt, we've kissed a few times, and we have a date on Friday . . . but does that, technically, mean I'm in a relationship?

I cast a quick glance at Jo, hoping she'll give me a thumbs-up or thumbs-down for what I should do right now, but her eyes are still glued to my phone. *Useless.* I think she's even screenshotting text conversations to forward to Gary.

I look back to Garrett and do a quick assessment of him: nice dark hair, well-trimmed beard, taller than me, an open smile. And overall, he's not setting off any alarms that make me feel like I should ask a security guard to walk me to my car when I leave here.

But the truth is, all I can think about is Jake. I like Jake. I want to date Jake, not this guy. "You seem nice, Garrett, which is why I feel like I should be honest and tell you that I'm sorta-kinda seeing someone."

Garrett gives me a kind smile and nods. He then reaches into the laptop bag that's slung over his shoulder and pulls out a pen. After grabbing a clean napkin, he writes his number on it and hands it to me. "Well, since 'sorta-kinda' doesn't sound like you've set a wedding date yet, here's my number. Call me if you find yourself in need of a fun date."

A voice I hate sounds behind me. "Hitting on my girl? Not cool, dude." When in the hell did Tyler Murray sneak up behind me? He drops his arm over my shoulder like he owns me.

Tyler pulls the slip of paper with Garrett's number on it out of my hand and tears it in two. Because, yep, that's the kind of guy Tyler is.

Garrett gives me a look that says he's worried about my intelligence for dating a jerk like Tyler. I flash an apologetic smile and wait for Garrett to walk away, planning to throw my elbow into Tyler's southern regions.

He knows me too well, though, because the second Garrett walks away, Tyler jumps back with a big grin. "You were going to hit me, weren't you?"

"Why are you saying it in the past tense? The threat is still real."

Tyler is still very much the same man who moved to New York five years ago. He's wearing a dark-gray suit that hugs his toned body. He's tall with blond hair and green eyes (yes, we look like siblings, and that truly freaks me out). And he's still got the same slithery smile. He openly scans my body and then raises and lowers his brows. "Well, shoot, Eves. You look even better than the last time I saw you."

I roll my eyes and turn around to return to my seat next to Jo. "Go away, Tyler."

He chuckles and tries to catch my arm, but I'm faster. "Wait. Don't you want this phone number? I'd be willing to paste it back together for a kiss."

I would tell him he could kiss my butt, but he would likely just treat it like an innuendo and say something that grosses me out. "Nope. Don't need it. And now you've filled your douchebag quota for the day, so you can scurry on back to the vermin hole you climbed out of." Charlie and I are weaving in and out of tables, and unfortunately, Tyler is keeping pace with me.

"Why don't you need it? Have you finally decided to marry me after all?"

When I walk up, Jo hands me my phone and, before she realizes Tyler is right behind me, says, "Jake texted you something sappy again, and I asked him to send a picture of his backside." I know she's kidding, so I don't press it. At least . . . I hope she's kidding.

But I really wish that she hadn't just mentioned Jake's name in front of Tyler. It's not that I think Tyler is some crazy guy from the movies who will kidnap me and stuff me in his trunk until I agree to marry him, but I do know that he's enough like my parents to go to extreme manipulative measures to get what he wants. He's always been that way. It's why he's such a good attorney.

"Wait, who's Jake? Don't tell me my Evie Grace has a boyfriend," Tyler says, coming to stand far too close to me. He's like a pimple. I just want to pop him—or punch him, or step on his toes, or slap him—but I know that if I do, he'll just get more inflamed and annoying. Best to ignore him and wait for the breakout to pass.

"I'm not yours, Tyler, and I never will be. Now leave me alone and find someone else to bug."

"Come on, Eves. You know we'd be good together."

"Do you seriously not think it's completely bonkers to marry each other just because you own your dad's portion of the business now?" I'm asking because I genuinely want to know. He and I have never seriously discussed this and part of me hopes there's a sliver of a heart beating inside his chest.

"I think it makes sense. You know this life better than anyone else. You know what it takes to be a good wife to a man like me, and I know that you look ridiculously good in a cocktail dress. So, yeah . . . I'm willing to sign that contract."

"You mean marriage certificate?"

"Same difference."

"Go away, Tyler."

He chuckles like he hasn't heard a word I've said. Like he thinks I'm cute for turning him down. I swear, if he pats my butt like he did last time he came to visit, I will tear his favorite limb right off his body.

"Tell you what. If you're so worried about it, let me take you out. I'll wine you and dine you, and if you're lucky, I might even f—"

"If you finish that sentence, I promise you I will dump this drink all over that fancy suit of yours."

His eyes widen like I've just threatened to shoot him. Then he relaxes back into his sleazy grin and tugs on his suit lapels. "Your parents want this, Eves, and so do I. So, don't think that by me walking away right now, I'm giving up. I'll find a way to show you that us being together is the right choice." He tries to kiss my cheek as he passes by me, but I turn my head away. And *whoa,* someone should tell that man that a spritz is all it takes. He is a walking bottle of cologne.

"Oh, I hate him," says Joanna once Tyler is out of earshot.

"You and me both." I turn around just as Tyler makes it to the far end of the restaurant and stands in line to order. I smile a big blinding smile and call out to him so the whole restaurant turns and looks. "Oh, Tyler! I forgot to say that the ointment you had me pick up for you is on your desk at work! The pharmacist said it should clear your rash right up but that sex is not advised for the first three weeks!"

I have the privilege of watching the scumbag's mouth fall open, and the woman in front of him in line (whom he had just been checking out) turn her shoulder firmly away from him. Even from this far away, I can see his face turn beet red. And then, just as I had hoped, he steps out of line and leaves.

"That was too satisfying to watch," Jo says and gives me a high five.

I should feel satisfied too, but I don't. Because the only take-away I have from this whole situation is that I have no idea what sort of relationship I have with Jake, and I really need to figure that out. Are we exclusive? Is *he* dating other people?

A minute ago, I was thrilled about my date with him. Now I'm feeling nervous. I can feel a big fat DTR on the horizon. It's always awkward. But it needs to happen so I can know whether or not I should pocket phone numbers from cute strangers in the future.

CHAPTER 23

Jake

It's Friday, aka a major day for me.

Not only is today the first time my daughter will spend the night away from home since being diagnosed with epilepsy, but also tonight I will have my first date with a woman other than Natalie in about eleven years.

As I'm searching through my closet for something to wear, I realize how out of touch I am. I think my mom got my birth certificate wrong, and I'm actually one hundred years old instead of thirty-three. Do I wear a T-shirt? Do I wear a tux? A tux is probably a little much.

Okay, breathe, Jake. You know you can't wear a damn tux.

I've just put on a shirt I hate when I hear Sam scream from her bedroom. I've never run faster in my entire life than I do on my way to her room. I'm expecting to find her in a pool of blood on the floor.

Nope.

But I do find her in a pool of clothing. Her dark, wide eyes look up at me, and she says, "I have nothing to wear!" *What? How can we be having the same dilemma?*

"What do you mean? I see lots of clothes."

"Dad!" She rolls her eyes and sounds way too exasperated with me for stating a fact. "These are all day clothes. I don't have any cute PJs! All the girls are going to have the perfect slumber-party PJs, and I'm going to have to go in these old stained polka-dot pants that are way too small for me!"

This is catching me completely off guard. I had no idea that fashionable PJ attire was a must-have to attend an eleven-year-old's slumber party.

Although . . . now I feel like I should have known this. I've seen the cheesy teen movies.

I sigh and look at my watch. "Okay. We have an hour until I have to get you to Jenna's. Grab your stuff, and we'll swing by the store on the way and get you some new PJs."

"And a bra."

"What?" I'm going to have a full-on panic attack now.

"Dad, I'm almost a teenager!" *Hardly.* "All the other girls who will be there have already been wearing them. It'll be embarrassing if I'm not."

My gut instinct is to pull the emergency lever and shut this whole thing down here and now, because I'm having trouble breathing. My daughter is almost a teenager, and she's wanting to wear bras, and up next is the sex talk that I don't feel at all ready to give her. But after I give myself a mental slap, I remember that I've been training for this very moment. A man doesn't watch all seven seasons of *Gilmore Girls* for nothing. I know to stay calm. Don't panic. Stop, drop, and roll. Basically, do anything besides make my not-so-little girl feel uncomfortable about her changing body.

Channel your inner Lorelai Gilmore. I will not be that single dad that sucks.

"Got it," I say with a firm nod and start ticking things off on my fingers like it's no big deal. "New bra. New PJs. And probably a new toothbrush because I'm guessing you don't like that princess one I bought you last time?"

She smiles, and I feel like I can sigh with relief. And then she looks at my chest, and she scrunches her nose. "And a new shirt for your date. I hate that one."

"Perfect. Meet me downstairs in five minutes."

I go back to my closet, change into a plain white tee that's good enough for shopping and dropping her off at her friend's house, then hustle downstairs. Sam and Daisy are already waiting for me when I reach the bottom floor. It's then that I notice something in Sam's eyes that I saw in my own the last time I looked in the mirror.

We stare at each other for a long minute, both of us heavy with emotion. We are moving on with our lives, not letting the obstacles of this year hold us back.

I pull her in for a hug, and she doesn't resist. "It's okay. I'm a little scared too, kiddo."

"You are?" she asks, sounding relieved.

"Yep. But we're both going to do great. The first steps into change are always the hardest."

She pulls out of my hug and picks up Daisy's leash. "I wish Evie could help me pick out my new bra. I don't really know what to get, and I'm guessing you don't either."

Should I be worried that she's wishing for Evie right now and not her own mom? I probably would be if I didn't completely get it. Natalie basically abandoned her. It's hard to want someone who doesn't seem to want you back. Evie, however, has been more invested in Sam's life over the past several weeks than Natalie has been all year.

I would love to be able to call Evie right now and beg her to go with me and Sam to pick out a bra. I bet she would be perfect in that role. I've no doubts that she would make Sam feel special and grown-up without making it awkward like I probably will. Yet Evie and I haven't even been on a real date yet. I can't call her.

But maybe I can at least text her when we get there about tween bra sizes. Would she think that's weird?

> EVIE: OMG. I loved my first bra. Get her a white one and a gray one so she has something to wear with both a light and dark outfit. Size: small. No underwire and nothing with the words "push-up" unless you want to have a heart attack. And whatever you do, get in and get out as quickly as possible without saying anything remotely close to "My baby girl is growing up so fast."

So . . . I guess she doesn't find it weird.

I drop Sam off at Jenna's house with a backpack filled to the brim with turquoise-and-white PJs that have some kind of sequined koala face on the front of the shirt and the words *Don't wake me until noon* on the back. She talked me into not only a white and a gray training bra but also a pink.

All in all, I think I've crushed the single-dad thing today.

When we pull up in front of Jenna's house, Sam tells me I can stay put in the truck. I suggest dropping her off a block away so she can walk back—that way, no one will even need to know she has a dad. And she just replies with a simple, *Not this time,* like it wasn't even a joke and she was really contemplating it.

She's in for a treat if she thinks, for one second, that I won't be sitting a row behind her at the movies on her first date.

Sam jumps out of my truck with Daisy in tow and her bag

strapped on her back. She darts toward the house with one of her friends who has also just told her parents to keep the car running and drive off as soon as her feet hit the grass. But my kid—the good one—pauses and looks over her shoulder at me. She comes sprinting back and jumps up onto the running board of my truck to kiss my cheek through the open window. "Love you, Dad."

"Love you too, Sam. Have fun. Call me if . . ." I let the statement dangle because, somehow, I'm afraid that if I say the words out loud, I'll be responsible for a seizure if she has one.

She smiles and nods. "I will."

And then my little girl goes into her friend's house for her first ever slumber party. My heart squeezes painfully. I'm glad now more than ever that I had the forethought to plan a date to distract me tonight.

I put the truck in drive, and I'm headed home to get ready for my date with Evie when my phone buzzes with an incoming text. A text that makes my heart drop into my stomach.

NATALIE: Headed back from Hawaii soon. Thinking of coming
to visit when I get back. Hug Samantha for me. <3

CHAPTER 24

Evie

Jake asked if I wanted him to come pick me up for our date, but I thought it would be silly for him to come all the way over to my place and get me, only to drive right back to his house. We went three rounds until he gave up and let me call an Uber. But he was adamant that he was going to pay for it.

The Uber pulls up in front of Jake's magazine-worthy farmhouse, and I'm still in disbelief that I even get to go inside this home, let alone date the man who owns it. (I'm not after Jake for his money or his belongings, though—I'm after his abs.)

Charlie and I get out of the Uber, and I tug down the hem of my floral-print midi dress. I even took the time to curl my hair in long, loose waves. Sure, they'll fall over the course of the next hour, but for now I'm feeling like a walking ad for a beachy-waves hair product, and I wonder how I got so lucky to not wake up with a zit today. Life is on my side.

Everything feels too good. I'm still waiting for that hammer to drop while also trying to be more optimistic like Jo suggested.

I ring the doorbell and count the seconds it takes for Jake to answer the door, using the frantic beats of my heart as a guide. *Ten.*

As he's opening the door, my nervousness ratchets up, and I wonder if it's too late to play ding-dong-ditch and hide in the bushes. Yes, too late. He's seen me. And *oh boy,* do I see him.

"Hi." His voice is so sultry and warm, and that one word holds so much promise. He puts the guy from the restaurant's paltry little *hi* to shame. Jake is so tall and muscular, and he's wearing a form-fitting, slate-blue shirt. A sexy day-old stubble covers his jaw. His jeans are dark and trim, and I'm sure that he has them tailored to fit him like a glove. I like this look on him. No, I love it.

"Hi yourself," I say, and *nope,* sultry doesn't sound good on me. I sound drunk and like I have a throat bubble.

I'm just considering jumping into the bushes again when Jake steps out to where I'm standing and slides his arm around my waist. He leans down and brushes my cheek with a kiss from his deliciously scratchy jaw and whispers in my ear, "You look beautiful."

Well, okay, then. I guess I'll stay.

He releases me to pat Charlie on the head and then takes my hand, pulling me inside. I smell herbs and spices and hear a Leon Bridges song playing softly from the speakers in the ceiling. It doesn't escape my notice that he's put on the very album I was listening to the night he came over.

The lights are dimmer than normal, and my body is hyperaware that Sam is not home, and this is officially *Jake the Man's* house and not *Jake the Dad.* My nerves are humming, and buzzing, and ping-ponging with excitement, and suddenly I don't know what to do with my hands. There are no pockets on this dress, so I'm forced to clasp them behind me.

"Come on in. I'm just finishing up a few things." He goes into the kitchen, and I follow a few paces behind him, afraid to say anything.

Someone please tell me what to do right now! I've stood in this kitchen dozens of times. I've spent the last few weeks talking to Jake every single day. But this feels different. The air is different. It's rich with anticipation. It's whispering memories of the night in my apartment.

It's been a long time since I've gone on a date. Even longer since I've been on a date with a man I liked. Or a man who looked and acted like Jake. No one should look that sexy holding a ladle and stirring a pot. He's a safety hazard.

I decide to give in to my awkwardness and plaster myself in the farthest corner of his kitchen. The cold marble cuts through the fabric of my dress and stings at my lower back, but I don't care. I'm not moving.

"How was Sam when you dropped her off?" Sam seems like the safest conversational avenue.

Jake taps the wooden spoon against the side of the pot and sets it down. He takes note of me standing all the way across the room and smirks. "Great. She looked so happy running in with all her friends. I'm glad I let her go." He goes toward the fridge and pulls out a bottle of white wine. How did he know that was my favorite? "Want a glass?"

"Yes!" I didn't mean to shout that.

He smiles and pours but stays put where he is. "Here you go."

He holds the glass out in front of him but doesn't take a single step toward me. I know what he's doing. It's a bribe to get me away from my private island, and I have no choice but to comply if I want that wine. And I do want it.

I slowly move closer, making him smile. "Why are you so afraid of me tonight?"

"I'm not," I croak. But I am. I totally am.

My nerves are sizzling because I don't know what to expect from the night, or what he expects. We are two adults on a first real date, and let's face it, there's been a lot of tension building up between us lately, and I just don't know what he's thinking is going to happen tonight. What do I want to happen?

When I get within arm's reach, he slips his hand around to my lower back and pulls me closer. My hips land against his, and he grins playfully. "Fell right into my trap," he whispers in my ear.

I like being trapped with him.

He smells so good tonight—like he used a bodywash with descriptive words on the bottle like *mountain* or *rain*. Somehow, the scent acts like a truth serum, because when he asks me to tell him what's going on in my head, I do.

"I'm nervous." I look up and meet his tender blue eyes.

"Me too."

"Really?" Somehow, that surprises me because he seems so put together and sure of himself. He *always* seems that way. Like a sturdy tree that's been there for hundreds of years. You know that if a strong wind blows, it won't knock it over.

"I changed my outfit three times," he admits with a cute, guilty look.

I grin and relax a little more into him. "You didn't."

"I did." His voice is warm and rich.

Something changes between us, and I can feel the moment we both realize that we are completely alone in this house and no one will burst in and interrupt a kiss this time. Chills fly across my skin as Jake brushes my hair away from my face and neck and then leans down. But he doesn't kiss my mouth. No, that would be way too obvious a choice for him. Instead, Jake passes right by my lips and goes to my neck, placing a light, lingering kiss right below my jaw. His lips melt against my skin, and his scruff tickles my neck where he's placing slow, hot kisses.

I tip my head back to give him a better vantage point. His kisses are lazily moving up toward my mouth, and as much as I'm loving this slow torture, I hear a bubbling sound on the stove. "I think something is boiling, Jake."

"Mm-hmm," he murmurs against my cheek.

"Is that a bad thing?"

"It's fine." He's in a sexy haze again.

"Are you sure? Because—" I don't get to finish my thought.

Jake's lips take mine, and all thoughts of dinner are behind me. In fact, I don't think I ever need to eat again. I'll just stay here and keep kissing Jake for the rest of my life, and I'm pretty sure that will be enough to sustain me.

He presses me back into the counter, and together, our kiss feels like a deep exhalation. Like life has turned fuzzy around the edges and nothing else matters anymore. Except, he's too tall. I hook my arm around his neck to pull him down to me, but Jake responds to my dilemma by picking me up and setting me on the counter in front of him. He stands between my legs.

My greedy little fingers run all over the tight ridges and valleys of Jake's shoulders. I'm making a mental map of his body, unable to believe that I'm even allowed to touch this work of art. He should be boxed up and sent off to a museum where he can be adequately appreciated. I lace my fingers in the back of his hair and breathe in his clean scent. Jake's lips move, both soft and fierce like the tides of the ocean, and I fall into them and swim.

I can hear something on the stove bubbling into a frenzy. It perfectly mirrors our kiss. I wind my arms tightly around his neck. *You're not going anywhere.* He takes a handful of my dress and tugs me closer. I slide my tongue against his lips, and just like a three-Michelin-star chef, I'm able to taste the notes of everything he's been cooking.

Viciously possessive thoughts run through my mind. *He's mine. Only mine.*

And now I'm kissing him with the intent to brand him. I want everyone to be able to look at Jake and see my kiss planted across his lips. Maybe Jake can read my thoughts because suddenly he's slowing things down. That delicious bite of his hand is lightening up, and I can tell he's putting on the brakes.

He slowly pulls away, and I can't open my eyes. They are too heavy and lust-filled to function properly yet. He cups my jaw—thumb tenderly caressing my cheek.

"I still think slow is a good idea, Evie. Even if I'm struggling with it." The way he says it, though—with a low, raspy voice—knots my breath and instantly makes me wish we were still kissing.

But with my eyes shut, I nod my head in agreement because *I am* in agreement. He's been through a heck of a lot over the last year, and I respect him immensely for trying to protect himself emotionally. And if sex tangles him up too much too soon, I don't want to press it. Honestly, I feel the same way. My heart gets attached way too quickly when physical stuff gets involved. And if he's not sure about us yet—I don't want to make that leap.

Lucky for me, kissing him is a top-tier experience in itself.

I open my eyes and find Jake giving me a lopsided grin. He knows the effect he's just had on me, and he likes it.

"Slow," I repeat back to him like English is not my first language and I'm trying to commit this new foreign word to memory.

He smiles wider and shakes his head a little, stepping back and taking his fantastic body with him. With the new, cool air comes a little bit of embarrassment. I can feel that my lips are swollen, and my cheeks are warm, and just a minute ago Jake felt the need to remind me that we should take things slow . . . which means he was aware of how much I want him. That I had my blinker on and was ready to change over to the HOV lane. *Move over, slowpokes.*

Then again, I felt how much he wanted me too. His blinker was definitely on. And although I'm perfectly happy taking things slow with him, I also need some clarity.

"Jake." I catch his hand before he turns away. "What are we?" Oh gosh, it's out there now. *It wouldn't have hurt to lead up to it a little more, Evie.*

His brows pull together, and a thoughtful expression clouds his eyes. "What do you mean?"

"I know this is only our first date, but . . . I guess . . . I don't know." A+ conversational skills are happening over here. Really top-notch stuff.

The problem is, I'm scared. I'm scared that making him *define the relationship* will scare him off. Not only is he wonderful, but he hasn't seemed scared of my disability at all. Granted, he hasn't seen an episode from me yet, but I have to think he would be tender and understanding, given how he talks about Sam and her seizures. I don't want to spook the best man I've ever met.

"You want to know where this is going?" he asks, and I can't tell if he sounds hesitant or not.

"Yeah. I guess I do."

He bites his lips together and nods. He turns away, and I worry that maybe I've annoyed him. But when he shuts off the burner and takes whatever has been furiously boiling off it, I realize he's just getting settled in. He takes both of my hands, pulling me back up against his warm, solid body. I wrap my arms around his waist. I like this. I like that I get to do this. It feels natural and new—but also like we've been doing this forever.

Jake eyes me and fills his broad chest with air, then sighs. "I think our title would be dating. I like you. You like me. We're making out in the kitchen but not going too fast too soon."

If I'm doing this, I'm really doing it. "That's still vague. What kind of dating?" I frown in thought. "I'm asking because a guy at a restaurant asked me out earlier today, and I didn't know if I should accept or turn him down, because I wasn't sure what this thing between us is. I know we are dating, but are we exclusive? Are we casual? Are we seeing other people?"

Jake's brows pull together tightly. I can't tell if he looks upset or is just giving it a lot of thought. *Guarded* is probably the best description. "You got asked out?"

I nod.

His eyes are fixed on me—unrelenting and not giving away an ounce of what he's thinking. And then all at once his expression changes to something lighter. He shrugs, and suddenly he's never had a care in the world. "We should be non-exclusive. Casual."

Oh.

Is it wrong that this is not where I was hoping this heart-to-heart was going?

"Casual?"

"Yeah." He smiles softly. "Like I said, I want to take this slow with you. We should just have fun and keep things light. Date. Get to know each other. But by all means, feel free to go out with other people." He leaves my side to pull two plates down from the cupboard.

I'm staring at him numbly, trying to decide if I'm okay with this or not. But of course he wants to be casual. He's just come out of a long relationship, and he needs some time to explore his options. It makes sense. I support it for him. The problem is how it makes *me* feel.

I'm not particularly comfortable in a non-exclusive relationship. It takes a lot for me to trust and open up to people—to be vulnerable with them emotionally and physically. I'm not sure that I like the idea of growing close to a man who's keeping his options open. Maybe this means we're in different places in life? I thought we were both feeling the same connection, but maybe it's just attraction on his end.

Geez, this sucks. I'm crushed even though I have no right to be.

I hop off the counter, just needing to escape and have a minute to let my frown loose.

Jake is moving casually around the kitchen, looking just as cool and collected as he did at the beginning of the night, and I'm pretty sure my shoulders are dragging on the floor as I walk.

"Be right back. I need to wash my hands before we eat." No one can argue with good hygiene.

Except I think my voice might have trembled, because Jake looks over his shoulder with an inquisitive expression. I don't wait around for him to ask me if I'm okay. I turn on my heel and make a mad dash for the bathroom, shutting the door behind me. I lean against it and give myself the freedom to pout for a minute. *Just one little indulgent pity party.*

My mind bounces from that devastating kiss to his proposal of a casual relationship back to the kiss.

While I'm in here, I buy myself some more time by actually going to the bathroom. It's when I'm seated on the porcelain throne that I realize my obnoxious and never-nice friend, Aunt Flo, has arrived early for her visit. *Perfect! Just wonderful timing.* Because guess what? I know for a fact that I don't have any tampons on me because I forgot my purse at home.

I want to groan at the injustice of the last half hour. Thankfully, this isn't my first rodeo. It's not glamorous, but I know what to do here. I wrap toilet paper around my hand a few times until I've made a scratchy and uncomfortable pad for myself to tuck into my underwear until I can get home.

I don't know if I'm relieved or disappointed that this date has to end early. On the one hand, I'm happy that I'll have more time to think over the *casual* proposition, but on the other hand, I'm also sad to leave Jake. I've missed him this week.

CHAPTER 25

Jake

I've been nervously pacing the kitchen, waiting for Evie to come out of the bathroom. I have a bad feeling in the pit of my stomach that the conversation we just had did not come out in my favor. It might have just been in my head, but she seemed spooked before she went to the bathroom.

When I hear the bathroom door open but Evie doesn't come right into the kitchen, I round the corner and find her in the living room. She has Charlie's leash in one hand and her cellphone in the other. She's looking down and typing on it, but when I enter the room her wide green eyes shoot up to me and she offers an awkward smile.

"Oh hey, yeah, so I'm really sorry, but it turns out I've got to cut our dinner date short." *What?* "I had something come up, and . . . it's kind of important. Well, actually it's *super* important, and I have to take care of it right away. I'm really sorry."

Jake, you dipshit! I knew that I played it too cool back there in the kitchen.

When Evie told me she was asked out by some random dude, I

freaked out inside. That situation is exactly why I've been hesitant to date someone younger than me. But then I thought about it and realized she had given me the perfect excuse to have my cake and eat it too. I could date her. I could enjoy time with her. I could kiss her. But as long as I never plan to commit to this woman, I'll be okay. I can't lose someone I never really had, right?

I don't love the idea of a non-exclusive relationship (hate it, actually) but I thought maybe it's the best option for me when I'm scared to death of committing to someone only to open the possibility of her leaving me too.

But right now, seeing her frantically typing on her phone . . . I'm thinking that I made a mistake.

"Don't go," I say, reaching out to cover her phone with my hand. "Or . . . at least give me two minutes."

Her eyes hit mine, and there is a look of finality in them that makes my stomach twist. "Definitely not. I need to go."

Wow. I must have really butchered that conversation more than I realized.

I'm now desperate. I tried to play it cool earlier, and clearly that didn't work, so now it's time to let it all hang out. "Evie, that was an act back there. I panicked when you said someone else asked you out. I was trying to be chill, but the truth is, I really like you. I like you so much that it scares me. The last woman I cared for left me high and dry after nine years of marriage. I'm still a little banged up and scarred. I want to have a relationship with you because I think you're incredible, and gorgeous, and smart, and . . ." She looks so shocked right now that I'm worried I'm coming off a little stalker-ish, but I keep going because I've opened the gates and the truth is all flooding out. ". . . way too good for me. But I have a lot of baggage, and honestly, I wouldn't blame you if you want to split right now. But I hope you don't because I'm so tired of holding back from you, and I'm ready for something real ag—"

"Jake!" Evie cuts off my long-winded monologue with a small chuckle. I don't really know what's funny about what I just said—laying my heart out on the line like that and all—but she chuckles nonetheless. "You didn't have to say any of that." She shrugs and shakes her head. "I'm not leaving because I'm mad or offended. I'm leaving because I just started my period early, and I don't have any tampons with me."

Oh my god. Her words sink in with the same effect as a sedative. My shoulders relax. *She's not upset.* "You started your period?"

She nods, a tense smile on her mouth.

I stare, blinking at Evie and trying to wrap my mind around this new turn of events. Evie is not upset. She never was. I didn't have to pour my heart out to her. She was fine with casual.

She clears her throat and folds her arms. "So, can I call an Uber now? Since . . . you know, I still don't have any tampons with me?"

"Oh." I snap back to life and take her phone out of her hands and toss it onto the couch. "No."

She sighs. "I don't think you fully understand my predicament."

I grab her hand and take her with me to the guest bathroom. Once inside, I open the linen closet, revealing three shelves fully stocked with every kind of maxi pad and tampon known to man—or woman. I wave my hand over the selection like I'm Vanna White.

"Ta-da," I say and then feel like a dork. Is it weird to be proud of your selection of feminine hygiene products?

She's amazed. "Why do you have a closet full of pads and tampons?"

"My sisters are never prepared, and I got sick of making tampon runs when they would come over to hang out or watch Sam. I decided to just stock my house. And it'll come in handy when Sam starts one day."

She laughs and stares at the closet. "I've never been so jealous of anything in my life. I'm cheap and always buy the smallest boxes possible, like I might not get a period next month." She pauses and looks at me hesitantly. "Was that TMI?"

I laugh. "Evie, I have four sisters, a mother, and a ten-year-old daughter, and I was married for nine years. I'm very aware that you have a period, and I'm not at all squeamish about it. You don't have to be either. Ever. *In any capacity*." I hope she understands my meaning with the last part.

She quirks a brow at me. "Are you about to give me a speech on feminism and how I should be proud of my body and its functions?"

I let my gaze travel the length of her, and when my eyes meet hers again, I drop my voice low. "You should definitely be proud of your body."

She shoves my chest with a guttural laugh. "If anyone but you said that to me, it would immediately give me the ick."

"So, what you're saying is, I can deliver a line better than any other man in the world?"

"Okay, get out."

I agree, but not before leaning down to kiss her once, softly on the mouth. "We're good?"

She smiles and brushes her wavy hair behind her ear, and I swear she's the most beautiful woman I've ever seen. "We're great. But we're going to have a whole different problem soon if you don't get out of here and let me steal one of these tampons."

"If you're lucky . . . I'll even let you take home a whole box."

She pretends to shiver. "I thought you didn't want to be my sugar daddy?"

"I'll be whatever you want me to be, Evie Jones," I say in a serious tone, because I am dead serious. In that moment where I thought she was going to walk out my door and out of my life, I was ready to take out a billboard and announce our relationship to the world if that's what she wanted.

"Jake." She catches me before I leave. "I really am happy to take things slow for you. We don't have to label it yet. But I'm probably not going to go out with anyone else while we're seeing each other because that's just how I work."

I release a breath. "That's actually how I work too. But I didn't want to scare you off."

She smiles. "How about we just agree from here on out to say what we're thinking? Truthful from the start about what we need?"

"That sounds . . . incredible."

CHAPTER 26

Evie

It's 9:30 and Jake and I have moved outside to swing on his porch. The night is warm, and the stars are bright against the black backdrop of the sky. We leave the porch lights off and decide to swing with the moon as our only light. It's romantic and quiet and still.

When we sit down on the swing, Jake reaches over and pulls me closer, wrapping his arm around my shoulder. I've learned that he's an affectionate man, and I still can't believe I get to know that about him. I also like his deodorant. I briefly wonder if I could get away with using some before I leave without him noticing. That's creepy, right? I might do it anyway.

Jake picks up his phone again and checks the screen. He's had that thing glued to him all night, and if I didn't know the real reason he was checking it so much, I'd be worried he was waiting for a better offer to come along from someone else. But I don't say anything about it because I know that he's just worried about Sam.

It strikes me how different this first date is from all the others I've been on. Not only have we already made out in the kitchen and discussed my menstrual cycle, but usually on a first date I would *maybe* be holding his hand with about twelve inches still neatly placed between the sides of our thighs. I'd be very hesitant to show any real part of myself to him because I don't do that until I think someone's worthy of that honesty. But as it is, Jake has me tucked in so close to his side that I'm pretty much sitting on his lap, and I'd be willing to tell him my deepest, darkest secrets if he asked.

I feel like a little bunny rabbit as I nestle closer to his absurdly defined obliques and sigh with contentment inside my burrow.

"Sam's going to be just fine," I say when I catch him checking his phone again.

"I know."

"Do you?"

"No. I'm lying. If you weren't here to tether me to this porch swing, I'd probably already be in my truck, halfway to Jenna's house to get her back."

I reach across him and lace my fingers with his. His hands are calloused and warm. "Just say the word and I'll handcuff you to this swing."

He looks down at me with a big fat smirk. "Oh really? So, now I know you're a butt girl *and* a little kinky."

I poke him hard in the side, and he laughs. "You wish."

How is it so easy with him? It's not supposed to feel like this. We're supposed to be awkward and uncomfortable, and I'm due my usual SOS text to Jo where she'll then call and say my house is on fire and I need to come put it out. But I don't feel like sending that text this time.

Instead, I'm rubbing my thumb across the back of Jake's knuckles and wondering if he'd be scared if I asked to go ahead and move in. Truth is, I'm falling head over heels for this man, and it's scaring me to death. He wants to go slow. And I want to punch the gas. I feel safe with Jake, and the sensation is entirely new for me.

But I've watched enough movies and dated enough jerks to

know that something is probably waiting around the corner to jump out and bite me. Maybe I don't have to take a turn at all, though. No corners. No dark hallways. And I definitely don't have to walk through any creepy doors that would have the audience yelling, *Don't go in there, you ding-dong!*

I straighten a little and pull my knees up on the swing to be more eye level with Jake. "Let's play a game to distract you from worrying about Sam."

He picks up my legs and drapes them over his lap. "What sort of game?" His blue eyes are sparkling, and my whole body flushes. I can see his mind working, and it's not fair. These mixed signals are torture. We're playing tug-of-war between *fast* and *slow*, but I can't keep up with who's tugging for which end. What happens if we both give up?

Chills race along my arms, and I dust them off with my hands.

"It's called the honesty game."

"So, truth or dare?" Would he quit talking like that? In that deep, sexy, husky tone that's dripping with innuendos?

"No." I tug on the *slow* side of the rope. "Just the truth game. It goes like this: one of us asks a question, and the other answers truthfully."

He nods thoughtfully. "Yeah. So, just basically talking, then? I don't think you can call it a game if one of us isn't daring the other to take off their clothes and jump in the pool if we don't want to answer the question."

I gasp and give him a big poke in the side again. "You wouldn't! I thought you were a gentleman."

He chuckles and grips my legs as he squirms away from my tickling pokes. "No, *you* said I was a gentleman, but I never confirmed it. I would definitely enjoy daring you to skinny dip."

"But you *did* say you wanted to take this whole thing slow."

"Want? No. Will? Yes." Why am I let down by that? I want to smack myself with a ruler. *Behave, Evie.*

Except now Jake is massaging my feet and I am putty in his hands. In fact, I'd really like for those hands to climb higher over my legs. For him to take me up to his room. To forget brakes even exist, because if he's this good at a foot massage imagine all the possibilities! I think I'm half in love with him already.

"Are you feeling okay? Need a heating pad or anything?"

Never mind. It's full-on love.

"I'm okay, thanks." What I really want is to get inside Jake's head and learn everything I can about him. I think the idea of the truth game freaked him out a little, and that's why he was sidestepping it with a joke. But guess what? I like to wave at the relationship *no-no* stop signs as I'm speeding by them. "First question: Why did you get divorced?"

He chokes on a laugh. "Wow. You didn't waste any time with that one."

"I like to live on the dangerous side."

Jake takes in a full breath and lets it out. "Can I just take off my clothes and jump in the pool instead?"

Not picturing that. Not picturing that. Not picturing that. Shoot. I pictured it. And *yep.* I'm debating letting him do it now. "No. You've gotta answer."

He winces and then settles back against the swing, busying himself while he talks by rubbing his hand up and down my leg. Not distracting at all. "All right, here it is. I didn't really date in high school. I was more focused on my grades and sports than girls. My mom likes to say it was because I was a really great kid—but actually, it was because I didn't think any of the girls in my grade were hot."

I laugh and give him ten points for honesty.

"When I graduated and started college, I met this really vibrant woman. She was"—Jake takes on a distant look that wrenches jealousy from my heart, but I decide to chill—"very pretty and had a sort of larger-than-life attitude. She was so charming and fun, and I fell for her fast and hard. I proposed after only a month of dating, and she said yes. I really thought it was love at first sight, but I've since learned that it was more attraction at first sight and I was too inexperienced to understand the difference. We set the wedding date for six months after I proposed, and she was already two months pregnant with Sam on our wedding day."

"Whoa." My smile is heavy. "That's a lot of change to go through in college."

"Yeah. It was intense. But somehow we made those first few years work. Even had some great moments. We had that newlywed bliss phase where it felt like nothing could stop us. And then I graduated from college, and Natalie, Sam, and I moved to Texas so I could work at a big-box architecture firm. Natalie decided to drop out of school right after she had Sam, so she never finished her business degree. After about five years of marriage, things started to get really rocky. I decided that I wanted to branch out and open my own firm—and also that I missed my family and wanted to be closer to them.

"We came back here to Charleston, and money was really tight for the first two years of getting my firm off the ground. Natalie grew restless, so she started spending more and more time at the gym and with new friends. One of those friends introduced her to an improv club, and that's when I learned she had apparently wanted to be an actress her whole life and had put aside the dream to have Sam. That was news to me, and before I knew it, we were never seeing each other anymore. Natalie would still spend time with Sam, but not much. She was always gone and doing things with friends—and later I learned that it wasn't so much a friend as someone she was cheating on me with.

"Before I realized that, though, I felt guilty, thinking that maybe Natalie was so restless because she gave up her dreams to stay home with our daughter while I went after mine, so I started taking over the brunt of the parenting responsibilities.

"Things just got worse, and she became more and more distant. . . . It was like she had mentally made her decision but was still living with us anyway. Finally, two years ago, she told me that she'd met someone else who could give her the life I couldn't, and she was moving to Hollywood with him to go after her acting career." Jake finally looks at me. "But it turns out, I wasn't the only one who couldn't give her the life she wants. She's had three serious relationships since our divorce." He puts bunny ears around the word *serious*.

"Jake. I'm so sorry." I don't know what else to say. I imagine there's no words that can fully soothe the ache of someone you loved leaving you. "You and Sam deserve better than that."

He shrugs. "Sam does, for sure."

I take his hand in mine. "You do too."

His hand is tense, his body radiating discomfort. "I'm not so sure, Evie. I wasn't perfect. Sometimes I wonder if I had hit the brakes early on with her, taken it slow and given her time to become who she wanted to be, maybe things would have been different." *I'm beginning to see why he's so adamant we don't rush things.* "As much as I hate her for her choices sometimes . . . I understand her need to be happy away from me. To have her own life. But I'll never understand her choice to exclude Sam from her life too. I mean, she makes money and has a great apartment in California that she's never once invited Sam to."

I can't understand it either. Sam isn't even my daughter— technically isn't anything to me besides a sweet little girl I helped match with one of my dogs, as well as the daughter of the man I'm sorta-kinda dating. But already she's carved out a special corner of my heart. If I have to say goodbye to this family in the future, it's going to hurt like hell.

"Like you said . . . it's one thing for Natalie to realize her path needed to move away from you. But there's no excuse for abandoning her daughter, especially during one of the most difficult times in Sam's life. And I know you want to beat yourself up a thousand different ways for how you could have been better to Natalie—and maybe you really could have done more to support her early on—"

"Don't pull your punches."

I smile. "But I'm trying to say, I've seen what kind of man you are, and you're the kind that learns from your past and improves for your future. You always make things right. That's such a special quality, Jake."

There's a lot more I'd like to say—but right now I get the feeling he just needs someone on his side who can scoop him up off the ground, dust him off, and say *try again*.

But then again, maybe that's just me being selfish, because I really want Jake to try again . . . with me.

"Thank you," he says quietly, and it breaks my heart to see the heaviness he carries on his shoulders. So, of course I need to say something to try to lighten it just a little. "But you know what, at the end of the day, even if everything around you is crumbling . . . at least you can know you have a great butt."

Jake barks out a laugh and shakes his head at me. "You and butts."

"Yours is especially bubbly. How did you get it that way? Tell me now, are they implants? I won't think less of you."

He gives me a wry grin. "I'll never tell, Butt Girl."

"*Oof.* That's not going to be my nickname."

I'm now one hundred percent certain that if Jake and I make this work, he's going to buy me a mug for Christmas that says *I like big butts and I cannot lie*. I'll worry about that bridge when I have to cross it.

"Yeah, I heard how it sounded after it came out." His playful smile dips into one more vulnerable. "So, now that you know all the baggage I'm carrying, do you still want to date me?"

I feign a look of contemplation for a second before my eyes shift to him. "I'm in," I say, and then I lean in slowly to place a soft kiss on his mouth. I hear him take in a breath, and his hand lands on my jaw. But then, before things get too interesting, he groans and breaks the seal of our lips. He's smiling and shaking his head. "Oh no you don't. You're not going to distract me out of my turn."

"Shoot. I thought that was going to work." I lean my shoulder against the swing. "Fine. Do your worst."

"Tell me about your relationship with your parents." *Ouch*. So, this is how it feels when someone goes right for the kill.

I scrunch my nose and try to decide where to start. Fifth-grade talent show, when my mom scolded me all the way home for missing the high note and coming in third? Nah. Instead, I tell Jake what it was like growing up in a house with parents who only care about money and status. I tell him how the only time my mom ever showed me any affection was when we were in public and a woman who appeared to have better domestic skills was watching. "And now they are trying to freeze me out. If I'm poor enough and hungry enough, they think I'll come to my senses and marry Tyler. But the joke is on them, because I know how to make a pack of ramen noodles last a whole week."

"Which reminds me, I grilled an extra steak for you to take home." He just keeps getting better.

"Careful. I'm like a stray cat. If you feed me, I might keep coming back."

"That's what I'm hoping for." He smiles, and my stomach turns inside out.

"Anyway, I just decided that if I'm never going to be good enough for them, I might as well have them be disappointed in me for doing something I love rather than living a life that makes me feel like crap."

He reaches up and runs his hand through my hair. The look on his face says he's wanted to do that all night—maybe even since he met me. "Evie, you're an incredible woman. I'm sorry your parents don't recognize that."

I'm not good with compliments. It's either because I'm not used to hearing them or because I've heard so much criticism over the course of my life that I can't believe the good things people tell me, but either way, I want to throw my hands up and bat away those compliments like I'm Babe Ruth.

"Eh. I'm messy, and forgetful, and I don't like greens."

Jake's eyes grow serious, and I'm sure he's about to convince me of all the reasons he thinks I'm wonderful, so I stand abruptly and smooth out my dress. "It's getting late. I better call an Uber. Charlie's getting antsy."

Jake lifts his brows and glances around me. I follow his gaze to my traitorous dog, who's curled up in a comfy little ball by the porch railing. "You're right. He looks super anxious."

"Yep. This is how he manifests anxiety. He looks chill, but believe me, inside, he's fit to be tied."

Now run, Evie.

Jake grabs my hand and pulls me to a stop. "Why are you getting squirmy again?" He stands up and invades my space.

"I'm not," I lie. I'm squirming because Jake is the first man in a long time that I've wanted to look into my eyes and convince me that I mean something to him. I really can feel myself falling for him, and falling in love with someone on a first date is definitely not *slow* material.

"Stay with me tonight," he says quietly. *Well, that's definitely not going to help anything either.* "Not for sex. I just mean, stay here tonight. We can stay up all night talking, or watching a movie, or whatever. I just . . . I won't get many chances like this to spend time with you without Sam, and I want to take advantage of every minute I get."

I should go home. I *should not* stay.

Ohhhhh, but I want to stay. Staying sounds like a dream. And Charlie does look awfully comfortable. What kind of a heartless person would I be to wake my sleeping pup when he looks that comfy?

Jake squeezes my hand, willing me to agree. I'm opening my mouth to do just that when our attention is distracted by the sudden buzzing of his phone.

He lets go of my hand and darts to his phone. Noticing the number, his eyes flash worry at mine. "It's Jenna's parents."

"Answer it!"

He puts the phone to his ear, and I can see the worry and dread filling his face. "Will. Is everything okay?" He listens for a minute, giving away no hints of what Will is saying. I wish I had asked him to put it on speaker. Is Sam okay? Did she have a seizure?

There is a silent panic I've never felt before welling up in my heart.

Jake mumbles a few *mm-hmms* and then says, "I'll be right over." He hangs up, and his shoulders relax. "She's fine. She didn't have a seizure, but she wants to come home."

I sigh, feeling deep relief. What is this feeling? I'm worried about how my heart seems to be tying itself to not only Jake but also his daughter. "Whew. That's good."

He gives me an apologetic smile, and I already know what he's going to say, so I hold up my hand. "Don't apologize. I was going to decline your offer to stay anyway."

He gives me a look that says he doesn't believe me one bit. "Yeah, okay."

"I was! Jacob Broaden, I am a southern woman of great moral principle. If you think I can be easily seduced by your pretty blue eyes, you'll be . . . exactly right. I was absolutely going to stay."

He laughs and wraps an arm around me, pulling me close to him. "Come with me to get Sam. I can drop you off at your apartment after."

"You sure?"

He smiles and nods slowly before releasing me. He helps me gather all my things, and Charlie, and the extra food bag that looks suspiciously less like "an extra steak" and a lot more like a full bag of groceries. I should turn him down, but . . . I don't want to. I think I even see the box of tampons I opened earlier on the top, and I smile to myself.

CHAPTER 27

Jake

Evie and I pull up outside of Jenna's house, and the door immediately flies open. Out come Sam and Daisy, waving to Jenna's parents, who are decked out in ugly matching robes and slippers. They have their initials monogrammed on them (the robes and slippers), and they are giving Sam a pitying look as she barrels toward my truck.

I open the door and get out to help Sam and Daisy in and then wave back at Will and his wife, Beth.

Beth calls out, "So sorry you had to come all the way here in the middle of the night, Jake." *Okay, well, it's ten o'clock, so not exactly the middle now, is it, Beth?* "We tried to get her to stay, but she wasn't having it." Beth's voice annoys me for some reason. I think it's because she's looking at Sam like she thought it was a bad idea to invite her in the first place. It's a pitying *I-told-you-so* look. As if my daughter is the first young girl in the history of girls to want to leave a sleepover early.

"No problem, Beth. I was glad to come get her."

"Oh," she says suddenly, tilting her head to get a better look inside my truck as I hold the door open for Sam and Daisy. "Sorry, I just noticed you have a friend with you." She's squinting hard, trying to get a good look at Evie, but I just shut the truck door so the tinted windows will cut off her view. Not because I'm in any way ashamed to be seen with Evie but because I've always found Beth—queen of the school rumor mill—obnoxious. I don't want her to have access to my life and twist what's been a perfect night with Evie into anything other than that when she blasts out false information on her PTA group text.

"Night! Thanks again," I say, opening the driver's-side door and slipping in quickly.

The moment I pull away from the curb, Evie leans over to me and says quietly, "Silly robes, right?"

I wish I could kiss her right now, but I don't know how Sam would feel about that. "You don't like the matchy-matchy couple style?"

She grimaces and shakes her head before turning her whole body around in her seat to face Sam like she always does. It's not safe in the least, but it's sweet, so I don't say anything about it. "How's it going, darlin'? Everything okay?"

I was literally opening my mouth to ask that very question. Why do I like it so much that she beat me to it? I close my mouth and look in the rearview mirror to catch Sam's answer, but her downcast expression worries me.

"I'm sorry, Evie. I tried. I really thought it would be fun. But . . . I just couldn't stop feeling scared and wanting to go home."

"Oh, Sam. Why are you apologizing to me for that?"

She shrugs. "Because I know that that's why I have Daisy—to make me feel more comfortable and keep going on with my normal life like you do with Charlie. But even though I had her by me, and I knew she'd do her job, I just kept feeling scared that I would have a seizure while I was sleeping. I felt nervous and didn't like it." She pauses and looks at me now. "I'm sorry I put up such a big fight to go, Dad."

Her words pierce me. She thinks I'm going to be disappointed that she came home?

No way. I think she's brave as hell for even fighting to go in the first place. Once again, I'm about to say all this when Evie unclicks her seatbelt and climbs over the center console to get in the back with Sam. For a split second, her butt is in the air beside me, and I have to remember to concentrate on the road.

She settles in beside Sam and wraps an arm around her shoulders. The sight shakes me. I'm speechless.

"Listen to me, hon, and remember this for the rest of your life: it's always okay to go home. Anytime you feel uncomfortable or scared, never worry about what anyone else is going to think if you call your dad and have him come get you. Your house is a safe place, and you love being there, and that's something to be proud of, not embarrassed about."

A car honks at me, and I realize I've sat through most of a green light listening to Evie give my daughter the best speech I've ever heard. I kind of just want to roll down my window and wave the jerk behind me to go on by. I'm clearly having a moment.

"You're not disappointed in me?" Sam asks Evie, not me.

It also strikes me that Sam is not even questioning why Evie is in the car. It's like she knew she would be. Like she's a part of our life now. How do I feel about that?

Evie squeezes Sam. "Never. I'm so stinking proud of you for even giving it a try. Do you know that it took me a whole six months with Charlie before I felt brave enough to go anywhere without a friend with me? But there was nothing wrong with that either. We all find our bravery at different times, and that's perfectly fine."

Sam smiles and settles her head on Evie's shoulder. Evie kisses the top of Sam's head and brushes her hair away from her face.

The sight is tearing me up inside. In my little rectangular mirror, I see the most perfect picture of a woman who doesn't have to be here, caring for my little girl who adores her, and their service dogs on either side of them.

Evie connects with Sam in a way that I will never be able to. This should upset me, but for some reason it relieves me. Maybe I won't have to do everything on my own after all. Maybe Sam will get to have a mother who cares for her like she deserves.

And dammit.

Those thoughts do not sound casual. They sound a lot like commitment.

CHAPTER 28

Evie

The morning after the best date of my life, I'm trying hard to focus while training a handful of our volunteers in the techniques of walking with loose leashes. They're going to have to teach these skills to a new batch of puppies, and it's important they know what they're doing. But I can't keep my brain from wandering back to last night and how it felt to sit on Jake's counter and kiss him.

"Evie, is this okay?" asks a volunteer.

"Yeah, it's fine," I reply, still in a daze until I realize that the pup is practically dragging the woman across the lawn to chase a butterfly. I snap into action, gaining both the puppy's and the volunteer's attention, and quickly run back over the instructions on how to get the puppies to mind their manners on the leash.

We go on and on like this for a time, and I can't seem to keep myself from checking my phone every couple of minutes to see if Jake has texted me. I'm quite literally pathetic. I've gone from an independent woman to a needy girlfriend overnight. Actually, I'm not even his girlfriend. Just a needy girl with a Texas-sized crush on the guy she's seeing casually.

Finally, the workday is over, and I'm on my way home. I feel so let down from not hearing from Jake that I think my arms are actually dragging on the ground as I walk. There's sad music playing in my head, and I'm just about to break out in a melancholy ballad and let my hands drag across a field of wheat when I hear my phone ringing in my purse.

I pause on the sidewalk right outside of a bakery and pull out my phone. I don't even look at the caller ID because I'm certain that it's Jake. I think we have that special telepathy that couples get when they've been together a long time.

"Helllloooo." My flirtatious tone is dialed up to ten.

"Evelyn Grace, why do you sound like an inappropriate phone operator of some sort?" Ugh. Mom. Apparently, Jake and I do need a little more time for those superpowers to kick in.

"How would you even know what one of those ladies sounds like, Mom?"

She's quiet for a second, and I take that opportunity to give myself a point in the book of Evie versus Melony I started a few years ago. My therapist says it's not healthy, but what does she really know anyway?

Mom apparently doesn't have a good rebuttal for that question, so she decides not to answer it. "I'm sure you're busy petting puppies, so I'll make this quick." I think she has a tally book too and is probably adding a tick to her column right now, but she would be wrong. That one didn't even hurt, because *ha ha,* the joke's on her, I already did my puppy petting this morning, and it was a lovely way to spend my time as well as an important part of socializing the new pups.

I decide to sit on the bench outside the bakery to finish this chat instead of continuing my walk home, because I have a feeling that I'm going to need some carb therapy after I hang up. "Very kind of you to consider my time," I say and lean over to pet Charlie's head.

"I'll cut right to the chase. I want you to come to the house for dinner Wednesday night."

"Umm thanks, but no thanks."

"If you would have let me finish, you would have heard why I want you to come to dinner."

I wince and shut my eyes because I can smell a Melony Jones special coming down the line: a fancy dinner that costs more than my entire week's worth of groceries, dessert that melts in my mouth, and a big helping of manipulation on the side.

"I would like for you to come to dinner because your dad and I have decided to make a sizable donation to your little dog business." Yep. There it is.

"Actually, our dogs are pretty large," I say, but Mom doesn't snicker because I don't think she knows how to laugh at a joke. Jo would have laughed. I let out a long sigh and decide to be serious to get this over with faster. "A donation would be great. Feel free to make one at the benefit."

A family is walking by me, and I can see that they so badly want to stop and pet Charlie. Most people are pretty good about not storming up to pet him without permission. But occasionally, I get a few who don't understand that he is a working dog and will get right down on the ground and start loving on him without my consent. It's hard. Not only because it usually makes me have to stop whatever I'm doing but also because it distracts Charlie when I need him to be his most alert. But I try to give everyone as much grace as possible since I know it's difficult to ignore a dog as adorable and fluffy as Charlie.

Luckily the family passes right by me without stopping and I can breathe a little easier.

"Well, of course we will make a donation at the benefit, but we would also like to make a special donation separate from the fundraiser." Oh, Mom. I wish so badly she would stop trying to pull these puppet strings all day. I'm tired of dancing for her.

I'm halfway tempted to turn down her offer, but I can't. We're desperate for the money. More money means more dogs we can give away to those who need them. I would feel terrible knowing that I had to turn someone away who couldn't afford the high ticket price of our dogs because I was too insecure to have dinner with my parents. "And I'm guessing there is no way you would consider just mailing us a check?"

Mom makes a scoffing sound. "You know, Evelyn, you are starting to sound rather ungrateful for my offer. Maybe we won't give an additional donation since it sounds as if you're not in great need after all."

I sigh so loudly I'm sure it sounds like a windstorm on Mom's end. Looks like I'm going to be dancing Wednesday night. "Should I wear tap shoes or ballet shoes for my dance?"

"Excuse me?"

"Never mind. I'll be there. What time?"

I can practically hear the wrinkles creasing around my mom's mouth as her lips form a smug smile. "Dinner is at seven. And please, for heaven's sake, be punctual. We will have a few other important guests at dinner who I'm sure would be more than happy to pull out their checkbooks if you make a good impression. So, come wearing that winning smile I taught you back in your pageant days and a dress with a hemline that hits below the knee." There is no doubt in my mind that this is all one big trap. I wish I knew what it was so I could be prepared before I get caught in it.

"I'll be sure and pick up my nun costume from the dry cleaner."

"Evelyn Grace, don't you da—"

I hang up, and my phone immediately starts ringing again.

"I wasn't serious. I don't even own a nun costume," I say, standing up and starting to walk home. I don't feel like eating my feelings anymore. My stomach is twisting too uncomfortably now that I know I have to go to my parents' house for dinner.

"That's too bad. I bet you'd make a sexy nun."

It's Jake!

"Ha! We do have telepathy."

"What?"

"Nothing. What's up?" I realize I'm practically skipping down the sidewalk now. That's what the sound of Jake's voice does to me: turns me into a skipper.

"I was just calling to see if you have plans Wednesday night. And before you say anything, I know I'm supposed to wait forty-eight hours before asking you out on a second date, but this is Sam's fault. She wants you to come over and watch a movie with us. It has nothing to do with me wanting to spend more time with you."

I stop skipping and groan because now I'm doubly upset that my mom has manipulated me into going to dinner. "I wish I could, but I just made dinner plans that night."

"Oh. A hot date?" he asks in a playful tone, because he knows it's not that. I told him I wasn't going to be seeing anyone else while we figure out what this is between us and he's doing the same. I feel good about it—so does he.

"Far from it. I'm being forced to go to a dinner party at my parents' house because they are evil overlords who have too much money."

"Gotcha. Okay, so do you want some company, then? I can have June stay with Sam." He's offering to go with me? I didn't even really give him a valid reason, and he's willing to go with me anyway.

"It's going to be torture."

"Will you be there?"

I laugh. "Yeah."

"Then it'll be worth it."

Yep. I'm a goner. I am no match for this man. He makes me feel wanted and valued in a way that I didn't even know was possible. As scary as it is, I'm starting to picture a future with Jake. One where, after forty years of marriage, he still pinches my butt in the kitchen.

Charlie looks up and sees my dreamy expression and shakes his head at me. I think he really is getting jealous now.

"All right, then, yes. I'd love for you to come with me."

We continue to talk for my whole walk home, and before I know it, I'm lying on my couch and twirling my hair around my finger while Jake tells me about his day. Yes, he's made me a hair twirler too. I'm fully aware of how annoying I am to be around now.

Finally, he asks for details about what he should wear Wednesday night and what time we need to be leaving my house to get to my parents' place. I tell him six-thirty, to which he replies, "Great. I'll be there at six-fifteen so I can mess up your lipstick a little before we go."

I'm having so much fun in this flirty bubble with Jake that, at first, I don't even realize that Charlie has suddenly stood up and come to sit in front of me, staring. It's not a normal stare. It's a direct look that he only ever uses when he needs my attention most. My chuckle dies out, and dread takes its place. I know this look. I've seen it many times.

"Hang on, Jake," I say, and I think he can hear the worry in my voice because he starts asking if everything is okay. I ignore him and focus on Charlie, who is now whining, and I know it's not because he needs to go potty.

Annoyed that I'm not acting on his signals, Charlie takes his alerting to the next level. He gently bites the hem of my dress and starts tugging me. I blow out a breath through my mouth, because now I'm certain that Charlie is alerting me of an oncoming seizure.

I know what he's telling me to do. "All right, buddy, I'm coming," I say to Charlie, and I follow our usual procedure and get down on a clear spot on the floor. I probably could lie on the couch or my bed, but I'm always worried that I'll convulse myself out of the bed and hit my head on the floor. Living on my own, I like to be more careful than not when it comes to my seizures. So, I lie on my back and take a deep breath. It doesn't matter how many times I've gone through this, though, it never gets less scary.

"Jake."

"What's wrong, Evie?"

"Charlie just alerted me. I'm going to have a seizure." My voice shakes even though I'm trying so hard to put on a brave face. I'm going to be okay. Charlie will watch out for me. Once I lose consciousness and begin convulsing, I know that Charlie will move me onto my side to keep me safe. He'll go push the button on the wall that calls Jo and then come back to stay with me and lick my face to bring me back to consciousness faster. Even now, he's going to the fridge and using the tug rope to pull it open and retrieve a water bottle for me for after the seizure.

When Jake speaks, he sounds as heavy as I feel. "How long do you think until it starts?"

"He always alerts me ten to thirty minutes before an episode."

"Okay." I hear him rustling papers around frantically. "I'm on my way from the office, so it won't take me long to get there."

"What?!" I start to sit up, but Charlie doesn't like it and tugs me back down. I comply. "Jake, you don't have to do that. I'll be all right. I'll call you later, once everything passes."

"Evie." His voice is deep and means business. If my heart rate wasn't already high from nervousness, it would be elevated for a whole different reason. "I want to. Please let me come over."

Honestly, I'm contemplating saying no. I'm nervous. What if he gets here in time to see the episode? I've never filmed myself, so I don't know what I look like during a seizure, but I've seen it reenacted by mean boys in high school enough times to get a pretty good idea.

Jake has seen Sam's seizures, so it won't be totally foreign to him, but what if seeing me this way changes the way he feels about me? What if he's less attracted to me after? Or if he realizes that I'll just be more of a burden in his life?

These fears have all evolved out of past experiences.

The truth is, Tyler Murray and I dated from freshman to junior year of high school. And those jerks I mentioned who made fun of me for the way I convulsed during a seizure in class? Yeah, Tyler was one of them. Actually, first he broke up with me, and then he made fun of me with his buddies.

I never told my parents about that day in high school (and the weeks he spent reenacting my seizures in the hallway when I'd pass by) because I was too embarrassed—ashamed over something I couldn't control. Shame that never should have been mine to take on.

Later, when Tyler and I graduated, and before he moved away, he tried to get back together with me (most likely because by that point his parents were convincing him of the merit of marrying a Jones), and when I turned him down because of how he treated me our junior year, he said the teasing was all good-natured fun and he didn't mean any harm by it.

It didn't feel good-natured to me. He's never actually apologized for what he did. And I'm past the point of needing it. Tyler means nothing to me now and I care about his opinion as much as I care to eat dirt.

The problem is, the way I was treated in the past has stuck with me all this time, and I'm afraid that if Jake comes over and sees me in an episode, it will put an end to our relationship before it ever gets going. But then I remember my own advice to Sam. *If you think that these girls will be mean to you if you have a seizure, don't go—they're not worth your friendship.*

Jake is worth it.

I'm just about to tell him to come over when I hear Jake's keys jingle and he says, "Like it or not, I'm on my way."

I take a deep breath and shut my eyes. I guess that's that, then. I put my arm over Charlie and wait.

I had a seizure; I know that much. I feel a little foggy, and my arms and legs are heavy. I'm coming out of it, but life still seems like a dream where everything is fuzzy around the edges and doesn't make a lot of sense. I don't know how long ago I had it, but I know that I'm in the postictal phase and that I probably won't feel like myself again for a while. All I want to do is sleep.

Suddenly, I hear a voice. "Are we all clear, Charlie?" And I realize it's Jake. I peek open my eyelids, but they're so heavy. The nausea is pretty intense too, so I shut them again. "That was a good boy," I hear Jake say, and I picture him petting Charlie's head.

The next thing I know, there's warmth beside my body, and Jake's voice is close. "You're okay, Evie. I'm here, and you're safe. I'm going to move you up onto your bed so you're more comfortable, okay?"

I nod slowly because, really, that's all I can do at this moment. And then I feel Jake's hands slide under my body and he cradles me close to his chest. He's warm, and I wish I could stay in his arms forever. He's like a heating pad but even better because I don't have to plug him into the wall.

Jake lays me down gently on my bed and pulls my comforter up over me. The weight of the bed shifts, and although my arms currently weigh a million pounds, I reach out and find his hand. "Stay with me," I say quietly.

I don't open my eyes because my body is demanding I sleep. But then the bed sinks beside me and Jake's lovely warmth surrounds me. He smells like his cologne today. It's a clean, masculine fragrance that I hope never washes out of my linens. His big arm wraps around my torso and pulls me up close to him. I'm safe in his arms. He brushes a stray hair out of my face and tucks it behind my ear before he places a soft kiss on my temple.

I don't know how long he's been here. I don't know if he saw the seizure. But I do know that he's lying beside me right now and tenderly caring for me. He's not running for the hills.

CHAPTER 29

Jake

Evie is asleep in my arms, and I never want to let her go. I got here at the tail end of her seizure and in enough time to see her body jolting with movement. My heart broke for her. Charlie did his job perfectly, but now that it's over, I'm stepping in and holding her as close as she'll let me for as long as she'll let me.

Yeah, I'm doing great with this whole taking-it-slow thing. Completely casual. No strings attached. Just call me *Casual Friday* because I am so chill about our relationship, it's ridiculous. In no way am I stroking her long blond hair away from her face and contemplating proposing here and now. She smells so good too. Her soft curves are curled up against me, and my heart is splitting open. I'll be handing it to her on a silver platter before long.

When she told me she was about to have a seizure, it was like the world stopped spinning and all that mattered was getting to Evie as quickly as possible. It's the same way I feel about Sam. That protectiveness. The same worry.

Evie makes a little groaning sound in her sleep, and I wonder if she has a migraine. Sam always gets a migraine after her seizures.

But I see a water bottle with fresh condensation dripping down the side and a bottle of headache medicine on the bedside table. I know from talking to Evie and learning about all the ways she trained Charlie to aid her that he was the one to fetch her those necessities.

Has she taken the meds yet? I'll ask her when she's more coherent.

Charlie hears the groan and comes to stand beside the bed on Evie's side. He rests his head on the mattress and slices those big brown eyes up at me. I'm pretty sure he's telling me, *You're in my spot.* I get it. I'd be possessive too if I got to share Evie's bed on a daily basis. It's way too small, though. My feet are hanging off the bottom. She needs a king-sized bed like mine. Or maybe just mine . . .

What if I just packed up all her stuff and moved her into my house? *Good morning, love. Did you sleep well? Yeah, I changed my mind on the whole no-serious-relationship thing, and we're married now, and you have to live with me forever.* A tad too much of the *Beauty and the Beast* vibe.

As gently as possible, I shift Evie and myself over to the far side of the bed. She's totally out because she doesn't even stir the slightest bit. I give Charlie a nod, and he gets it right away. He jumps up on the bed and snuggles up under Evie's arm and stomach. Suddenly, we are a family, and I wish Sam were here too.

What is this? Why am I feeling this way? I'm out-of-my-mind scared that I'm about to get my heart crushed by this woman. I can't hide away forever, though, right? Sooner or later, I've got to give in and risk heartbreak. Evie feels worth it. And she hasn't given me a reason not to trust her so far.

I spend the next hour like this, watching Evie sleep (it's only slightly creepy) and trying to work through some of the insecurities that Natalie left me with. Evie may be stuffing herself inside Tinker Bell's house, but she's not fooling anyone—me, especially.

She's used to a different life. One of money and prospects and people who have a whole lot more to offer than me.

Natalie left me because she wanted more.

Evie's already had the kind of life that Natalie is chasing. She knows what she's missing out on. And although she says she doesn't want the kind of life she grew up with, what's to say she won't want it back later on? Sam and I can't go through that again.

I'm saved from my own thoughts when I feel my phone buzzing. I hurry and silence it before it disturbs Evie. She hasn't moved, though. Her soft pink lips are slightly parted, and her dark lashes are fanned against her cheeks. Her blond waves cascade around her, and I'm feeling so in awe of her that I'm glad I have to get up and talk to my sister on the phone. As carefully as possible, I extract myself from Evie's bed and slip out the front door.

"Hey, June," I say, answering my phone.

"How is she?"

Sam was already with June while I was at the office this afternoon. When Evie said she was about to have a seizure, I called June and told her I'd be later than I had originally planned because I needed to go be with Evie.

"She's okay. Resting now."

"I'm glad you're there with her," says June, and her concern makes me smile. She likes Evie a lot.

"Me too. And listen, what do you think about just letting Sam spend the night with you so I can stay here and take care of Evie tonight?"

There is a long pause. At first I think that maybe she disapproves. I should have known better, though, because I quickly realize that she's just taking a minute to stifle whatever celebration she's doing on the other end. "Eeeeek, you love her! I knew it."

"Stop," I say, hoping to put an end to her pestering before she gets out of hand. "I just don't want to leave her like this."

"Mm-hmm. Don't lie to me. You just want to be there when she's feeling better." She begins to sing, "Jake and Evie, sitting in a—"

"Is this going to go on for much longer? Because I need to head back in and help Evie."

She laughs. "Yeah, don't worry about Sam. I'll take good care of her." And do you know what? For the first time since Sam's diagnosis, I'm not worried. She's got Daisy now, and after today, seeing Charlie tend to Evie so diligently, I have more faith in service dogs than ever. Daisy will keep Sam safe until I get to her if something happens.

Later that night, I'm washing dishes in Evie's six-inch-wide sink when I hear her say, "You're still here."

I cut off the water and turn around to face her bed. She's sitting up, and her hair is all draped across one shoulder. Her eyes are heavy, and she looks more beautiful than ever. I lean back against the sink and cross my arms, smiling. "Did you think I wouldn't be?"

She looks down to pet Charlie and shrugs. "I didn't know."

Something about those words tears me up.

I uncross my arms and make my way back to Evie's bed. She watches me approach with worried eyes, and she pulls her covers up a little higher like she's naked under there. Which she's not. She's still fully clothed in her yellow sundress just like I found her. But I realize as I get closer that she does feel naked. I've seen her seizure, and that's making her feel vulnerable.

I climb onto the bed beside her, and it's hilarious how unsteady this little thing is. It sags heavily under my weight, and Evie notices with a grin. I lean my back against the headboard and pull her to my chest. "I'm not going anywhere," I say into her hair, and then I kiss her forehead.

We stay like that for a minute, and I can feel her quickened breathing against my chest. It's good to know that I have the same effect on her that she has on me. "How are you feeling?" I ask.

She tilts her chin up to me and wrinkles her nose. "I've been better." She then looks down to her hand resting on my chest, and she moves her index finger in a small circle. "I've also been worse."

I wonder if she can feel how hard my heart is beating.

Her smile grows, and her eyes peek back up at me, and yep, she can feel it and it's going right to her ego. She then lays her head right on my chest where her ear is perfectly centered with my hammering heart. It's a pointed move. One where she's saying, *Yeah, I know how you feel about me, and I like it.*

"I think you should know that I've not always been treated kindly for my seizures. Part of me expected you to bolt after one look at me on the floor."

My hand stills in her hair. "Who was unkind to you?"

"Too many to name. Don't get me wrong, a lot of people are sweet. Unfortunately, it's the hurtful comments that stick the most. And . . . I don't really feel up to talking it all through right now. But it means a lot to me that you stayed."

I hold her a little closer. "It's an honor to stay."

We spend the entire rest of the day like this until I force myself to go pick us up some dinner. When her stomach settles and her migraine subsides a little, we eat on the couch and watch reruns of *Friends* with her legs draped over my lap and my arm around her shoulders. It feels so right. So natural. I don't think I've ever felt this content in my entire life.

I think what we've shared together today has probably tied us together more than anything physical would have. Although, the night isn't completely physical-less. We definitely spend an entire episode of *Friends* making out on her tiny couch. It is sweet and appropriate (at least that's going to be my answer when June asks me about it later), and we both cut it off before anything more serious happens.

Sometime about midnight, Evie falls asleep beside me on the

couch. I pick her up and carry her to bed and climb in behind her. Charlie is once again on one side of Evie, and I'm on the other. It's not the most comfortable thing to sleep in jeans and a shirt, and the bed is so small that my ass hangs off the edge. But I couldn't care less. Evie is here with me. I can smell the coconut scent lingering in her hair and hear her taking deep breaths as she sleeps. This feels right, and I don't know how long I'm going to be able to keep convincing myself that we're just two people casually dating.

This feels a lot like falling in love.

CHAPTER 30

Evie

I can't stop smiling, and Jo notices. "Is it my imagination or are you glowing today?"

"I'm afraid I'm going to be glowing red if you aren't more careful with that curling wand." I inch myself away from the burning-hot hair tool hovering beside my face.

It's Wednesday and Jake will be here soon to pick me up to go to my parents' house for dinner. I told Jo about it, and she suggested she come over and help me get ready. But what I really think happened was she called me while I was still wrapped up in Jake's arms in my bed the other morning. My phone was going to buzz off my bedside table if I didn't answer it, so I did. That was mistake number one. Mistake number two was trying to whisper to Joanna so I didn't wake up the sleeping man beside me. But you guessed it, he woke up and leaned closer to huskily ask who I was talking to.

Want to take a wild guess what Joanna did before peppering me with one hundred and one questions? She squealed. Squealed like a little teenybopper at a Justin Bieber concert. "He's there with you, isn't he?! Oh my heavens, he's in your bed! It's only seven in the morning, so I *know* you aren't out of bed yet. Don't lie to me, missy!" She always calls me *missy* when she thinks her age will suddenly work as a rank card. Like she has the power to ground me or take away my phone.

"Oh, would you pipe down over there. I'll call you later," I said in a useless whisper because Jake was right there in my bed.

"*You better!*" she singsonged back to me before I abruptly ended the call, pleased to finally get to hang up before she had the chance.

It was so strange waking up with Jake beside me. I thought I was surfacing from the most wonderful dream where a strong, attractive man spent the entire day taking care of me and then snuggled me while we slept. And then when I opened my eyes, I realized a tan, muscular forearm was draped over my shoulder, and I nearly screamed.

Suddenly, the curling wand appears an inch from my face again. "Tell me everything that happened." Wow. Jo has a real interrogation-officer thing going on right now, and I'm a little terrified of her.

"Nothing!" I crane my neck as far back as I can without falling off the stool.

Joanna lifts a brow. "You're not holding out on me, are you? I know he was in your bed the morning I called. And no sense lying to me about it, because I already smelled your pillow, and it smells like Old Spice!"

"You smelled my pillow?!"

"Come on, Evie, didn't anyone ever teach you how to kiss and tell?"

I shake my head at her in mock reprimand. "Someone needs to teach you some manners."

She grins and picks up another section of my hair to wrap it around the iron. My hair is officially too long for me to curl myself, but I want it to be in pristine condition when I go to my parents' house later tonight. That way my mom can't say anything about how I should really try putting an effort into my appearance before I go out.

"Fine. You don't have to go into detail. But just tell me this . . . are you happy?"

I meet my own eyes in the mirror and take a long look. And yep, right there, reflected in my green eyes, is a spark of happiness I haven't felt in a long time. I feel cherished by Jake, and I'm starting to trust that feeling. "I am happy. Things are finally starting to come together in my life. Plans for the fundraiser are lining up nicely, and I'm hopeful that we're going to make enough to achieve our goal for the year. I'm seeing an amazing guy who truly understands me and my lifestyle, and I get to spend time with his adorable daughter who makes me feel . . ."

"Whole?"

I meet Jo's eyes in the mirror and nod. "Yeah. How'd you know that?"

She gently wraps my hair around the iron. "Because that's what happened to me three years ago when I met you." My heart swells, and all of a sudden tears are pricking my eyes. I sit very, *very* still because I despise crying in front of people.

Joanna unwraps a curl from the iron and sets it down, resting her hip against the counter and folding her arms in front of her. "Did I ever tell you that Gary and I couldn't have children?"

"No, you didn't."

"I don't like to dwell on it much. We found out back in the day before fertility treatments were as successful as they are now. The fact of the matter is a biological family just wasn't in the cards for us, and it was tough to realize at first, but we got through it and have had an incredible, lovely life together just the two of us." She smiles softly. "And then I met you and had the sudden distinct feeling that you were the missing part of our family I never knew I needed." She pauses as emotion clogs her throat. "I probably don't say it enough, but I love you, missy."

I feel my smile stretch across my face and reach out to take her hand. "You tell me every single day, Jo."

Her eyes are misty. "It's not enough."

Now my tears are falling too, and it's no use trying to stop them. "I don't know where I would be without you, Jo. I love you too. And you've been a better mom to me than mine ever has been. So . . . thank you for letting me be a part of your and Gary's family."

"You're welcome, honey."

We stare at each other for a minute, and then, as if we truly are mother and daughter, we both scrunch our noses at the same time and release each other's hand. "Right. Well, no sense making your mascara run right before your evening at the palace. Wouldn't want to give the queen anything to remark on."

I laugh and turn my eyes to the mirror to finish up my makeup. I'm pulling out all the stops tonight. Mascara. Eyeliner. Blush. It's all happening. Sephora would be so proud of me. "Oh, I'm sure Her Highness will find something to her distaste."

"I wish you'd bring me instead of Jake. I'd like to take that woman's hateful comments and shove them right up her snooty little—"

"Yeah, yeah, yeah, I know where you'd put them."

Jo gives me a mischievous grin and then leaves my bathroom. "I'll get your dress. Where is it?"

"On my bed," I call out to her, and then I hear her loud, overly dramatic gasp.

"Please tell me you're not going to wear this hideous thing."

I knew she'd hate it. It's a conservative little number I plucked from the sale rack of a department store. It's a plain navy pencil dress with a high neckline, and it hits me just below the knees. It looks like I should be walking into a courtroom with a briefcase at my side rather than going to a dinner party.

"But this looks nothing like you. Where's the color? Where are the flowers?" She sticks her head back into the bathroom, holding up the offending dress. "Oh gosh, don't tell me you got matching pumps to go with it."

"They're by the door."

"Why are you doing this?"

I sigh and stand up, taking the dress from her and walking out to lay it back down on my bed. "I know it's nothing like me. But I'm not trying to be me tonight. I'm just trying to get in, grab that check, and get out as fast as possible with as few mean comments stuck to my back as I can manage." It's probably a little cowardly of me, but I don't care. I'm tired of fighting my mom at every turn. Might as well play the game and blend in with their lifestyle until I can get back home and change into my sneakers and summer dress.

I peel off my clothes and slip into the dress, having Jo zip up the back. I spin around, and she gives me a begrudging smile. "Well, we can at least be grateful it hugs your curves."

I shake my head at her. "I promise I will burn this dress as soon as I'm done with this dinner party. How about that?"

"Okay. As long as you let Jake unzip it for you." She winks with a devilish smirk, and I swat her arm.

A knock sounds at the door, and Joanna and I both look at each other. She wags her brows and bolts to it immediately.

"Joanna, don't you dare ask him if we had sex the other night!" I say way too loudly just as she's flinging open the door.

I guess my door is paper-thin, because Jake smiles at Joanna and his dimples pop. "Sadly, we did not," he says, and my stomach flips over.

To say he looks amazing would be a gross understatement. He's wearing dark-blue slacks that cling to his muscular thighs and a white button-down tucked in with a brown belt. A light-gray suit jacket hugs his big shoulders, and his jaw is clean-shaven. I also think he must have called some kind of hair-and-makeup artist to come style his hair, because it's molded into a soft, tousled look that only a movie star should be able to achieve.

My mouth is hanging open at the sight of him, which gives Joanna immense pleasure. She chuckles and grabs her purse. "I think I'll just be on my way, then. Have fun tonight, darlin'!" She squeezes Jake's arm on her way out and then flashes a wide-eyed look back at me after she realizes he's all muscle.

Jake steps inside with a soft laugh and shuts the door behind him.

His eyes take me in, and they hitch on the curves of my waist before he shakes his head with a smile. He walks up to me and lightly sets his hands on those curves to tug me closer. "I think we might need to have a talk later about the whole *casually taking it slow* thing we discussed."

"Oh yeah?" I ask with a smile and a lifted brow, looking as cool as a cucumber and not at all like my stomach is exploding with butterflies.

His mouth dips to mine, and yep, I'm going to have to reapply my lipstick before we leave, just like he promised.

It's a good start to the evening, and I think dinner is going to be more bearable with Jake at my side. But really, I can't wait until it's all over and I get to have that conversation with him.

CHAPTER 31

Jake

"So. This is where you grew up?" I ask, staring up at the white three-story Charleston mansion that has a wraparound porch on every level. The house is obscenely big for this part of town. I now know it's possible for a home to look smug.

It's tucked off the main road, and we had to punch in a number for the large iron gates to give us access to the driveway. I can see a tea garden off the right side of the home, and the landscaping is so well manicured I wouldn't be surprised to see a staff of twenty on their hands and knees, cutting each blade of grass with golden shears.

I design homes for a living—often a lot like this one—but for some reason, knowing that this house is a part of Evie's history is leaving me a little dumbfounded. It's what this house represents. Wealth. Status. Power. Insecurity pokes me in the ribs.

Evie grabs my arm and tugs me out of my trance. "Don't look it in the eyes. That's how it traps you." She lifts up on her tiptoes and kisses my cheek and then drags me and Charlie up to the front door. I think he wants to be here just about as much as I do. "There are two rules tonight: stay close and keep that pretty mouth of yours shut," she says while nervously running her hands over her dress.

I think she was trying to go for a modest look with this outfit, but really she just looks like a hot businesswoman or librarian. I'm not going to let myself get distracted, though, because I'm pretty sure I should be offended right about now.

"Did you say keep my mouth shut?" Surely I didn't hear that right.

"Yep. Seal it up."

Huh. Well, yeah. Now I'm a little annoyed. Does she not think I'm good enough for her family?

She's still fidgeting with her clothes and fluffing her long blond waves (gosh, it's hard to focus when she's doing all that), and I've never seen her look so insecure before. She finally glances at me, and her furrowed brow softens. "What's wrong?"

"You just told me not to speak during this dinner."

"Oh!" She steps closer. I want to be annoyed, but her nearness does strange things to me.

I can see two future paths forming in my mind. One, we go inside and have a tense dinner with her parents. Two, I toss her over my shoulder, haul her off to my truck, and we peel out of here before anyone knows we were ever on the premises. She makes me feel greedy. I want Evie all to myself.

"Jake, I'm telling you not to talk for your own good. It doesn't matter how wonderful you are or how successful you are. If your last name is not Murray, they will eat you alive. They want me to marry Tyler, and so trust me, anything you say tonight will be twisted around in some way to bite you in the ass."

That makes sense. "They are really that serious about this Tyler guy?"

She nods, looking remorseful, like it's her fault somehow. "We are only here to get that check and run. The less we both say, the better. Are you ready?"

I feel like we are about to step into battle. Suddenly, I'm not prepared for this. Where's my sword? Where's my armor? All I've got is this stupid button-down shirt and slacks.

I nod. "I'll cover you. And if you get in over your head, squeeze my hand three times and I'll execute an extraction."

Her green eyes glow bright. "What if we get separated?"

I step a little closer and put my hands on her hips. "Don't worry. I won't let you out of my sight."

Evie's eyes glow and then fall to my mouth.

I'm bending down to kiss her when the front door suddenly flies open. Evie jumps, and I let go of her. We both look to the woman watching us with an expression that is somehow both bored and angry. It's hard to explain. Kind of like she hates me but also knows she can crush me at any moment.

"Wonderful," Melony says with mock enthusiasm. "You brought your friend."

It's in this moment that I wish Evie and I had already had the talk that's been rolling around in my mind all day. Because, yeah, that's all I am to her, technically. A freaking friend. *Not for long, Melony.*

"Hi, Mom. You look nice," says Evie, being really generous to her mom.

Melony's hawk eyes scan down Evie, and she sighs. "At least you're wearing something on your bottom half tonight."

You have got to be kidding.

Evie's shoulders lower and it's like I can see her caving in on herself. I hate seeing her like this. And I hate this woman for making her feel bad about herself.

"Evie looks perfect as always." I put my hand on Evie's lower back. It's not much, but since I can't shove Melony to the ground and then run off with Evie it'll have to do for now.

"Oh goody," Melony says with a vicious smile. "He's a hero."

Evie flashes an apologetic smile up at me and wraps her arm around mine. "Okay, let's just go inside, shall we?"

CHAPTER 32

Evie

I hate being in this house. It's wrapped in memories that I despise.

"Do you feel that?" I whisper to Jake as we follow Mom from the foyer into the parlor, where, supposedly, the rest of the guests have been waiting on us for the past fifteen minutes. I call bullshit. We were right on time! If they were waiting, it's because those snooty booties got here early.

"Feel what?"

"That plunge in temperature. My mom's heart is so cold it keeps the house at a chilly sixty degrees."

Jake laughs, which draws my mom's attention. She looks over the shoulder of her powder-pink linen dress and scowls. "I know you've been out of society for a while now, but try to remember your manners, Evelyn Grace. None of your jokes at the dinner table if you want to leave here with a check in your pocket."

"All you said was that I had to attend tonight to get the check. You can't change the rules now, Mom."

"As long as I am holding the pen, I can change the rules

whenever I like," my mom says with a lazy smirk as she pauses outside of the parlor threshold.

Everything looks exactly as it did the day I left home. Dark-chestnut hardwoods, cream walls, and expensive thick trim for the baseboards and windows. Plush rugs with various shades of slate blue, cream, and burgundy dot the floors, and in the center of the foyer, there is the same round antique table that would make Joanna Gaines salivate.

Mom's house has been featured in *Southern Living* as one of the most beautifully designed houses in Charleston. It's not at all my style. Everything is overdone. Overdecorated. It's not warm or inviting like Jake's house. And instead of smelling of vanilla and teakwood, I think the candles they burn here have wicks made from hundred-dollar bills, giving it the overall aroma of wealth.

Mom gestures with her hand for us to enter before her. She casts a disgusted look at Charlie, and I know she's annoyed that I brought him. I feel a familiar prickle of dread roll over me, and just as I'm considering kicking off my heels and running for the door, I feel Jake's hand slide into mine. I glance up at him, and he winks at me with a smile that makes my heart grow.

That's when I realize this night isn't going to be anything like all of the rest. Jake is with me. I have a sidekick. Someone to shoulder some of the weight and help me deflect the fiery scowls my mom will throw at me.

I'm lighter and more hopeful as we step into the room together. And then, as plain as day, I can spot the trap. Time to turn around and bolt again. In fact, I do. I spin out of Jake's hand and make a beeline for the door, but Mom catches my arm before I can escape, and I realize it's too late. We're toast. Done for. All good feelings are gone.

Mr. and Mrs. Murray are seated on a love seat, and Tyler is

standing by the beverage cart with something amber-colored already swirling in the glass in his hand. I hate when he drinks. It makes him more of an asshat. And handsier.

Apparently, my parents were hoping this would be a *family* dinner. Because that's what they want all of us to be: one weird, competitively dysfunctional family. I wouldn't be surprised if I looked in the corner and found a preacher gagged and tied until they're ready to force him into officiating a ceremony.

"I thought you said we would be having a dinner party with important guests," I hiss at my mother. She's no longer Mom to me. It's Mother from here on out. I knew she was underhanded, but this is too much. Forcing me to eat and be merry with people whom I have clearly been avoiding.

She's got her fake pageant smile on and that disgustingly sweet voice that gives me chills. "Of course I did. Because these are the *most* important guests, dear. It's been much too long since you've seen Tom and Amy." She's spinning me around, and old habits really must die hard, because I'm pasting my fake smile on too, even though I really want to stomp on my mother's foot and yell *NEVER!* before running out of the room.

I just keep reminding myself, though, to not rock the boat tonight. Get in. Grab the check. Get out.

"Evie, how nice to see you again!" says Amy Murray. She's as feline as I've ever seen. The only woman who could ever give my mom a run for her money. Keep your friends close and your enemies closer, right? Mom and Amy act like friends; they keep everything southern sweet, but there is an unspoken code between them that says, *If you double-cross me, I will destroy you.* "Tyler, dear, come see Evie! How long has it been since you two have seen each other?"

My eyes meet Tyler's, and he's smirking like the devil as he looks at me and Jake. I feel a chill settle over me, and I'm worried that

Tyler is in on this trap. I fall in line beside Jake, and suddenly I feel his hand tap mine in a silent question. My answer is to take it firmly in mine.

"Actually, Tyler and I already ran into each other a week ago. By the way, how's that rash treating you these days, Tyler? I hope it's all cleared up."

"Evie Grace, always such a jokester," says Tyler, rounding the love seat to come stand in front of Jake and me. He's wearing a suit that I'm sure costs upward of five thousand dollars. He sticks his hand out toward Jake, giving him his most winning (vicious) courtroom smile. "I don't think we've met. I'm Tyler Murray. Longtime friend of Evie."

Looking on, you might think this is polite. No way. This is a strategic power move, because now Jake is forced to let go of my hand to shake Tyler's.

"Jacob Broaden. Guy who's lucky enough to be dating Evie," says Jake, and I cringe because he's already broken my second rule. *Keep your mouth shut.*

Everyone in the room chuckles like they've already somehow rehearsed this little skit before we arrived and know their cues.

Dad swoops in out of nowhere. "You'll have to be more specific than that, Jake. Any number of men could boast that same title." Umm, that is so not true. Not even a little.

My smile tightens, and I look at Jake, afraid that he's going to be mad about what he's heard, given his past relationship with his wife. I know he's skittish. But when I look up, he gives me a reassuring smile and wraps his hand around my hip. "I'm just grateful to have made the cut."

We all continue on with small talk for a few minutes about the law firm and how much Tom misses being in the thick of the action. After that, they spend a solid ten minutes gloating over Tyler and all of his achievements and the cases he's won since taking over at the firm. I want to gag. Tom and my dad then volley back and forth about whose golf swing is better while my mother and Amy gossip about Cathey's new nose. All in all, everything is mind-numbingly boring—just the way I like it. No boat rocking tonight, and Jake and I get to sit quietly and observe.

It's when we sit down to dinner that I realize we have exactly enough place settings for everyone. That's odd. I never told Mom that Jake was coming with me. I look up and notice that Tyler is staring at me from across the table. Staring like a serial killer final-izing his plans. He raises his glass to his mouth, smirking and never breaking eye contact. My heart rate picks up speed, and I can feel that he has something up his sleeve. Something that I'm not pre-pared for but he is. Something everyone at this table is prepared for, because there is an extra place setting here. Oh crap. *This* is the trap. They knew I'd bring Jake. Planned on it.

Suddenly, Tyler's gaze cuts to Jake, and he sets down his glass. "You own your own architectural firm, do you not?" Now, how did he know that? I sure didn't tell anyone in my family, so how in the world would Tyler know that? *Shoot.* My parents must have had Jake investigated. (Because Melony and Harold do not rely on Google.)

I glance around the table and notice how it looks like everyone is running their lines in their head, waiting for their cues again.

"You're right, I do." Jake's smile is so kind and open and I hate these people for baiting him. He's completely oblivious to the knife they are about to plunge into his chest. I put my hand on his thigh under the table to warn him, but he doesn't get the hint.

"Ah, yes," my dad says from the far end of the table. "Evelyn told us all about it. She went on and on about how proud she is of you for owning such a successful company." I did not! I look at Jake and hope he will feel my thoughts meld with his. *This is a trap! Something is afoot!* "I've got to say, I'm impressed by you, Jake. To own God-dard Smith is something to be proud of."

WHAT?!

Jake's brows twitch together, and his smile dims. "Oh . . . uh— I don't own Goddard Smith, sir. My company is Broaden Homes."

My father looks at me with a put-on frown that could win him an Oscar. "Why did you tell me he owned Goddard Smith, then?" Oh, he's good. They're all good. Sitting here, acting like this wasn't a battle strategy to drive a wedge between Jake and me while also making him feel belittled.

"I didn't say anything of the sort!" I flash my eyes to Jake next. "I really didn't. I never told him you owned that company. In fact, I haven't told them about you at all!" Oh. But that just made things worse, didn't it?

Jake's smile is oh-so-tight now, and I can see that he's trying his best to not let this situation eat at him. I touch his arm, and he whispers, "It's fine."

It's not fine. I can tell it's not.

"Evelyn Grace, tell Amy all about your wonderful little service dog company." *Now it's a wonderful company, is it?*

"Oh yes!" says Amy, eyes twinkling in rehearsed anticipation. "You know, a few girls from the club and I were just saying that we need a new little project to keep us busy. And from what your mom says, it sounds like your company could use a few patrons." She pauses. "Or . . ." *Blink. Blink. Blink.* She turns her doe eyes to Tyler. "Actually, Tyler might be just the person for the job."

"Tyler?" I don't bother to keep the disgust from my voice.

"Well, yes! Who better than him? I'm sure that he could drum up all kinds of high-profile sponsors for you with all his connections from New York. You two could get together and brainstorm through a game plan. You would be happy to work with Evie to further her company, wouldn't you, son?"

Gag me. Do they really think I don't see through this charade?

"I'd love to help you with your company, Eves," he says in a way that sounds like he's undressing me with his words.

I give him a tight-lipped smile. "Thanks, but I've got it all handled. Our benefit is tomorrow night, and I already have lots of big companies signed up to donate services and items for everyone to bid on. So, yep. Don't need your help."

"A benefit?" Tom steps into his part now. "We didn't hear anything about a benefit. Is it open to the general public?"

Oh, shoot.

"Well . . . no. It's by invitation only."

"Surely we are invited, though, and our invitation just got lost in the mail."

"That's exactly what happened, isn't it, Evelyn?" says my mother. "Because you specifically called me and asked for their address a few weeks ago. And are you and Tyler still going together like you two talked about?"

Okay, so first, Mom is manipulating me into inviting Tom and Amy to the benefit, and now she is flat-out lying about me and Tyler. Where to start?

One quick look at Jake, though, answers that question for me. "I—no. I'm going to the fundraiser with Jake. He's my date. He and I are going together." How many more ways can I say this? Jake + Evie = Together.

My mother pouts and turns a brokenhearted smile to Tyler. "Oh. I'm terribly sorry, Tyler. I hope you'll be able to find a date on such short notice." Unbelievable.

"I'm sure he'll be just fine calling one of the many girls from his little black book and asking them to leave their Barbie dream houses for the night." Hang on. He isn't even invited to the fundraiser! Did I just get tricked into inviting him too?

"Don't be jealous, Evie. You know you're my number one choice. Just say the word and I'll go with you."

I'm gritting my teeth so hard they're close to shattering. I glance at Jake and he's already looking at me with an expression so hard to read it could be an instruction manual from Ikea. "Like I said, I don't need you to go with me, Tyler, because I'm going with Jake. The man sitting right here beside me."

"Right. Sorry, man. I didn't mean to make you feel weird."

"You didn't," Jake says, but his voice is so hard that it's clear he's annoyed.

"Oh, Jacob, you'll have to excuse all of us." My mom's voice grates on me. "We tend to go on and on about Tyler and Evie because . . . well, there's no other way to say it, but we've all been waiting for the day they finally get back together and tie the knot."

Honestly, I'm shocked. I shouldn't be, but I am. I knew my family was capable of some manipulative shit, but this is so out of bounds. *"Mother."* I use that title as a warning. I'm about to lay into her at this table in front of everyone when my dad pipes up, blotting his mouth and setting his napkin down.

"Come on, Evelyn. Enough is enough. It's time you stop this hippie lifestyle of yours and get back to real life. Tyler is your future. No offense to Jacob, because I'm sure he's working very hard in his business, but he can't give you the life you're accustomed to by owning a small-scale *residential* architectural firm. But Tyler can give you the life you deserve right now, and he's willing to do it. I'm sure he would even bankroll your little dog business too, if it means that much to you."

"Don't you remember how good together you two were in high school?" asks Amy, jumping in with a smile that I want to smack off her face.

"It's true, Eves. We were great together, and I'd like for us to be a *we* again. What do you say?"

Is this really happening? Please tell me this is just a nightmare, and any minute now I'm going to look down and realize that I'm not wearing pants. I'll wake up in a cold sweat and then immediately call Jake, and he will make me feel better by laughing and saying it was just a dream, because in real life we would never be so ignorant as to willingly set foot in my parents' house. I feel so silly for trusting that this was ever about her giving me a check for the company.

I don't want to look at Jake. I'm so humiliated by the way my parents are treating him, especially when his parents were so kind and welcoming to me. But I do, and his expression breaks my heart further. His jaw ticks. His eyes cast down. I can feel him slipping away from me.

I want to cry right here at the table. This night had started out so well for us, promised so many things, and now here we are, sitting at this table, and a wall is being constructed between us for all to witness, just like they planned.

And now I'm pissed. I shoot up out of my seat and make the legs scrape painfully loud against the floor. Good! I hope they leave a big ugly scratch! "That's it. We're leaving."

Jake stands beside me, but his movements aren't as full of fire as mine are. I grab his hand and Charlie's leash, and we start walking from the room, hearing everyone's protests behind us. I then whirl around and level each of them with a searing glare. "For the last time, I'm not going to marry Tyler. And all of you should be ashamed of yourselves and the way you treated me and Jake tonight. Consider yourselves uninvited from the benefit, and uninvited from my life. Lose my number."

"Evelyn Grace," my mother says, fire blazing in her eyes. "Are you forgetting about something?" She's referring to the check she's trying to dangle in front of my face.

"Keep it. I don't want your manipulative money supporting my company anyway."

I grip Jake's hand tighter and race us through the house and out the front door like we just robbed a bank. The second we've put enough feet between us and the enemy, I drop Jake's hand and turn around to face him. "I am so sorry! I had no idea they were going to gang up on us like that. It was a trap, and I should have seen it coming!" He's not meeting my eye. He's looking over my head into the distance, and I can feel that wall between us grow taller. "Jake, please look at me." He does, but the look in his eyes says things have changed. My heart squeezes painfully.

I'm desperate to get him to understand that I do not share my family's opinions, so I put both of my hands on his face to hold his attention on me. "Everything they said was a lie. They are master manipulators, and you can't trust anything that comes out of their mouths. Please believe me. And I swear I didn't tell them you own Goddard Smith . . . because I don't even care what company you own. I just want you."

Jake doesn't say he wants me too. He doesn't say everything is okay and that he trusts me. His eyes are meeting mine, but I don't think he's really even seeing me.

"I don't know anymore . . ." is what he says before pulling away and walking toward the truck.

My arms fall back to my sides. "Where are you going?"

"To get in the truck and take you home."

"So, that's it, then? We're just done talking because you decide we are?"

He pauses and turns to look at me—but he looks so hollow it scoops my heart out too. "Believe me, Evie. You don't want me to keep talking right now because I will say lots of things that I'll regret. I just endured an hour of so much belittling of both of us that my blood is boiling. I have a lot to think about."

"Jake!" I say, taking a desperate step toward him. "None of what they said was true. Are you worried because of Tyler?"

He grimaces at hearing Tyler's name and shakes his head. "No. That guy's a tool, and I know you'd never go for him."

"Then what is it? And why are you looking at me like that?"

"Like what, Evie?"

"Like you've already said goodbye to me!"

Jake holds my gaze for a minute, and every breath I take sounds excruciatingly loud in my ears. His jaw flexes, and he breaks eye contact to look down. "Maybe I have. I heard them in there; they don't think I'm good enough for you. And . . . I'm not entirely sure that I don't agree with them."

"No," I say as an expelled breath. "That's not true! You're so much better than those people, and I don't want the life they have!"

"Maybe not now." His eyes meet mine with a new look of fire and determination. "But what about in two years? What about when you start missing your old life? When I don't make as much money as you need? Or have the connections you need? What then, Evie?" I hate the way Jake just said my name. It was like a jab to my stomach.

"And just when have I ever given you the impression that I'd be that way?"

"*This* is the opposite of what I need right now." He gestures toward the house and then between us. "Sam and I need support and stability. We need someone we can trust. And . . ."

I shut my eyes. "Don't say it."

He holds my gaze for the span of three breaths and then quietly says, "And I don't know that that person is going to be you."

He turns and gets in his truck and starts it. I stand there motionless, feeling like I've just been hit with a stun gun. I feel angry and hurt and betrayed. But it's odd because I know that's exactly how Jake feels too. The selfish people in that house accomplished exactly what they set out to do, and my heart is shattered.

I look back up at my parents' house and spot Tyler watching us from the window. He sees me looking at him and raises his glass in a mock toast. I wish I had a brick I could throw through that window.

I'm not quite sure that I'm welcome in Jake's truck right now, but I also know that there's no way in hell I'm going back into my parents' house and asking for a ride.

I look down at Charlie, and his big chocolate eyes promise me that I get to order in a dozen cookies and eat them all when I get home. At least Charlie is always there for me.

CHAPTER 33

Jake

I dropped Evie off at her apartment after a completely silent drive home where I acted like a brooding jerk. It wasn't intentional, and now that I've had a minute to myself I completely regret the way I treated her. But after everything that took place in that house, I couldn't get a handle on my emotions. It was like every single one of my fears was boiling to the surface of my skin and I just wanted to claw it off.

As I'm driving home in the dark, I still can't quite pinpoint the moment it all went south. One minute, Evie and I were united and I was happy to be her shoulder to lean on during a difficult night, and the next thing I knew I needed a stretcher to carry me off the field of a game I epically lost.

I pull up in front of my house and cut the engine but don't get out of the truck. I sit here numbly, thinking over everything that just happened. My hands scrape over my face and hair and then I groan as a sinking feeling fills my stomach.

I played right into those people's hands and then self-sabotaged.

Away from Tyler's haughty smirk, I can see it all clearly. They said exactly what they needed to push my buttons and hit me in all my sore spots. How they knew what my sore spots were is a little frightening, but I guess that people with as much money as them can accomplish just about anything they want to. Tonight being evidence of that.

Why did I listen to them? Deep down, I know that Evie doesn't want their life. She doesn't fit into that manipulative elitist world any more than I would fit into one of Sam's training bras. And yet . . . I let them get into my head.

I'm still raw from Natalie. And hearing them confirm my biggest fears that I'm not good enough for Evie and she'll leave me and Sam just like Natalie did, well, it undid me. I wanted to run away with my heart clutched in my hand to keep it safe.

But I was wrong. I overreacted. And I pushed Evie away.

My only hope now is that Evie will forgive me and forget all the accusations I tossed at her. I slam my palm firmly on the steering wheel once, replaying every awful thing I said to her. There was so much hurt in her eyes. Betrayal. I sided with those people over her, and now I'm fearful she won't forgive me. I wouldn't blame her either.

I'm getting ready to put my truck in reverse so I can drop at Evie's feet and grovel for forgiveness when a movement on my porch catches my eye. I forgot to turn on the porch lights before I left the house, so I can't see who it is. For a split second, hope soars in my chest, and I think that it's Evie. But then I remember she can't drive, and there is no way she could have called an Uber and beat me here.

Maybe I should be worried that it's a robber. But I haven't heard of many criminals who like to leisurely swing on porches before breaking and entering, so I think I'm safe in that regard. Curiosity has me putting the truck in park once again before I step out of it.

Only after I approach the porch do I remember the old saying *curiosity killed the cat.*

"What the hell are you doing here?"

"Not exactly the welcome home I was hoping for, but hello to you too." Natalie, my ex-wife, is smiling and swinging on my porch like she never left me. Like she has spent every day of the past few years caring for our daughter beside me. Like she belongs here.

She doesn't.

"This is not your home. We're not friends. And I sure as hell am not going to banter with you. Now, tell me what you're doing here."

Her smile fades, and she stands up to walk closer to me. I take a step back because every cell in my body is attuned to how angry I am at her and is acting like an opposing magnet. I don't want her anywhere near me.

"I thought it was obvious. I'm here to see you and Sam." She looks over my shoulder like maybe I carry Sam in a backpack or something. "Where is she, by the way?"

I so badly want to say something snarky like *Maybe you'd know if you had cared enough to stick around and be a part of our life.* But I don't because I've already been a jerk once tonight, and I don't feel like being one again.

"She's spending the night with June."

Natalie makes a disgusted face. "With *June?* I hope you're not letting your sister rub off on Sam."

I bite the side of my cheek so hard that I taste blood. In an attempt to not lose my cool with Natalie, I turn around and unlock my front door. "You lost the right to make parenting decisions when you left and stopped coming back. And if you have any hope of talking to me about whatever it is you're doing here, you'll want to talk nicer about my sister, who has sacrificed an enormous amount of her life to help me raise my daughter."

I go inside the house and Natalie is practically biting my heels; she's walking so close to me. She slips in behind me before I can stop her.

"You're right; I'm sorry. I shouldn't have said that." Natalie looks around the house. She's wide-eyed as I turn on the lights. *Oh, right.* This is the first time she's been in here. I was in the process of building this house when she left, so she never got a chance to enjoy it. It's a good thing too. It gave me and Sam a clean start. A place where we could move on and not have to be plagued with memories of what our life was like before in that old house.

"Wow, Jake. This house is gorgeous." She smiles at me, and I try to squint to see the woman I used to love. But nope. She's not there anymore. Natalie is as beautiful as she always was, but there's a distance now behind her eyes. Layers and layers of a new person I know nothing about. And don't really care to know anymore either. If it weren't for our daughter, I wouldn't even be engaging with her now.

"So, you're here to see Sam?" Finding an end to this conversation would be nice.

Her shoulders slump. "You don't have to be so gruff with me. I know I messed up, okay? I've been too distant . . . and I know it's not fair to Sam."

I cross my arms. I've fallen for her wounded-bird act before. It ended with Natalie splitting in the middle of the night once again and me holding my daughter while she cried the next morning, trying to convince her that her mom's leaving had nothing to do with her.

"Are you implying that you want to be part of Sam's life again?"

She tips a shoulder and gives a light grin that I realize is supposed to be flirtatious. She starts advancing toward me. "And yours."

Not even if hell freezes over.

I shake my head and give Natalie a sharp look that tells her not to take another step in my direction. "First of all, you can't just do this, Natalie. You can't leave us with barely any contact for two years, then surprise me on my front porch late at night, hoping to play house whenever you want to. You needed to call, give us some notice, and I would have arranged for you and Sam to spend some time together. I've never kept you from her; you're the one who abandoned her, and I don't know if *she* will even want to see you. Second, you and I are done for good, so let's get that out of the way now."

"Arrange a time for me and *my daughter* to spend together? You've got to be kidding me, Jake. Sam is just as much my daughter as she is yours, and I have a right to come and see her whenever I want to."

"Really? Because it seems to me that if she was just as much your daughter as she is mine, you would have known when she had the flu . . . or when she won first place in her school talent show . . . or been there when she was diagnosed with epilepsy. I don't remember seeing you sleeping beside me on the floor in her room." I'm fighting hard to keep my voice from raising, but I don't know how much longer I can stand in front of Natalie and keep it even.

I'm pissed the hell off.

Natalie doesn't seem to sense that every muscle in my body is flexed with anger, because she steps closer and tries to press her hand to my chest. I shrug her hand off and take a retreating step back.

Her brows furrow. "Jake, I know that I haven't been the mom that I should be for Sam. I'm so sorry. It's just that auditions have been demanding and I didn't want to miss out on any opportunities. But I'm sorry I left you to deal with this all alone. I'm here now, though, and I've changed. I'm ready to be a family again."

I laugh, but it doesn't sound nice. "Just when did this change take place? On your flight back from Hawaii? And what did your boyfriend have to say about you wanting to become a family woman again?"

The long lashes I used to think were so beautiful drop down to my chest. "He and I broke up this week."

"I see. So, you think you can just use us as stand-ins until better options come along?"

Her eyes shoot back up to me. "Jake! What a mean thing to say. I'm here because I want to be with you and Sam." *For now.* But it won't last.

This is all so eerily similar to how things played out during her last "I want to be a better mom" trip, I bet I can quote word for word what she says next. Except this time I will not be inviting her to stay with us, and ignorantly pretending to be a family again until she decides to split at two A.M. with another bogus excuse.

"I want to be a mom to our daughter again. To parent with you and share the responsibility!"

"Are you planning to move back from Hollywood?"

"No. But I can make it work in both places."

I wish I could believe her. I really do.

I force a deep breath and relax my muscles. "Tell you what, Natalie. You rent a hotel room and stick around here for one whole week, and I want you to call and talk to Sam every single one of those days. If you can do that, I'll think about letting you spend more time with her. But what I won't do is let you jump in and out of her life whenever you want and crush her little heart more than you already have."

I haven't gone to court to fight for full custody of Sam yet—but I will if I need to. So far, Natalie has never seemed interested enough to warrant it.

"But, Jake! It's late. You really want me to go get a hotel room right now?" She tries to grab my arm as I pass her, but I pull it out of reach. "Surely I can stay here with you. I mean . . . we were married, for God's sake."

Is she actually implying we could sleep together tonight if we want to? I can't begin to understand what has happened with Natalie, but I know for sure that she is completely unrecognizable to me now.

I head toward my room to pack a bag. "You can stay here tonight since Sam is with June," I yell while quickly tossing a few pieces of clothing in a duffel bag.

When I return to the living room, I see that Natalie is already lounging on my couch with a glass of *my* wine in her hand, looking like she owns this place.

She sees my bag and frowns. "*Wait*. You're leaving?"

I nod and go to the front door because I'm not falling for any more traps tonight. "Yep. I told you, Natalie, we're over. I'm not staying under the same roof as you."

She shoots to her feet, looking angry, and crosses her arms. "Who is she?"

I sigh and pause only long enough to turn the thermostat up to eighty degrees. If she's going to stay here, I don't want her to be comfortable. I know it's petty, but I allow myself this one little shitty indulgence. "*She* is none of your business."

"So, there is someone?"

"Sure is." I'm not about to tell Natalie that I'm really going to my parents' house to sleep tonight. I want her to know I have moved on and there is no hope for us. "Check-out time is at ten A.M. If you're not out by then, I'll send June over."

"You're going to sic your sister on me?"

I smile. "Definitely." Maybe I'm being a little too much of a jerk now, but I'm so over this day that I don't even care anymore. I'll deal with Natalie more like an adult tomorrow when the sun is up and I'm not fresh out of the emotional wringer from Evie's family.

"I mean it—stick around for a full week and you can see Sam if she wants. But not before then."

Natalie shakes her head and starts to spit a rude comment at me, but I don't fully hear it because I shut the door and walk toward my truck.

Once I'm down the road a little way, I let out a full breath, feeling like I just dodged a semi that had every intention of running me over. My heart is raw. Emotions twisted up into a confusing knot. But if anything, this encounter with Natalie has only confirmed how I feel about Evie. I can trust myself to spot someone who isn't going to be good for me and my daughter now. I can trust myself enough to move on. And I can definitely trust Evie—she's never given me a reason not to. Her word has been as solid as gold and her heart as soft and warm as her skin.

She's nothing like my ex-wife, and I'm ready to stop letting my hurt get in the way of what I know will be a very good thing between us.

But then her face flashes in my mind, and I remember how badly I left things with her. It's *me* who has to be better for her. *Damn, I hope it's not too late to fix this.*

I try to call her on my way to my parents' house, but she doesn't answer. After two attempts and after I park my truck in their driveway, I get a text from Evie: I don't want to talk tonight. I'll call you when I'm ready.

CHAPTER 34

Evie

I didn't sleep a wink last night. Not one teeny-tiny microscopic minute. I went back and forth between deciding to return Jake's call or printing out a picture of his face so I could draw devil horns and a mustache on it. I would have too, but I remembered I don't own a printer.

I probably made two hundred laps around my apartment, cleaned out all three of my cupboards, vacuumed under the cushions of my couch, folded all my panties into neat little triangles, and matched my socks.

Finally, the sun came up and I decided I was ready for Jake's apology—and that big jerk *does* owe me an apology. And only because he's not normally a big jerk am I giving him a little slack. I also know firsthand what it's like to be on the other end of a Harold and Melony Jones Special. They whisper words in your ear that sound so true and real. And poor Jake got hit where he's most hurt: in the I'm-not-good-enough pants.

I drank a whole pot of coffee between the hours of three A.M.

and six A.M. in preparation for a talk with Jake. I made an entire pros and cons list of why I should give him another shot and why I shouldn't. There was nothing on the shouldn't list.

So, now that it's an acceptable time to be awake and doing things, I blow-dry my hair, put on my favorite sundress that makes me feel powerful and confident, and call an Uber. Charlie and I climb into the car twenty minutes later and set out for Jake's house. My knee bounces the whole way, and I *know* that my Uber driver notices, because she keeps giving me looks that say she's afraid I'm going to pee in her back seat.

Honestly, I'm so nervous and caffeinated that I just might.

It's when we are pulling up to his house that I start to wonder if this was a bad idea. Should I have texted first? Maybe he wasn't calling last night to apologize but rather to tell me to come get a hair scrunchie I accidentally left at his house or something.

I imagine Jo pinching my arm and telling me to get out of the car to help me get moving. I have a man to make things right with.

Charlie and I walk with determined strides all the way up to Jake's door. I ring the doorbell, and as I wait for him to answer I have a flashback of the first time I rang this doorbell. Not unlike that day, I want to throw up in the bushes.

I have my speech all rehearsed:

Jake. Hear me out. I know that you think I will miss my old life, but that couldn't be further from the truth. I hate everything about my parents' society, and I left it for a reason. I want you ... all of you. I don't want to share you with anyone else or pretend that we don't have strong feelings for each other. Because I know we do. And you also owe me a big apology for—

The door opens, and a woman stands on the other side. A woman with shiny dark hair, beautiful full lips, a tight (pretty much see-through) tank top painted over her very intimidating body.

She's not wearing a bra. And . . . she's not wearing pants either. She looks as if I just woke her up, and . . . that's because I did.

No, no, no.

Now I really think I'm going to be sick in the bushes.

"Can I help you?" she asks, looking mildly annoyed.

She's annoyed?! *I'm* annoyed! Who is this woman? Did Jake seriously call a random woman to come hook up with him last night because he was so angry with me? And after all his bullshit about needing to take things slow.

The thought sours in my mouth. *He did.* That's exactly what he did.

"I—" I have no idea what to say to this woman. I'm so hurt. I'm afraid I'm going to melt right here on his porch, and then that will be the end of me, and someone is going to have to come mop me up. "I was just . . ."

"Looking for Jake?" she asks with a taunting smirk. "He's not awake yet."

Of course he's not. Clearly, he had a late night.

"Okay." I wish I had something better to say or do than just stand here smiling like a depressed Ronald McDonald statue. But I'm clearly in shock and my body has no idea how to respond. I never imagined Jake would be that kind of guy. I thought he . . . I thought he had real feelings for me.

"Do you want me to go wake him up for you?"

"No!" I'm backing away from the door now, squeezing Charlie's leash in my palm and wishing I had superpowers that would teleport me out of here as quickly as possible. And erase all those happy memories that are painful to think about now. "That's not necessary. I'll just . . ."

I don't finish my sentence. Instead, I sprint back to the Uber, and luckily I'm able to catch the girl before she drives off. I practically dive into the seat and then yell, "Drive!" like I'm in the movie *Baby Driver.* I expect her to squeal the tires as she puts the pedal to the metal, but of course she doesn't, because nothing in my life is going my way anymore.

"Are you okay, lady?"

"No. I'm not. Please just drive."

"Where to?"

"Anywhere!" Tears are now running down my cheeks. "Mexico! Let's go to Mexico."

"I can't drive you to Mexico." *Seriously?* Where is this girl's sense of sisterhood? I would settle for just a smidge of empathy.

I let out a big puff of air and then just tell her the address of Joanna's house.

Because right now . . . I need a mom.

CHAPTER 35

Jake

I woke up to a text from Evie that said, In case it isn't obvious, we're done. Lose my number. It was so startling and unlike her that I tried to call. She sent it right to voicemail. And normally I'm not the kind of guy to keep trying to get ahold of a woman when she isn't interested, but something about her response was so odd. Concerning.

I went by Evie's apartment, but either she wasn't home or she just didn't want to talk to me, because my knock went unanswered. I sent her one final text, saying, I know I messed up big-time, but I'd love the chance to apologize if you'll let me. Please, Evie.

It all went unanswered.

I'm not quite ready to give up yet, though. Tonight is the bene-fit, and since I know she'll be there, I intend on going and groveling at her feet. Respectfully, of course. And hopefully without making a scene that will embarrass her. But now I'm convinced there's something else going on here that I'm not realizing yet. I can feel it in my gut, and I need to see Evie's face to make sure everything is okay. I *will* fix this.

After driving by my place and making sure Natalie is gone, I pick up Sam from June's house. When we walk through the door together, the smell of Natalie's perfume knocks into us both. I'm thankful I told Sam that Natalie is back in town and didn't try to hide it. On the way here, I gave her a very delicate and stripped-down version of what happened last night. *Your mom came in for a visit last night and I told her it wasn't a good time because you were with Aunt June.*

Sam silently processed this information the whole drive home, and I didn't press her on it. But now, as she walks through the door and smells her mom's scent, her eyes well up with unshed tears.

"I don't want to see her," Sam blurts from her spot, rooted at the front door. Her nostrils flare. "And it smells like she dumped her perfume all over the place in here."

I grit my teeth because I thought the same thing. I have no doubt Natalie doused our furniture with the stuff—probably trying to get back at me for not staying with her last night. A selfish move, like always.

"Do you want to go outside and sit on the porch?" I take Sam's overnight bag off her shoulder and set it by the door. She doesn't hesitate a second before turning on her heel and barreling out the front door. She sits down on the front steps instead of the swing.

I take a second to think through what my next move should be. What do I say to Sam about all this? She's still so young, but she's not naïve. How much do I protect her from the truth while also giving it to her in the amounts she needs?

Evie's words from the night we picked Sam up from the slumber party echo loudly in my mind: *Your house is a safe place, and you love being there, and that's something to be proud of.*

I have done my best to make sure our house feels safe physically and emotionally for Sam, and last night Natalie violated that. My daughter doesn't want to set foot in her own home because the mom who should have always made her feel loved and cared for, but instead abandoned and hurt her, filled her safe haven with her damn scent. So, even though I'm not sure what to say, I know what I won't be saying. I will never force my daughter to see her mom—or anyone—who hurts her.

I sit down gently beside Sam on the porch and wait for her to talk when she's ready.

She hugs her knees to her chest. "I don't want to see Mom."

"And I won't make you."

She cuts her eyes to me, a tear streaking down her face. "You won't?"

"No. It's your choice if you want to let her back into your life or not. I told your mom that before I would even consider letting her see you again, she had to call and talk to you on the phone for a week. But only if you wanted to."

Sam's gaze drops to her little pink Converse shoes, and I note that she has Natalie's long lashes. "I don't know if I want to or not. I just got used to her not being here. And . . . I don't want to talk to her again and get used to her if she's going to leave."

My chest squeezes. "That's understandable. I would feel the same way. And it's okay if you need more time before talking to her again. It's okay to make her wait until you're ready."

"But . . . what if while I make her wait . . . she gets tired of it and leaves?"

Tears press against the back of my eyes. I hate that she has thoughts like this and that it's a valid concern.

I put my arm around Sam's shoulder and tuck her into my side. "If she leaves again, she's missing out on an opportunity to have a relationship with the best person in this entire world." Sam snorts a little laugh. "I'm serious, Sam. I'm so honored to be your dad. You are funny, and kind, and brave, and strong. I love you and you can trust that I will always fight for you to have the incredible life you deserve. It's you and me against the world."

"Promise?"

I give her my pinky and she loops hers around it. "Promise."

Sam and I spend the rest of the afternoon together playing in the pool while I let the house air out from Natalie's perfume bomb, and then we watch a movie and eat Sam's favorite junk foods. I don't hear a peep from Natalie all day, and the closer I get to the fundraiser gala the more hesitant I feel to leave Sam. At least I can take comfort that my mom is staying here with Sam tonight, and there's no way she'll let Natalie through the door if she shows up unannounced again.

"Don't you need to go get ready?" Sam asks from beside me on the couch.

I frown at the time on my phone. "Uh—I'm not sure I feel like going. I'm having so much fun with you I might just stay home."

Yes—I need to go see Evie, but Sam comes first in my life. And if she wants me to stay home with her, I will.

But Sam laughs at me. "Dad, we spent all day together. I think we've had plenty of hang-out time." *Oh great. My kid is already over me.* "Besides, Grandma said that after you leave she and I are going to do some online shopping for new school clothes."

I raise my eyebrow. "Oh, she did, did she?"

"Yes, she did," my mom says, rounding the corner from the kitchen and proudly sticking her nose in the air. "Now, quit trying to encroach on my Sammie time. Get out of here and go support Evie tonight."

If she'll let me through the doors.

CHAPTER 36

Evie

I stand outside the venue where the benefit is being held and try to suck my tears back into my body. I've been crying all day, so I'm pretty sure that without the help of all the concealer I slapped on I would look like I've been punched in both eyes. Apparently, whoever made up the phrase *time heals all wounds* meant *a lot* of time, because with every hour that has passed today, my wounds have only grown deeper. My heart hurts, and I wonder if it's possible for an organ to physically split down the middle just from emotional turmoil.

It's silly, but . . . I really thought Jake would end up being *the one*.

Too bad he just ended up being *the one* to sleep with someone else when I made him mad.

Even still, it doesn't make sense to me. The picture the woman painted when she opened that door this morning doesn't line up with anything Jake has been telling me since we started talking/kissing/seeing each other. But maybe he was lying. Maybe he really is into casual sex. He just didn't want it with me.

Great, more tears.

"Nope. Uh-uh. No more tears from those pretty green eyes," says Jo, rushing up beside me to hand me a tissue. "You look too pretty to waste your night thinking about that frog leg for one more second!"

I spent the whole day today at Joanna's house, lamenting everything that happened over the last twenty-four hours. Her advice was that we try out a new Pinterest recipe she found, where you boil lemon and various items that belong to an ex-boyfriend and then pour the "juice" into a spray bottle and go spritz that person's house to bring them bad luck. Or maybe it was to keep the flu away . . . I can't remember because I was too busy ugly-crying into a pillow while she explained it.

"I know, I'm trying to quit, but I can't. This is the worst night to have to host a fundraiser."

"Or it is the best night to host a fundraiser. Because now you get to look gorgeous and keep yourself busy all night. And who knows, maybe you'll find someone new here tonight too."

"I don't want anyone new."

"You're right. Too soon. But I'm just saying . . . I think I saw a Calvin Klein model walk in earlier, and if Gary didn't make such good chili, I think he might be in trouble."

Gary chooses that moment to walk by us. He gives Jo a little pat on her rear and then winks at me. "Chili is just an innuendo."

I cringe. "Yeah. I figured."

"I'm going on in. Y'all coming in soon?"

"Right behind you, honey," says Jo with adorably pink cheeks. I thought I had finally found a man who would make my cheeks rosy like Jo's even after years and years of marriage. Nope. And now the waterworks are happening again.

You are a strong, independent woman, Evie. You don't need a man to be happy. Time to move on.

Jo gives me one more pitying look. "Okay, okay, let's get you inside so everyone can see your handsome date."

Charlie is ridiculously cute in his bow tie. I bet Jake would have looked horrible in a bow tie. But when I walk into the venue and look around the warm, glitzing room, I spot Jake standing by a cocktail table, one hand in the pocket of his black suit pants and the other holding a glass of something bubbly—and man, am I disappointed to see that he looks freaking amazing in a bow tie.

"What is he doing here?" I whisper angrily at Jo, who follows my gaze to Jake.

Her eyes widen, and she looks back at me. "I don't know, but you can't tear him apart here. There are lots of people watching us right now, and if we both go all crazy ex-girlfriend on him, there's no way we will get any sponsors."

I sigh, knowing she's right. "Fine. I'll deal with him and then get him to leave."

"Are you sure you don't want me to do it?"

"No. I can handle him."

I think Joanna notices the way my eyes are trailing down his body in that fine-looking suit, and maybe a smidge of appreciation shows on my face, because now she's stifling a grin and humming a *mm-hmm*. "You just go deal with him, then. Make sure you lock the bathroom door before you do, though."

I turn my saucer eyes at her. "Joanna!"

She just laughs. "But for real, Evie. Hold your ground no matter how good that man looks. If he treated you badly, he doesn't deserve you." I nod and she walks away to go mingle with the many guests already gathered.

I steel myself and then turn to look at Jake again. He's on the opposite side of the crowded room, but then he sets down his glass and moves slowly through the center of the venue toward me. My heart races, and I have to remind myself that I now hate him. *I do. I hate him.* I don't want a man who's not going to cherish me—who's going to sleep with other women to make himself feel good when we've had a fight. No, I don't like this man anymore.

I don't like his dimples when he smiles.

I don't like his tousled hair.

I don't like the way his muscles fill out that suit.

Okay, I like all of those things, but those are just physical attributes. And muscles aren't forever, my friends.

I decide that Jake is not going to have all of the upper hand here, so I lift the front hem of my floor-length evening gown and begin to meet him in the middle with Charlie at my side. Jake's eyes scan over me as we approach each other, and I can see that he likes the way my black satin gown is clinging to my curves. He hasn't even seen the plunging back yet.

Eat your heart out, Jacob Broaden.

We stop right in front of each other in the center of the room, but Jake doesn't make a move to touch me. *Smart.* He can probably read the murderous scowl on my face and knows I'll bite if he does.

"You look"—his eyes rush over me again—"gorgeous."

His flattery is not going to work on me. I cut right to the chase. "Why are you here? I told you we're done."

"I'm your date."

"You most certainly are not my date. Not anymore. Not after . . . last night." Those last two words come out in a whisper because I know my voice will shake if I try to say it at my normal volume.

Jake's shoulders sink a little. "Evie. I've been trying to call you all day. I'm so sorry. Can we go somewhere and talk?"

I shake my head. I don't want to hear anything he has to say. *You slept with another woman last night. I saw her with my own eyes.* That told me everything I needed to know. "I'm busy tonight, and I need to focus on the event."

His lips press together, and he nods slowly. "Of course. I understand. Maybe after?"

I look away from him toward the tables where vendors are set up. A few couples are starting to slow dance near us, and everyone else is beginning to mill around the room and place their bids on various vendors' items and services. We have a live string quartet playing in the corner, a cocktail bar where all proceeds go directly to Southern Service Paws, and later in the night there will be a sit-down dinner. All in all, everything is going well, and I'm hopeful that it will be a success.

"I won't have time," I say, giving Jake my best cold shoulder. "If you'll excuse me, I see a few people I need to speak to."

I brush by him as I walk away, and I wish so badly that my whole body didn't hum from this small connection of our bodies. I want to lean into him. I want to lift up on my toes and press warm kisses up his neck all the way to his mouth. But I don't . . . because I am done with Jake.

For the next hour, I try to pretend that Jake doesn't exist. I laugh too loudly with guests, I check in on all the vendors and am pleased to see that every clipboard is nearly full with bids, and I field about a thousand questions about our company and Charlie, who has been dutifully standing at my side all night.

I'm exhausted from keeping up this fake smile, and I just need a minute to myself to let my mask fall off. I look down at Charlie, and I can tell that he is exhausted too, so I do something that I very rarely do and hand off his leash to Joanna, who is sitting at a table with Gary and a few other guests. I'm going to let him have a five-minute break to lay at Joanna's feet while I get some air, and then he and I will face the rest of the night together.

I open the main doors and let the fresh air wrap around me and fill my lungs. I wish it were cooler, but it's the middle of July, and even after sunset it's still a balmy eighty degrees out here. I move toward the side of the building and cross my arms, staring at nothing in particular.

My thoughts wander to Jake. He's been hanging around, which means he might try to talk to me again. I hate that I'll have to tell him not to attempt to contact me anymore. But I mean business—I'm not playing around with my heart. I'm not sure I'd ever be able to fully trust him again. And yes, I know that, technically, we were both keeping it casual, but what Jake did was just sleazy. He had told me he wasn't going to sleep with anyone else while we were seeing each other, and I like to be able to take people at their word.

I'm pulled from my thoughts when a warm hand suddenly lands on my lower back. I turn, thinking I'll meet Jake's eyes, when instead I'm faced with Tyler's annoying smirk.

"Ugh," I say, pulling away from him. "What are you doing here? I thought I made myself clear that you were not invited tonight."

"I know not to take your temper seriously." He starts advancing toward me until he has me backed up against the wall of the building. His hands move to rest on my hips, and I try to push him away, but he doesn't budge.

"Get your hands off me, Tyler!" I say, feeling more annoyed than frightened.

"Just give me one chance to show you what you're missing." He's dipping his head down while I'm still trying to squirm out of his grasp and away from his lethal-potency cologne.

But I'm so tired of this. I'm tired of feeling like my voice isn't heard. Like my opinion means nothing to my family or Tyler and his family. It's time to *make* them listen. I don't wait for him to magically become an upstanding man and make the right decision on his own. I kick my knee up right between his legs, hitting him as hard as I can in the crotch.

He grunts in pain, falling two steps backward while holding his junk. "Dammit, Evie. You didn't have to kick me in the balls!"

It's now that I notice Jake rounding the side of the building and spotting Tyler doubled over and moving away from me. He immediately puts two and two together and shoves Tyler hard to the ground—so hard I'm sure Tyler's tailbone is going to be bruised along with his other parts. "Apparently she did, jackass, or she wouldn't have needed to kick you like that." I guess he came outside in time to hear what I said.

I storm up beside Jake and hover over Tyler. "Listen to me. Don't you ever try to kiss me like that again. And this is the last time you will ever try to pursue me. I've made it perfectly clear that I don't want you anywhere near me, and from now on you will respect my decision or I will take out a restraining order against you. Am I clear?"

Usually, this is where Tyler would say something sarcastic in reply, but I think the kick to his balls has momentarily stunned him because he nods and silently struggles to his feet. He doesn't apologize—predictably—and I don't make him because I'm so done with this man I just want him gone. For good.

As Tyler skulks away to his fancy BMW parked by the curb, Jake looks like he's about to call him back and force an apology, but I put my hand to his chest and tell him to leave it be.

Jake lets out a breath as Tyler peels off, then he turns his head and pierces me with his gaze. "Are you okay?" His voice is so tender it nearly melts me right here on the sidewalk. "Did he hurt you?"

I shake my head and finally let the tears roll down my cheeks. "No. But you did."

He looks like I physically stabbed him. "What can I say to make this better, Evie? I'm so sorry for everything I said outside your parents' house. I let your family get in my head for a minute, and I acted like a selfish jackass to you. I'm so sor—"

"This isn't about what happened at my parents' house, Jake!"

His head kicks back, and his brows dip together. "I don't understand, then."

My mouth falls open, and I let out a sad mock laugh. "Did she not tell you I came by?"

Jake blinks a few times. "Evie, I have no idea what you're talking about. Came by where?"

"Your house, Jake!" I hurl my words at him as hard as possible. It feels good. "I saw her. The beautiful brunette with amazing boobs, standing in your doorway in her underwear! I saw her, Jake! How could you turn around and sleep with someone right after dropping me off at my house? I thought we had something special, but—"

"No! Evie . . ." He shakes his head vehemently. "That's . . . that's not at all what happened. I didn't sleep with her. In fact, I slept at my parents' house last night."

What in the freaking *hell* did that man just say?

"You . . . didn't sleep with the woman at your house?"

Jake's face cracks into a tentative smile, and he shakes his head slowly. He opens his mouth to explain but is cut off by the sound of his phone ringing in his pocket.

"I've got to answer this; it's my mom. But I'll explain everything in a minute. Don't go anywhere, okay?"

I nod and wrap my arms around myself because the past twenty-four hours have felt like a roller coaster, and I'm not sure I'm off the ride yet.

"Mom? Everything okay?" He pauses, and I watch as a heavy expression settles over his face. He stays perfectly frozen.

Something in me knows. "Is it Sam? Is she okay?"

He nods, and I didn't realize that I had walked up to him and wrapped my arms around his middle, but apparently I did because his hand is wrapping around my shoulder. He mumbles a few replies to his mom before he says he's on his way and hangs up.

"Sam had a seizure," he says, squeezing me like he needs my support to stay standing. "But she's okay. Apparently, she went upstairs to get her PJs on, then Daisy rushed back downstairs and started alerting my mom. Sam did fall, but it was on the carpet, and Daisy rolled her on her side just like she and Sam practiced. She stayed with Sam and hasn't left her side since the seizure ended." I see Jake's eyes welling with tears, and I hold him tighter. "Daisy made sure she was safe."

I smile. "Good. That's so good, Jake."

He nods and his jaws flex. "I need to get home to Sam, though."

"Right, of course." I let go of him and look back toward the venue. "Let me just go get Charlie, and we can leave."

"We? You're going to come with me?"

I freeze, hoping that wasn't presumptuous of me to invite myself along. "Oh, I'm sorry, you probably just want it to be family—"

"No." He cuts me off and gently takes my hand, raises it to his mouth, and lays a soft, slow kiss just under my palm. "I want you to come with me. But I know you have the fundraiser going on here and probably need to stay. Also I haven't fully filled you in on what you saw this morning."

I smile. "First, you and Sam are most important to me. Joanna can handle the fundraiser just fine without me. And second, you can explain it on the way to your house."

A slow smile spreads across Jake's mouth, and then, before I have time to breathe, he tugs me closer to him and captures my mouth with his. His hands are on my jaw, then sliding down my neck and shoulders and bare back to press me up closer to him. His lips shift gears back and forth from tender to firm to demanding, and I'm just trying to keep up. The kiss doesn't last long enough, but it certainly does enough damage that I touch my fingers to my swollen lips when we part. I blink, feeling drugged, then start walking. Jake turns me around so I'm actually headed in the right direction.

"Right. This way. Okay, so I'll just be right back."

CHAPTER 37

Jake

E vie and I got home about twenty minutes ago. We both raced up the stairs together to get to Sam's room. She was still on the floor when I got there, with her head resting on Daisy. This was the first seizure my mom has been around for, and she wasn't sure whether it was safe to move Sam to her bed or not.

Sam is in the postictal period of her seizure, and I know that, like Evie's seizure the other day, she won't feel or respond like herself for a while yet. Her episode progressed normally and didn't last too long (Mom was able to time it, thanks to Daisy coming to get her when it began), so I felt good about letting her just rest here at home and not taking her into the hospital. I drop down to my knees, though, and brush her hair away from her face to plant a kiss on her forehead. She smiles and mumbles a "Hi, Dad" that feels like an instant balm to my heart.

"Hi, kiddo. We're here now, and you're safe."

She hears me say *we,* and Sam's eyes peek open and instantly find Evie. Her little hand reaches up and Evie takes it, coming to kneel down on Sam's other side. In short, Sam is surrounded head to toe by people who love her.

Evie adjusts so that her legs are curled up beside her, her fancy evening gown draped around her, and she leans in closer to Sam to continually brush her fingers across my daughter's hairline in such a motherly way. It's a sight that will likely stick with me until the day I die.

"Do you want some water, darlin'?" Evie asks, and Sam nods.

I go downstairs and try to catch my breath while I fill a glass with water for my daughter. It's been a heck of a day, and the minimal amount of sleep I got last night is catching up to me. Once the water glass is filled, I set it on the counter and unbutton my cuffs to roll up my sleeves.

My mom walks into the kitchen and comes around the island with a look that tells me to brace for a good old-fashioned southern-mom bear hug. That's exactly what she gives me. I squeeze her small frame back, kiss the top of her head, and thank her for taking care of Sam tonight.

Finally, she pulls away and smiles up at me, patting my cheek like she's a hundred-year-old senior citizen in a nursing home rather than the spunky fifty-seven-year-old mother that she is. "I'm gonna get going."

"Are you sure? I can make you some tea or something. . . ." I'm not even sure if my mom drinks hot tea (or if I have any in my pantry), but it seems like a comforting thing to offer after the evening she's just gone through with Sam.

She looks at me with that same smile that I'm just now realizing is heavy with hidden meaning and shakes her head. "I'll make some tea at home with your dad. I love you, Jakey. Go be with your family."

Ah. My family. So, that's what was with the secret smile.

"You know we haven't even had the let's-be-a-couple talk yet, right?"

She shrugs, slings her leather purse over her shoulder, and heads for the door. "Doesn't matter. My eyesight is twenty-twenty and I know what I see. And what I saw up there was a family." With those parting words, she leaves the house.

I can just picture the self-satisfied smirk she'll be wearing during her whole drive home. She loves leaving a house on a monumental final thought.

I should be rushing back upstairs to get to Sam, but the truth is I just need a minute to myself to breathe and soak up everything that's happened today, and I know that she's safe with Evie. For the first time this year, I don't feel alone in this parenting job. Someone who I can trust is upstairs right now, taking beautiful care of my daughter. And apparently, thanks to Natalie, I almost lost Evie.

After allowing myself five full breaths and a moment to run my hands through my hair, I head up the stairs with Sam's water. I crack open her door and pause in the doorframe, letting the picture before me steal the last bits of my heart. Evie has moved Sam up onto her bed and tucked her in. Daisy is on one side of Sam, and lying on Sam's other side is Evie, with Charlie at her feet. Her black silk gown is a sharp contrast to Sam's unicorn bedding.

She looks like a movie star home from receiving an Oscar, skipping the after-party in favor of tucking her daughter into bed. She's singing a quiet, sweet version of "Over the Rainbow," and I have to try very hard not to drop down onto one knee here and now.

My mom is right. This feels like a family.

That thought would have scared me last week, but now it fills me with hope.

Evie must feel me watching her, because suddenly she looks over her shoulder and finds me. A slow smile blooms on her face. I cross the room and set Sam's water glass on her bedside table. It looks like Evie has already put Sam to sleep, so I nod toward the door. Evie carefully extracts her arm out from under Sam, looking like she's been doing it every day for the past ten years of my daughter's life, and tiptoes with me out of the room.

I leave Sam's door open so I can hear her if she calls for me and take Evie's hand to silently pull her back down the stairs to the couch.

CHAPTER 38

Evie

Jake's house at night is my favorite place in the world. He has the kind of lighting that can be dimmed in every room of the house, so right now the house is blanketed in a soft, warm glow. A candle is lit on his coffee table, filling the air with my favorite vanilla and teakwood scent, and everything is peaceful and still.

Jake tugs me toward his couch and then, without dropping my hand, dives onto it, landing on his back and pulling me down on top of him. We both laugh as we settle into a comfortable position, where our feet are intertwined and I'm lying half on the couch, half on Jake. He has one hand cradling mine and is kissing every single one of my fingers, as his other hand lightly brushes circles on my back.

It's so romantic, I'm aching.

"Jake," I say, somewhere between breathlessness and a reprimand. "We need to talk. . . ." I try not to smile as he pulls me up a little closer so that we're face-to-face. He tucks his hand into my hair, and his gaze lands on my mouth. He gives me a half smirk and mumbles against my lips, "I don't want to talk."

I know that look. *Sexy haze.* The man is half-drugged on the feel of my body, and I know that if I have any hope of figuring out what's happening in our relationship, I need to drop a tray of ice cubes down his shirt. Or maybe his pants . . .

He leans up just enough to take my bottom lip between his. *Okay, so I guess I need some ice cubes too.* "Jake!" I give the worst protest anyone has ever heard and halfheartedly pull away. He tugs me back, and his grin nearly undoes me.

"All right, let's talk," he says as he's kissing the spot right under my ear. "What do you want to talk about?" He laces kisses down my jaw, and . . . *poof.* There goes my desire to talk too. I give in and press my hand to his chest to give me better leverage.

Fire lights his eyes, and I dip down, slanting my mouth over his. Our lips dance for only a minute before Jake breaks the kiss and sits up abruptly, sliding all the way to the opposite end of the couch.

He's all mussed and rumpled when he looks at me. "We really do need to talk. I owe you explanations. And apologies. But I can't do that with you on top of me."

"Can I at least sit next to you? I don't want to have a serious conversation over walkie-talkies."

"Are you going to behave, Miss Jones?"

"Maybe . . . maybe not."

His grin tilts and he pats the seat beside him. "I'll take my chances."

I slide over and there's no way to do it without it looking suggestive. Jake watches me, barely containing his laugh. "Okay, I'm here."

"You're here." He takes my hand and laces our fingers together.

"Who was the woman I found at your door this morning?" I ask, because I've decided we're just going to cannonball right on in. We were going to talk about it in the truck on the way here, but Jake's dad called to make sure his mom had gotten ahold of him, then Jo called me with a question from one of the vendors. Our conversation had to wait.

He nods firmly. Down to business. "That was Natalie."

My shoulders droop. "Natalie? As in, Sam's mom and your actress ex-wife Natalie? The lady with the body like a goddess?" Images of Natalie and her absolutely incredible boobs assault my memory. Without really thinking, my gaze drops to my own flat-chested self, and all of my insecurities I like to pretend don't exist bubble to the surface.

"Hey," Jake says, touching under my chin to tip my gaze back up to his face. "You're perfect, Evie Jones. Don't second-guess that for even a second."

"But . . . she's so—"

"It doesn't matter what she is—she isn't anything to me anymore. I don't have any feelings or lingering attraction to her. And please know that I would never *ever* sleep with someone else when I told you I wouldn't. That's not how I operate."

"I didn't think you would. . . . That's why I was so shocked to see her. Why was she here?"

He runs his thumb over my knuckles. "When I got home last night, she was on my porch. I didn't know she was coming or else I would have told you. But we talked for a few minutes, and she said she wanted to be a family again. I obviously have no interest in that, so I went to my parents' place for the night. The end."

I angle a little more toward him. "*She wants to be a family again? How do you feel about that?*"

Jake must hear the shrill tone of my voice because he laughs and scoots closer to put his arms around me, completely wrapping me up. "Evie, Natalie and I are over. Her telling me that made me feel nothing but angry. It wouldn't be the first time she's said it, and she didn't mean it the last time either."

"And if she did mean it?"

"I would like for her to step up and be a mom for Sam, but that's it. We'll never be a family again. I don't want that. And sadly, I don't have high hopes of her becoming a good mom for Sam either. In fact, I told her that before she could see Sam again, she had to stay in town for one week and call every day."

"What did she say to that?" For Sam's sake, I hope she agreed. That little girl deserves a good mom in her life.

"Well, she texted me during the gala saying she was sorry but she heard back about an audition and would be flying to Hollywood in the morning."

"I'm so sorry, Jake. I know that's going to be hard to tell Sam."

He scrunches his eyes shut like he hadn't even thought of that yet. "So damn hard." He breathes deeply and I angle up to kiss his cheek.

"I hope for Sam and Natalie's sake that one day she really will get her act together. But until then, I'm not going to let her hurt Sam any more than she already has."

I touch his jaw and feel his five o'clock shadow beneath my palm. "You're a good man, Jacob Broaden. Sam is lucky to have you."

He looks down at me, and his gaze pins me in place. "Evie. Let me be perfectly clear with you now. I don't want something casual anymore and I'm done with going slow." He adjusts himself to face me, and his big hand raises to cradle my face, making my hand drop to his shoulder. "I want Jake and Evie. Stupid kissing profile pictures. Cute nicknames for each other. I want *serious*. Exclusive. Us. I don't want anything less than planning months out for a vacation and obnoxious Christmas cards that have you, me, Sam, and the dogs on the front. Can you handle that?"

My skin is tingling, and my heart is racing. It's trying to leap out of my chest and jump into Jake's lap. In fact, yeah, it turns out it wasn't my heart doing that—it was my body. I scoot up onto Jake's lap and wrap my arms around his neck, smiling down into his face.

I hover an inch from his mouth and then narrow my eyes. "Do we have to wear matching robes?"

A rumbling laugh breaks from his chest, and his head tilts back as he squeezes me a little tighter. He doesn't answer my question, because with his head tilted back like that, it gives me a perfect shot at his neck. His skin is warm against my lips as I place kiss after kiss along the long column of his throat.

I make it up to his mouth, and his gaze is sultry, and passionate, and full of . . . "I think I love you, Evie. Is that okay?"

There's no way to keep from smiling wide as I touch the corner of his mouth with my thumb. "More than okay. Because I think I love you too, Jake." I dip my head, and his lips caress mine for a luxurious, top-of-the-line, special-edition kiss.

Just as it's heating up again, we both hear a soft little voice on the stairs. "Ew. Are you guys kissing?"

Jake and I break apart and both wipe at our mouths in case my lipstick is everywhere it shouldn't be. "No . . . We were just . . . just . . ." He looks at me, but what in the heck is he thinking I'm going to do to help this? He's been a parent for ten years, and I've only been a mom to a golden retriever.

"Just looking for something in my eye!" *Nice one, Evie.*

"Through your mouth?" *Okay, maybe not so great after all.*

I can see Jake trying so hard to contain his laughter. He rubs his hand firmly across his face and mouth and looks back up at Sam. "We'll stop kissing. Are you feeling better, kiddo?"

I scoot off his lap, and Jake stands and walks to Sam.

"A little," she says, coming down the stairs with Jake's help. Daisy is right behind her.

Jake brings her over to the couch, and without hesitating even a second, Sam sits down beside me and curls her little body up next to mine. I wrap my arms around her and hug her close. I don't know who is benefiting from this connection the most in this moment. I feel like my heart is physically expanding. It's making room to accommodate all of this new love.

Jake disappears into the kitchen for a minute and then comes back out with a bowl of popcorn. He sits beside me, sets the bowl in my lap, and drapes his arm behind me to rest over my shoulders and let his fingers dangle over Sam's, effectively snuggling both of us at the same time. Charlie and Daisy both come over to hunker down at the foot of the couch, draping over our feet. Jake turns on a movie, and we spend the rest of the night just like that. Snuggling, laughing, stealing kisses when Sam isn't watching, and eating popcorn.

I hope with all my heart that this is what every day of the rest of my life will look like. And later, after Sam falls asleep and Jake carries her back up to bed, I wait for him by the door.

As he walks down the stairs, the sight of him with his rolled-up shirtsleeves and suit pants honestly takes my breath away. He has stepped right out of *GQ* magazine to stop just in front of me. He takes my hand. "Are you leaving?"

CHAPTER 39

Evie

"I was—until I remembered I don't have a car. Or a license."

His grin slants. "I guess you'll just have to stay, then." He pauses. "If you want."

"Hmm." I pretend to mull it over while simultaneously inching closer and putting my hand on his chest. "Is this a formal invitation?"

He brushes my hair back from my face as I angle it up at him. "It is. Stay the night with me, Evie."

"Okay."

"Okay?"

"Are you going to repeat everything I say?" I ask, recalling our afternoon in the hallway when he first asked me on a date.

"No, I'm going to take you to my room now and wow you with those incredible basics I told you about at your place."

"Don't set my expectations so high," I say as he slides his hand slowly around my lower back and guides me down the hallway toward his room. *His room.*

It takes us ages to make it there because we stop every foot or so to kiss. He presses me against the wall and circles his tongue on the base of my neck. I push him to the adjacent wall and unbutton his shirt, pulling it out from the waistband of his pants. He drops the strap of my dress off my shoulder and kisses the skin it was hiding. And then he repeats the process all over again after walking another foot.

I run my fingers down his bare abs and then count them with my lips.

By the time we make it to the door, his hand is skating up my thigh, dragging my dress up with it. I hook my finger through his belt loop and pull him into the room, then Jake closes and locks the door behind us.

This is really happening. *Finally.* There's been so much buildup to this moment that we make quick work of each other's clothes. They're tossed all around the room, and only when I'm in Jake's glorious bed with his amazing body spread out over me do I ask, "Is it killing you to not immediately tidy up the room? Do you want to take a break to fold the clothes into neat piles?"

He laughs against my rib cage. His teeth scrape lightly over my skin. "As if I could care about anything in this moment besides you."

I gasp as he proves it.

We're all hands and lips and tongues and teeth. It's frantic and luxurious all at once and worth every bit of the torturous wait. We take the night to love each other. But the most wonderful part of all is waking up and knowing it wasn't a dream. It wasn't a mistake. And it wasn't something that's going away.

Jake Broaden is all mine, and I'm never letting him go.

EPILOGUE

Two Years Later

I wake up to the feel of Jake's mouth against mine. Turns out, I love being kissed first thing in the morning. This is the way Jake has woken me up every morning since we married nine months ago. "Rise and shine, Sleeping Beauty," he murmurs in my ear.

I peek one eye open and take a long look at his muscled, tan chest beside me and then to the clock on my phone. I groan because I know that I have no time to spend in bed with Jake this morning. "You let me oversleep."

"Mm-hmm. You need all of it you can get." His hand lands on my swollen stomach as he kisses my cheek.

"I also need to get to the venue to unlock it in time for the vendors to get set up." Our first fundraiser was such a success that we decided to make it an annual thing. This will be our third year of the gala, and thanks to all the vendors who donate their services, we exceed our fundraising goal each and every year. Not only is it a great way to support the organization, it's also a great way to look at my hot husband in a tux.

Jake's voice turns husky, and he starts nibbling at my earlobe.

"Let Joanna do it." Joanna technically retired a few months ago, but the poor thing was bored to death and driving Gary nuts. Unsurprisingly, one week after she retired, she signed up as a volunteer for Southern Service Paws. I think she's putting in more hours now than she was before, but since I'll be going on maternity leave in two months when our baby boy is born, I don't mind. In fact, I'm downright grateful.

"I know, but I want to be there. I *like* my job, remember?"

"I know something else you like," he says, undeterred.

But *I* won't be deterred today. So, I roll my eyes and push him away halfheartedly. He laughs and reaches out to drag my body up close to him again. So greedy. I lay my head on his chest and Jake and I both feel our baby boy kick him in the side, making us laugh.

He looks down at my round stomach and shakes his head. "You're not even in the world yet and you're already taking your mom's side? I thought I would have at least one of my kids on my team."

It's been a dream building a life with Jake. Not always perfect—but I wouldn't want it to be anyway. I like a little mess here and there. We took our time while we dated. Got to know each other and fell in love more every day. And on our one-year anniversary, Jake took me to the coffee shop where we first met and he proposed. He actually rented the whole place out after hours so he could fill it with flowers and lights. We had chocolate chip muffins for dessert. It was the easiest *yes* I've ever said in my life.

Jake was understandably hesitant when I told him a few months after we got married that I was ready to add to our family. He still carries a lot of guilt where Natalie is concerned in that department, and he didn't want me to feel stuck like she did. It took some time and a lot of conversations for him to really trust that it's what I want—and I love him all the more for his concern.

In the next moment, Sam busts into our room, and I'm *oh so glad* that I had put a stop to Jake's advances.

"Morning!" she says with a cheery smile and a bouquet the size of her head in her hand. She approaches the bed and sets them on the bedside table. "These are for you, Mom."

That's another wonderful part of this life. Sam calls me *Mom*, and it still melts my heart every time. This girl and I have bonded like we were always meant to be mother and daughter. Natalie still hasn't been in the picture much, and I know it hurts Sam more than she lets on, but I've been trying my best to ensure Sam knows she has a mom who loves her more than life. Because if my relationship with Jo has taught me anything, it's that the title of mom sometimes has nothing to do with sharing the same blood. I would do anything for Sam, go to the ends of the earth and back for this kid, and I will aways do my best to make sure she knows it.

But also, I'm going to have to have a talk with her about opening the door to flower-delivery strangers first thing in the morning without a parent present. For now, I smile and sit up, sending a questioning glance to Jake. He sits up too, and the sheet falls off his chest. When am I going to be immune to this man's incredible body? I'm betting never.

"Don't look at me," he says. "I was saving my flowers to give to you after the fundraiser tonight."

I frown and pluck the little white card from the bouquet and tear into it.

> *Evelyn Grace,*
> *We're proud of you. See you tonight.*
> *Mom and Dad*

"What man with a death wish sent my wife flowers?" asks Jake.

I numbly hand him the card. "They're from . . . my parents."

Sam jumps on the end of the bed to pet Charlie, who absolutely adores her. As it turns out, my dog's love and affection is pretty cheaply bought. Sam devotes five minutes a day to throwing a tennis ball with him in the yard, and he is putty in her little hands. I'm not mad about it.

"What's it feel like to read those words from your parents?" asks Jake after his eyes scan the card.

"I don't know yet. It's still hard to trust that they mean it. But I'm trying to let it sink in."

Shortly after Jake and I married, my dad had a massive heart attack that almost killed him. Something happened to my parents after that experience. It was a wake-up call for them. I spent more time with my dad than ever, because for one, my mom needed the help. And second, because my dad really seemed to see me for the first time. He listened when I talked. He wanted to know about my life—apologizing for the parts he missed out on because of how closed off he'd become to our family. My mom warmed up to me too, in her own way. I wouldn't call us best friends, but she's kinder to me and has finally accepted my need to live a different life than theirs.

I thought I had somehow warped into a new dimension the day my dad told me he had given up his position at the law firm. That it was taking up too much of his life and he never realized until after the heart attack just now much stress it was putting on him. He still has part ownership, but he fully stepped down from any day-to-day work. Instead, he and Mom have started checking things off their bucket list with all of their free time. They travel. They started a book club with their friends. They're cute sometimes.

And they've been trying their hardest to mend their relationship with me. I won't lie; I wish that it hadn't taken a heart attack to make them see my importance, but I know that beggars can't be choosers. I've been cautious in letting them into my life, but so far they've proven that their motives are pure.

They've even been trying to get to know Sam (with me or Jake always nearby) and seem to want us all to know we are a part of their family. Mom is still snooty, but she's getting better with every passing day. I went to lunch with her last week and she didn't even mention it when I was three and a half minutes late. My hope is that, soon, we will have a real relationship and that they'll be better with my children than they were with me.

Oh yeah, and this pregnancy has been a miracle in and of itself. I've had to grow accustomed to closer monitoring and *lots* of doctor visits (especially after seizures), but so far everything has gone smoothly. We are all hopeful that I will carry to term and have a healthy birth. The doctor has assured me that patients with epilepsy have safe deliveries all the time.

Jake leans in and kisses my temple. "Well, I love you, and I'm proud of you. And you can always trust that."

I smile and meet his gaze. "*That* I do know."

"Me too!" says Sam, squeezing my feet. She inches up in the bed to lie down on my pillow beside me and rubs my belly. "How's my baby brother doing today?"

Jake puts his hand on my belly too. These days, my stomach seems to be a public attraction. Even a random old lady in the grocery store rubbed it yesterday. Maybe everyone knows something I don't, and they are all being granted three wishes. "He kept his mom up all night last night, dancing circles in there, the little booger," I say.

Sam leans closer to my stomach and whispers something about joining forces to annoy me and Jake, but I tune out when I feel my husband's eyes on my face. I turn to look at him, and he and I stare at each other, lost in the same thought: *I can't believe this is our life.*

"I love you," he mouths.

"I love you more."

Two Months Later

Jonathan Timothy Broaden came into the world this morning around two A.M. He and I are both perfectly healthy, but send good vibes for Jake because I think he might be losing it from sleep deprivation. The poor man has cried more in the past twenty-four hours than I thought possible. I allow it, though, because I know he has so much love pumping through his heart that he can't keep it contained.

He's so wonderful, my husband. And so is my daughter. And my son. And of course, our dogs are superheroes that I will always adore. Which reminds me, I need to order their capes for Halloween.

I don't think this life of mine can get any better.

Except it does when I spot Jake walking into the hospital room with a chocolate chip muffin.

ACKNOWLEDGMENTS

First, thank *you*, wonderful reader, for making it this far. :) Without you, my stories would just be collecting dust in my imagination. Thank you for helping me bring them to life!

Thank you to my sweet beta readers: Ashely, Lesley, Kadi, Kari, Kasey, and Carina. You guys are my heroes for helping me find all the places my story needed to get stronger!

Thank you to my wonderful parents, Mark and Karen, for fostering my love of reading and always encouraging me to write the stories in my heart! I'm thankful for how much you love me and my girls. :) I would never have made it this far without you!

Thank you to Lesley Adams for letting me ask you a million questions about training service dogs and never once telling me to stop bugging you. :) Thanks for encouraging me to write this story and helping me make it accurate! Also, thank you (this includes you, Dave) for being amazing in-laws and loving us all so well! I'm so grateful to be a part of your family.

Thank you to my true inspiration, my husband's six-pack abs. :) Oh, also a huge thanks to Chris for being the best husband and dad in the world. I love you!

READ ON FOR AN EXCERPT FROM *THE ENEMY*

BY SARAH ADAMS

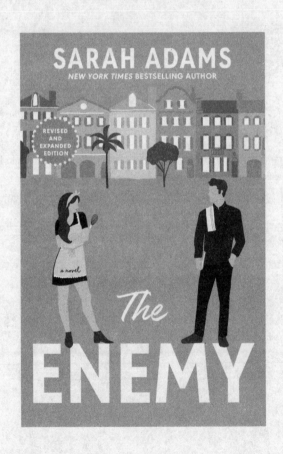

June

t's been twelve years since I've seen him.

Twelve years since his smug face leaned down to kiss me, stopped just before our mouths met, smirked, then turned and walked out of my life forever. That day, I stood stunned and awestruck. I wish I had smashed his toes. Instead, I closed my eyes as he went in for the kill. I cringe, remembering how I tilted my chin up, feeling a chill trickle across my spine at the thought of him kissing me after spending our whole high school experience trying to kill each other. I acknowledged defeat the moment my eyes fluttered shut. I hate that he won our war back then.

But tonight . . . tonight, I resurrect the battle.

And victory will be mine.

No longer am I that naïve little graduate, excited for a kiss from the enemy. I'm now thirty years old and majority owner of Darlin' Donuts—one of Charleston's top hotspots. My best friend, Stacy, and I opened the bakery three years ago, and we have been enjoying a nice bit of success ever since.

Not only am I the southern queen of the gourmet donut market but I'm also turning down men calling me up nightly for a date. Okay . . . nightly is a stretch. But it's definitely somewhere around three times a week. Twice a week. Once a week. Above average, okay?

Point is, I've got a lot going for me now. Career success. Tons of friends—because family makes the best friends, am I right? And I'm at least four inches taller than I was in high school (read: two inches). Best of all, I've perfected a killer winged eyeliner and paired it with a little black dress that has had men eyeballing me from across the bar all night long.

Sorry, boys. You can look, but you can't touch.

In short, I've made sure that tonight—the night I come face-to-face again with my archnemesis—I look the best I've looked in my adult life. Because mark the words coming out of my red lips: Tonight, I will crush Ryan Henderson under my black stilettoed feet.

He will see all that he has missed out on and weep on the floor, clutching my legs, begging me to give him the kiss he left behind all those years ago.

And *finally*, I hear the door squeak open. I wait, measuring the seconds passing by, the click, click, click of a woman's high heels drawing nearer.

Just a little closer.

Ugh. She passed me, choosing the far end of the row like a normal person. Why did I have to choose the middle?

"Hey there!" I call out. "Why don't you take the one beside me?"

Her clicks come to an abrupt halt, and suddenly I'm aware of how creepy I sounded.

Because . . . yeah, I'm currently sitting on a toilet with my fancy little cocktail dress hiked up to my hips and the telltale prickles of a woman who has had no choice but to sit on a toilet seat for far too long shooting down my legs.

"Uh, I think I'm okay with this stall." The woman is undoubtedly shooting off a frantic text to her date, saying if she's not out of here in five minutes, it was the woman in the middle stall who killed her.

I laugh, trying to sound as little like a serial killer as possible, because any minute now Ryan Henderson will be arriving at the party, and I need to be out there to see his ugly face first. (I'm assuming he's ugly because it helps me sleep easier at night.)

"Sorry, didn't mean to freak you out! I'm normal, I swear. Just out of toilet paper over here and was hoping you could slip me a roll."

"Oh." Her voice is still far away. She's not convinced I won't do something creepy if she comes near my stall.

Meanwhile, I'm sitting over here, air-drying on the porcelain throne, worrying I'll never feel my feet again, while Miss Barbie Heels makes up her mind.

I sweeten the pot because, apparently, I'm a black-market toilet paper dealer now. "There's five bucks and a half-used tube of red lipstick in it for you."

That got her moving. Moving right on out the bathroom door. Apparently, red isn't Barbie's lipstick color of choice, and she's decided she would rather risk a bladder infection than get near me. If I hadn't left my phone on the table like a potato, I could have texted Stacy and asked her to come bail me out. But noooo, I had to prove that I'm not obsessed with my phone like the rest of the world and leave it on the table.

Still, Stacy should be receiving my telepathic BFF distress signals. I've been in here forever. She should be worried that I've either been kidnapped or am suffering from some serious stomach trouble. Both of which would warrant an appearance from someone who claims to love me like a sister.

Stacy is also the reason I am having to be reunited with the man

I hate more than menstrual cramps. She and her fiancé, Logan, were high school sweethearts, and after over fifteen years in a relationship (yep, you heard me right) they are finally tying the knot. I would be over-the-moon excited for Stacy if Logan hadn't gone and asked Ryan to be his best man.

Although I think it's debatable, Stacy says it's customary for the best man to attend the groom's bachelor party, which is what is happening tonight. Actually, it's a joint bachelor and bachelorette party, because Stacy and Logan are one of those annoyingly in love couples who do everything together. They share a Facebook profile, order the dinner portion of every meal so they can split it, and even book overlapping doctors' appointments. So, it was really no surprise when they announced they were joining their parties together. We're all having one fancy bar crawl, and I can think of at least one hundred things that could go wrong tonight. But all of them happen to Ryan.

1) I slip a laxative into his drink.
2) I squirt superglue onto his seat before he sits down.
3) I set his car on fire. (Don't worry, I'll wait until he's out of it . . . maybe.)

I could go on and on, but you get the picture.

I can't, for the life of me, understand why Logan and Ryan have stayed close friends even after graduating and living in different states. Sometimes I wonder what Ryan has been up to this whole time, but I don't dare ask Stacy because I implemented a strict no mention of the devil rule a long time ago, and I refuse to break it. Both Stacy and Logan know that even the slightest slip of Ryan's name gets them put in the friendship doghouse for an entire week. Am I being petty? Yes. Absolutely. But I'm okay with it.

I've had twelve blissful years of Ryan-lessness. Well, almost blissful. That time, five years ago, when my fiancé cheated on me and I had to cancel my wedding sucked. Other than that, though, it's been twelve years of success without worrying that he will somehow swoop in and overshadow me. And if I could ever get off this toilet, I could go rub all my newfound success in Ryan's face.

Thankfully, I hear the door open again, and I sit up straighter, determined not to mess up my lines this time. Fate is on my side, as the woman chooses the stall beside me. Deciding not to risk it with chitchat, I cut right to the chase. "Umm. Hi. I don't mean to startle you . . . but the thing is, I've been in here for a while, and I was wondering if—"

I cut myself off when a hand shoots under the stall wall, clutching a bouquet of toilet paper. "Yeah, yeah, here you go."

Yes! Finally! See, now this is a woman I can appreciate. Soul sisters. Women who understand each other! I briefly consider giving her my tube of red lipstick and asking her to exchange numbers, but I decide against it.

Once all my business is complete, I emerge from the bathroom like I've been lost at sea for ten years. It's good to be back in the world. Are the Kardashians still famous?

I make my way down the dark, slender hallway toward the bar. The music pulses through my chest, and my heels pound the floor with the sure strides of a six-foot-tall *Vogue* model on the catwalk rather than the five-foot-two southern peach I am.

Right now I am all confidence—high on my own determination as I step out of the hallway into the trendy sports bar. I have no time to scan the room before I'm grabbed hard by the arm and yanked to the side.

"Ow! What the—"

"He's here," Stacy whispers loudly into my face. And WOW has she already had a lot to drink or what? I'm going to need to slip her a Tic Tac.

"Who's here?" But I know who she's talking about. I'm just getting into character with my false disinterest.

"Didn't you get all my texts?" She sounds frantic. It makes me laugh a little because I know that even though this is our first stop of the night, she's already a little tipsy. Stacy is a lightweight. And when Stacy gets tipsy, she turns into the star of a reality TV show. Which reality show? It doesn't really matter. A drunk person is the driving force in all of them.

"No, I left my phone on the table."

Stacy looks appalled. "Why'd you do that?"

"Because I was proving that I—it doesn't matter. How long has he been here?"

"About five minutes. He's standing over at the bar."

Nerves zing through me, because this is it. After twelve years, my archnemesis is once again standing in the same room as me, and I fully intend to squash him.

My little black dress is hugging my curves, and my loose-wave, honey-brown hair is tickling my spine. I've been saving this dress for exactly this occasion. It has a high neckline but low-cut open back, making it the perfect combination of sexy and sweet. The mullet of dresses, if you will. Business in the front, party in the back. Even better, the slender long sleeves cover almost all of my shoulder tattoo, leaving only the tiniest sliver of pale-yellow sunflower petals to peek out over my shoulder blade.

I take in one deep breath before turning around and scanning each man at the bar. I search. I search again. I search one more time because . . . "He's not here."

"Yes, he is," Stacy says in a matter-of-fact way that gives me a sinking feeling. "He's right there." She points toward the bar, and I whip my head around to her.

"No. He's. Not," I say through my teeth. "I don't see any ugly men with greasy hair and rotting teeth!" I'm doing that thing where

I'm yelling in whisper form with a smile still plastered to my face. It's scary.

Stacy doesn't back down from my intensity. She gives me a look that says, *This ends here and now.* "That's because Ryan is not ugly or greasy."

"But you said he was!" I sound so desperate now. I'm seconds away from breathing into a paper bag.

Stacy shakes her blond head, and if I weren't completely freaking out right now, I would tell her how pretty her new highlights look. "Nope. You always assumed he was, and I just never corrected you."

"Why! That's the kind of thing that you correct a girl about."

Her eyes go wide, and her mouth falls open. "You've got to be kidding me! The last time I tried to mention anything remotely complimentary about Ryan, you took my fifteen-dollar glass of wine and poured it into the restaurant's ficus!"

I did do that. And I stand by it.

"Now, like it or not, Ryan is here, and he's not ugly, greasy, or unhygienic, so it's time to put on your big-girl panties and woman up."

Right. She's right. This pep talk was good. I nod in agreement, trying to get hyped like those football players before they run out of the tunnel. I feel a new adrenaline coursing through me—an electric shock to my system that triggers my brain to switch into high alert. Because suddenly, the game—or rather, the opponent—has changed.

"Which one is he?" I go shoulder to shoulder with Stacy as my eyes cut fire across the bar.

"The navy suit with Miss USA draped over him."

Of course.

Of freakin' course.

ABOUT THE AUTHOR

SARAH ADAMS is the author of *The Rule Book, Practice Makes Perfect, When in Rome,* and *The Cheat Sheet.* Born and raised in Nashville, Tennessee, she loves her family and warm days. Sarah has dreamed of being a writer since she was a girl but finally wrote her first novel when her daughters were napping and she no longer had any excuses to put it off. Sarah is a coffee addict, a British history nerd, a mom of two daughters, and an indecisive introvert. She is married to her best friend. Her hope is to write stories that make readers laugh, maybe even cry, but always leave them happier than when they started reading.

authorsarahadams.com
Instagram: @authorsarahadams

ABOUT THE TYPE

This book was set in Hoefler Text, a typeface designed in 1991 by Jonathan Hoefler (b. 1970). One of the earlier type-faces created at the beginning of the digital age specifically for use on computers, it was among the first to offer features previously found only in the finest typography, such as dedi-cated old-style figures and small caps. Thus it offers modern style based on the classic tradition.